"I am willing to pay any price to save my brother," Shaw declared. "Even enter a den of vipers."

Merritt was disturbed by the nearness of his naked chest and the mat of gold hair that disappeared beneath the waistband of his breeches. "A word of warning, then." Her voice lowered to a whisper. "Take care that you do not anger this viper, or you will be forced to endure my venom."

His gaze fastened on her mouth, and a dangerous smile touched his lips. When she tried to pull back, he dragged her into his arms. "I think, viper, I might enjoy seeing you hiss."

Her eyes flashed. "May you be damned to eternal fire, Campbell. And your brother, as well—"

Her words were cut off with a hard, punishing kiss. This time she was prepared to do battle rather than give in. And Shaw was just as determined to dominate....

Dear Reader,

With close to three million books in print, Ruth Langan has clearly established herself as a popular writer. From historical romance to mainstream fiction, she has done it all, and we are very proud to continue to bring you her unfogettable historicals. This month's *Highland Heaven* is another in her dynamic continuing Scottish series from the author whom *Romantic Times* has described as "a talented author who never disappoints...." You won't want to miss it.

Our other titles this month include *Redwood Empire*, a reissue of the Western saga written by talented authors Ann and Evan Maxwell writing as A. E. Maxwell, the powerful story of a woman torn between a ruthless businessman and his renegade son; *The Saxon* by Margaret Moore, the sequel to her award-winning medieval, *The Viking;* and from contemporary author Susan Mallery, her first historical for Harlequin, *Justin's Bride*.

We hope you'll keep an eye out for all four titles, wherever Harlequin Historicals are sold.

Sincerely,

Tracy Farrell
Senior Editor

Please address questions and book requests to:
Harlequin Reader Service
U.S.: 3010 Walden Ave., P.O. Box 1325, Buffalo, NY 14269
Canadian: P.O. Box 609, Fort Erie, Ont. L2A 5X3

RUTH LANGAN
HIGHLAND HEAVEN

Harlequin Books

TORONTO • NEW YORK • LONDON
AMSTERDAM • PARIS • SYDNEY • HAMBURG
STOCKHOLM • ATHENS • TOKYO • MILAN
MADRID • WARSAW • BUDAPEST • AUCKLAND

ISBN 0-373-28869-7

HIGHLAND HEAVEN

Books by Ruth Langan

Harlequin Historicals

Mistress of the Seas #10
+*Texas Heart* #31
**Highland Barbarian* #41
*Highland Heather #65
*Highland Fire #91
*Highland Heart #111
+*Texas Healer* #131
Christmas Miracle #147
+*Texas Hero* #180
Deception #196
*The Highlander #228
Angel #245
*Highland Heaven #269

Harlequin Books

Harlequin Historicals Christmas Stories 1990
"Christmas at Bitter Creek"

+Texas Series
*The Highland Series

RUTH LANGAN

traces her ancestry to Scotland and Ireland. It is no surprise, then, that she feels a kinship with the characters in her historical novels.

Married to her childhood sweetheart, she has raised five children and lives in Michigan, the state where she was born and raised.

For Ally Aja Shrader,
our newest family treasure.
And proud parents Mary and Dennis.
And for Caitlin Bea and Bret,
loving sister and brother.

And, as always, for Tom,
the light of my life.

Prologue

Scotland—1290

The Highland meadow was filled with the clash of sword against sword, and the cries of men as they fell to the grass. The Highland peasants fought with a fierceness born of desperation, refusing to admit defeat, though their number had already been cut by half.

Desperate for victory, the leader of the invaders ordered his warriors to form a circle around the remaining ragged band of Highlanders.

Three of the Highland peasants stood head and shoulders above the others. The russet strands in their hair and beards proclaimed their Norse ancestors, as did their refusal to back down even against so great an adversary. All three proved to be fierce opponents, who would die before surrendering. With each strike of their blades, they shouted encouragement to one another.

"Hold, Modric. Do not yield."

"Aye, Upton. Nor you. See to Thurman."

"I'll see to myself. Watch your back, friend."

For a moment the leader of the invaders studied them through narrowed eyes, to determine who would lead and who would follow. Then, lifting his sword to the throat of Modric, he ordered the others to throw down their weapons.

"Nay," the Highlander shouted. "Not even for the sake of my life shall we concede. Fight on, men."

Modric was stunned to note that his words fell on deaf ears. With great reluctance, the others did as they were told, tossing aside their weapons in order to spare his life.

With a sneer the invader called to the women and children who had taken shelter in the nearby forest, "Show yourselves now, or you will witness the deaths of every man here."

Haltingly, the women and children emerged, though they knew what their fate would be. The women would be used cruelly until their captors tired of them and consigned them to a brutal death. The children would be taken away, to serve as slaves to these barbarians.

A beautiful, auburn-haired woman, heavy with child, emerged from the forest, leaning on the arm of a small boy. Suddenly a cry was ripped from her as she dropped to the grass in pain.

At his wife's tortured cry, Modric knew that her time had come. In desperation his fingers tightened on the hilt of the crude knife fashioned from stone that was hidden at his waist. Though it would be a meager defense against the invader's sword, he would do what he had to. With a cry of rage he sprang. His companions could do nothing more than watch helplessly as the two men engaged in a battle to the death.

While their cries and grunts of pain filled the air, the woman lay on the ground, in the throes of heavy labor. The grass beneath her gradually became stained with her blood. Her young son sat beside her, gripping her hand tightly.

Taking pity on her, one of the women found the courage to separate herself from the others and come forward to assist.

"The bairn comes too soon," the young mother managed to gasp as the midwife dropped to her knees.

"Nay, Cerese, the gods have always done things in their own time."

The midwife handed the boy a length of rolled cloth and whispered, "Dillon, place this between your mother's teeth and hold it there."

The boy did as he was told, all the while continuing to watch the vicious struggle between his father and the invader.

The sounds of battle were suddenly drowned out by the young mother's low, keening wail as a tiny, wrinkled infant slipped into the world and gave out a lusty cry.

The midwife lifted the babe in her arms and whispered, "A son, Cerese. Can you hear him? He shows no fear of the world he enters. And look at him. Though small, he is perfectly formed . . ."

There was another low moan and the midwife glanced down, surprised by the look of pain on the young woman's face. "What is it?"

"'Twas not like this before, when Dillon was born. Something is wrong."

"Wrong?" The midwife bent to the woman. At that moment another infant, with an equally lusty cry, made its appearance.

At once the midwife let out a shriek of terror and scrambled to her feet, backing away. "Two of them," she shouted. "Exactly alike in appearance. It is a curse from the gods. We must flee. We are all doomed."

The crowd of peasants fell back, crying among themselves, as though in the presence of evil. For all knew that the birth of twins was the work of dark spirits.

The invaders, too, shrank back, terrified of this sinister event. Their leader, seeing it, was momentarily distracted. That was all the time Modric needed to thrust his knife into the invader's heart.

The remaining intruders fled, racing across the open space to their waiting horses and disappearing deep into the forest.

The meadow became eerily silent. No birds chirped. No insects buzzed. Even the babbling of the nearby stream seemed muted.

For long moments, no one spoke. No one moved. No one made an effort to help the peasant or his wife, for all knew they were cursed.

Bleeding from his wounds, the Highlander stumbled toward his wife. With great tenderness he kissed both her hands, then bent to brush his lips over hers. "If I could, Cerese, I would take every one of your pains unto myself."

"There is no need, Modric." She touched a hand to his cheek. "The pain is gone. Now there is only great joy that our sons have been born."

He examined the two crying infants, so alike that even their lusty cries were the same. "Dillon," he called to his young son, "come welcome your little brothers. We will name them Sutton and Shaw."

The boy peeked at the two tiny red, mottled faces, nestled in their father's arms. As they began to wail, the boy's lips split into a wide smile.

"Do you not see?" the man asked, as he gave his wife a look filled with love. "You have given me more than beautiful, perfect sons. Their strange, mysterious birth delivered us from our captors. It is because of them that we are alive."

"'Tis true," came a hushed voice from the crowd. "Did you see how the invaders fled when they caught sight of the two bairns?"

The crowd began whispering among themselves. Soon the whispers grew into a murmur, and then into a roar as they realized that they had indeed been delivered from the jaws of death.

"It is truly a miracle," one of them shouted. "We have been touched by the gods. And you, Modric, have been ordained from above as our new leader."

His two companions, who had fought so bravely by his side, appeared thunderstruck. How could the fates have permitted Modric, of the Clan Campbell, to be singled out as leader? Had they not risked their own lives to save his? Was this, then, to be their reward for their loyalty? Must they now submit their wills to the will of Modric?

Like an insidious vine that chokes the life of its host, the first stirrings of jealousy began to take root, strangling whatever bonds the three had shared for so long.

Unaware, Modric lifted the boy in one arm and the infants in the other, and turned to face the people. Having forgotten their fear, most gathered around, laughing, shouting, cheering.

"Until now, my only desire was a chance to till the soil in peace. But for the sake of my sons, Dillon, Sutton and Shaw, I will accept the role of leader and agree to use my weapons in the defense of all. I pray I will be a good leader. But hear me well. Let the word go forth. One day it will be the sons of Modric—" his face shone with joy; his voice thickened with emotion "—Dillon, Sutton and Shaw, who will be hailed as great leaders among our people."

Those words were the final indignity.

Upton, hearing him, shouted, "I cannot swear loyalty to you, Modric. Though I have no wife or offspring as yet, one day my own sons will be equally strong, and equally capable of leading our people. I'll not have them bowing to another."

"Bow? I do not ask you to bow to me, old friend. Merely to stand beside me, as loyal man-at-arms. For the gods have chosen me to be your leader."

"'Twas not the gods who chose you. 'Twas these fools," Upton declared.

With a look of sadness, Modric turned to the other. "And you, Thurman? Do you stand against me, as well?"

His friend was clearly undecided. It was well-known that a man without comrades in these fierce Highlands stood little chance of surviving the hordes of marauders. He glanced toward the dark-haired woman who stood to one side. Seeing the look in her troubled eyes, he swallowed his pride, though it tasted as bitter as gall. The woman was not his, and it was whispered that her heart lay with another. But he knew that she could be swayed by his words.

"I will stand with you, my kinsman," came Thurman's response as he took his place beside Modric, to the cheers of the people. At once the woman crossed the distance to stand beside him.

The Highlander clapped a hand on Thurman's shoulder. But his sad, haunted gaze was drawn to Upton, who had long been his closest friend.

"I swear this, Modric of the Clan Campbell," Upton Lamont vowed as he pulled himself onto the back of a shaggy stallion. "Your progeny will live to curse this day. For one day our offspring will clash, and it will be mine who will emerge victorious."

With a last lingering look at the beautiful woman who stood with head downcast beside his friend, Upton Lamont disappeared into the forest.

Modric, of the Clan Campbell, became known as a fearless leader among his people. And when he gave his life for those he loved, his sons vowed to continue his legacy.

Chapter One

Scotland—1315

"Forgive me, m'laird. A messenger has just arrived from Edinburgh." Mistress MacCallum, plump housekeeper of the Campbell stronghold, Kinloch House, bustled into the great room. She was trailed by a lad whose soaked and filthy cloak bore testimony to his arduous journey through the Highland forests. The messenger paused at the laird's table and presented his missive.

Accepting it, Dillon said absently, "See the lad is fed and given a pallet, Mistress MacCallum."

"Aye, m'laird."

As they walked away Dillon studied the scroll, then glanced across the table at his wife. "Rob commands my presence in Edinburgh."

Leonora looked stricken. "Oh, Dillon. Have you not given enough? You fought nobly by Rob's side. You spilled your blood at Bannockburn. But the battles are over. Robert the Bruce has all that he desires. You deserve some peace."

Amusement danced in Dillon's eyes, and he turned to his cousin, Clive, who sat at the far end of the table. "Ever my loyal protector, is she not?"

Clive smiled sardonically. "Would you be brave enough to say that to Rob himself, my lady?"

"I would indeed, if he were here. But since he is so far away, how am I to do that?"

"You may tell him when you see him in Edinburgh," Dillon said with a laugh. "For you are commanded to accompany me."

She blinked. Then her tone turned imperious. "Commanded?"

He reached out to place a hand over hers. "It is a request, but since Rob is now king, it is actually a command. He desires our company at the festivities honoring our nation's independence."

"A royal command." Leonora relaxed. Having grown up with English royalty, she was not awed by the prospect of spending time in the company of the most influential men in Scotland. But since her marriage to the Scots laird, she had grown accustomed to the slower pace of life in the Highlands. She was as comfortable here as if she'd been born to it.

Dillon's young sister, Flame, however, was another matter. She had spent her entire life in the primitive Highlands, and the thought of a big, bustling city like Edinburgh sounded like a grand adventure.

"And what of me?" she asked. "Am I to be included?"

"I don't think—"

Before Dillon could voice his intentions, Leonora interrupted. "I think it would be a fine idea to expose Flame to a life other than this."

"And what is wrong with this?" Dillon spread his hands to indicate the tapestry-hung walls, the glowing candles, the elegant touches his English-born wife had brought to his Highland home. He nodded toward the rows of tables at which sat dozens of hardy Highlanders, enjoying a midday meal, while servants bustled about offering platters of steaming food. Since the defeat of the English at Bannockburn, life had grown peaceful in the Highlands. Or as peaceful as life could ever be in this rough, primitive land where clan still battled clan.

"Nothing is wrong with it—" Leonora pinned her husband with a look "—if you think the most important thing a young woman can learn is how to ride without benefit of saddle, and how to wield a sword like a man."

"Teaching Flame a woman's ways is your job," he remarked, "not mine." He glanced from his wife to his sister, intending to put an end to this discussion. But seeing the pleading look in Flame's eyes he quickly relented. Besides, the touch of his wife's hand had softened his resolve. "Very well. The lass can accompany us."

"And Clive?" Flame turned to her ebony-haired cousin, who had come to live at Kinloch House after the death of his father, Thurman. Because she was so tenderhearted, Flame insisted upon including this quiet, solemn cousin in all her plans. "Is he not invited, also? After all, Dillon, you said yourself that he fought nobly by your side."

"That he did." Dillon turned to his cousin. "Do you wish to attend the festivities in Edinburgh, Clive?"

The lad shook his head. "Like my father before me, I much prefer the simple life of the Highlands."

"Are you daft?" Flame asked. Then a slow smile crossed her lips. "Or has a female caught your eye?"

The dour young man flushed clear to the tips of his ears.

"Enough, Flame. Show some respect." Dillon pushed from the table and turned to his brothers. "Sutton and Shaw, come with me. There is much to discuss before I take my leave."

Sutton nudged his twin brother, Shaw, and said with a confidence born of years of training as a Highland warrior, "You need have no fear, Dillon. With my sword, and Shaw's prayers, Campbell land will be in good hands while you're away."

"Och. Ye've picked a fine time to leave for Edinburgh." Walcott Maclennan, whose bushy white eyebrows nearly obscured his lively dark eyes, was fairly dancing with indignation.

"What is the trouble, old man? You've known for days that we were leaving for Edinburgh." Dillon Campbell pulled himself into the saddle and glanced down at his grizzled old man-at-arms.

"Aye. And so does half the countryside, 'twould appear," complained the old warrior. "No sooner is the word out that the laird of Clan Campbell is leaving his Highland fortress unattended than the raids have begun again."

"Raids?" Dillon's attention was immediately diverted from the long line of horsemen awaiting his signal to depart.

Up ahead, his wife, Leonora, gave final instructions to the servants who accompanied the wagons bearing clothing and household items, before being helped into her saddle. Beside her rode Dillon's younger sister, Flame, who was impatient to begin her new adventure.

"Three riders arrived this morrow, all of them bearing news of flocks being stolen and huts burned," Walcott said. "Praise the Lord that no one was killed. But according to your cousin, Clive, the raids occurred on Campbell land. And all carried out in the dark o' the night by cowardly villains too afraid to show their faces. Some clans have placed a price of one hundred gold sovereigns on their heads."

"Is this true, Clive?"

The tall young man nodded.

"Where did these raids occur?"

"Breadalbane, Cawdor and Loudon," replied Walcott Maclennan.

The laird of the Campbells mentally calculated. "All within a night's ride of Argyll."

"And who in Argyll bears a grudge against the Campbells?" Clive asked.

For the space of several seconds the two men stared at each other.

"Upton Lamont," Dillon breathed. "Leader of the Clan Lamont."

"Aye." Clive studied his cousin carefully. "And who better to lead the raids than Upton?"

"He would be an old man by now," Dillon scoffed.

At the mention of age, the white-bearded warrior standing beside Clive stiffened his spine, as if to remind his young laird that he could still lift a sword with the best of them. "Not so old. Upton would be nearly the same age as y'er father, rest his soul. But as ye know, the two were mortal enemies. In y'er father's day Upton Lamont became known as the Lawless One. If the anger has simmered all these years, 'twould be a perfect way for Upton to avenge himself, when he thought y'er defenses were weak."

"Weak!" Sutton, having overheard, swaggered forward with all the confidence of a young stallion. "Let the word go out to all the countryside that Dillon has left the defenses of the clan in my capable hands while he is in Edinburgh. I challenge any man who thinks he can best me with sword, lance or longbow."

"Ah, ever the humble one," came a voice behind him.

Sutton turned and dropped an arm around his twin's shoulder. "I speak only the truth. My prowess is well-known."

"Aye," Shaw said with a laugh. "But of which skills do you boast? Your skill with weapons? Or wenches?"

"Well, since you have already pledged yourself to the Church, and refuse to show interest in either weapons or wenches, I decided it was up to me to do the work of two men."

Shaw's eyes danced with laughter. "So that is what drives you. You feel responsible for my share of the females, as well as my share of the wars. I'll remind you, I've spent a lifetime praying for that soul of yours."

"Which is why I sleep so soundly, knowing my brother has the ear of God Himself. I shall have all the sinful pleasures, and you shall atone for them."

Dillon chuckled. These two brothers, so alike in looks that only family could tell them apart, yet so different in nature, could always be counted on to make him forget his troubles. Sutton, emotional, impatient, was known throughout the countryside as a fierce, hotheaded warrior. When he wasn't fighting, he was bedding every beautiful maiden in the Highlands. Quiet, thoughtful Shaw, on the other hand, had pledged himself to the Church, and had agreed to leave within the year to live among the monks who had raised him and his brothers after the death of their parents. In the monastery of Saint Collum, he would take his first vows of poverty, chastity and obedience, while beginning his studies for the priesthood.

Dillon had no doubt that between them, these two young giants, who stood head and shoulders above even the tallest Highlanders, could handle any problem that might arise.

"I leave our people in your capable hands, my brothers. Sutton, pay a call upon Upton Lamont, and see if the old thief is hiding any flocks taken from our kinsmen. If he is, I charge you to mete out justice and see that the sheep are returned to their rightful owners."

"With pleasure," Sutton replied.

Seeing the dangerous gleam in his brother's eye, Dillon added, "But I would caution you to temper justice with mercy, Sutton. Lamont was a lad when our father was young. He'll be no match for the likes of a strong young bull like you. And I charge you, brother," he said, turning to Shaw, "to storm heaven with your prayers for our safe return."

"Aye, Dillon," Shaw answered. "And I'll pray for the lasses who live between here and Lamont's land. For Sutton will surely try to bed as many of them as he can."

"And what of me?" Clive challenged. "Shall I accompany Sutton to Lamont's fortress? Or do you trust only your brothers to lead in your absence?"

"Cousin," Dillon said gently, "if Flame is correct, there is a lady causing you great distraction lately. By absolving you of all duties, I give you leave to pursue her."

"And pray she does not meet up with Sutton," Shaw muttered, dropping an arm around his cousin's shoulders.

For a brief moment Clive's eyes flared with temper, before he visibly relaxed.

At once Shaw squeezed his shoulder reassuringly. "I jest, cousin. Whatever Sutton's flaws, he is an honorable man. He would never bed another man's woman. Would you, brother?"

"Nay. I have trouble enough keeping up with my own to ever consider taking on another's."

With a laugh Dillon signaled for the journey to begin. Amid a cloud of dust, two columns of horsemen moved smartly out, led by a standard-bearer, proclaiming to all who approached that this party was under the protection of the Clan Campbell. The columns of soldiers were followed by the women and servants. After them came the procession of wagons and carts laden with food and household goods. Dillon and more than a dozen of his finest soldiers, including his old man-at-arms, took up the rear.

As their party descended into a green valley and faded from sight, Sutton turned to Shaw with a grin. "As of now, brother, we are the lairds of Kinloch House."

He glanced up suddenly as a groom appeared leading Clive's horse. "You leave so soon, cousin?" To his brother he said laughingly, "You see? He cannot contain himself. Already he flies into the waiting arms of his woman."

Clive gave them both a wide smile before saluting smartly and riding off without another word.

Sutton turned away, draping an arm around his twin's shoulders. "Come, Shaw. The first thing I intend to do is order Mistress MacCallum to bake me her finest tarts. Thus fortified, I intend to seek out Upton Lamont and his band of cutthroats."

"You intend to ride alone?"

Sutton nodded gravely. "'Twould be dishonorable to leave the fortress unprotected while Dillon is away. Besides," he added, touching a hand to his sword, "I need only this to stand up to the Lamonts. I'll teach them the proper respect for the name Campbell."

It had been raining all day, beginning with a fine mist, gradually increasing to a steady downpour. Shivering in his cloak, Sutton dismounted and tethered his horse, then crawled to the top of a hill overlooking the Lamont fortress, Inverene House. The buildings, a timber manor house and chapel of dull gray stone, loomed out of the mists like shrouds. They were well fortified by nature, with steep, forested cliffs behind and a loch flowing in front, making a surprise attack impossible.

From his location it was difficult to see beyond the walls, but Sutton imagined that life inside Inverene House was much the same as life at Kinloch House. The laird would be supping in the great hall, attended by servants. But there the similarity would end. Old Lamont would be perhaps laughing at the poor peasants who had been boldly robbed of their precious flocks. If the old laird had carried out even half the raids attributed to him over the years, he was indeed a blackhearted lout.

Sutton shivered again and wished for a fire. Instead, he took shelter beneath an outcropping of boulders and devoured the last of the tarts Mistress MacCallum had baked especially for him. That done, he hunched deeper into his hooded cloak and waited.

It was a good night for thieves to ply their trade, he thought, glancing heavenward. Clouds obscured the moon and stars. Rain would mute the sound of hoofbeats. Peasants, weary after a day of backbreaking labor, would seek the comfort of home and hearth.

Aye. A good night for thieving. And a better night for catching them.

"Good even, Father." A beautiful, dark-haired young woman kissed the bewhiskered cheek and lifted a candle from the nightstand beside her father's bed.

"Good even, Sabina."

Across the room a slender figure straightened from the hearth, where a roaring fire had been laid. "I've added another log, Father. It should last until the morrow."

"Thank you, Merritt." The old man smiled as his younger daughter lifted a tangle of red curls from her eye before crossing to him and brushing a kiss across his lips.

The two young women fussed over the old man, setting a goblet of ale beside his bed, tugging the furs up to his chin, before taking their leave.

In the next room they went through the same ritual, except that the figure in the bed was small and slight, with a cap of shiny red curls and bright, inquisitive eyes.

"Here is the sword you requested, Edan." Merritt handed her little brother a weapon that was so heavy he could hardly lift it with both hands.

As her sister deposited a goblet of goat's milk on the nightstand she added, "Though why you'd want it, heaven only knows."

The little boy shrugged. "I like the feel of a weapon in my hand."

Merritt grinned at him. "Mayhap you would like a dirk, as well."

Edan reached beneath the covers and retrieved a jewel-handled knife, which glinted in the firelight. "Father gave it to me. He said it belonged to his father."

"Then I would say you are well fortified."

"Aye."

His two sisters laughed and tousled his hair before brushing kisses over his cheeks. With a wave of their hands, they walked from the room and drew the door shut behind them.

As they made their way to their own rooms, they could be heard calling out loudly to each other, "Good even, Merritt."

"Good even, Sabina. Sleep well."

"If ye've come for the gold…" The peasant shuffled to his feet at the sight of the one known as the Black Campbell.

"Aye." A cloaked figure snuffed out the single candle, plunging the hut into darkness. "And to hear news of the latest attacks."

The peasant was grateful for the gloom that hid his discomfort, for his news was, as usual, not what the other would welcome. "We've done as you bade, m'laird. Your secret pastures are filled with sheep and horses taken from y'er enemy. But we cannot rid ourselves of these cursed Avengers. Each time we succeed in securing fresh bounty, they discover our hiding places and retrieve them from under our very noses. There are some in the Highlands who hail them as chivalrous warriors."

There was an ominous silence, before the leader said, "Then we shall use their reputation for our own purposes. Commit even more evil deeds, and spread the word that all are the work of these Avengers. That will free us to do as we please, without fear of retribution."

The peasant's eyes lit. "Ye are indeed blessed with a facile mind."

"Aye. And a restless sword. So see that you follow my instructions carefully, or you will feel its sting." His voice lowered. "Now hear me. I have a most urgent chore for you and your men."

The peasant listened intently as his leader spoke of old enemies, of ancient hatreds, of the latest who must die. But, though the peasant claimed few loyalties, the name of his victim shocked him, for it was one he knew well—Sutton Campbell. A short time later the two left the hut and disappeared in opposite directions of the dense forest.

* * *

The night was black as pitch, with no moon or stars to ease the darkness. Through the misty rain, a large, flat-bottomed boat moved silently across the loch. Even before it touched the far shore, two cloaked figures jumped over the side into the water and secured the boat, then led their horses from the boat to the marshy shore. As soon as they had pulled themselves into the saddles, the horses took off at a run.

Sutton sat up and rubbed his eyes, cursing himself for having fallen asleep. Straining to see into the darkness, he watched and listened. Already the sound of horses' hooves was fading into the distance. Drawing his cloak around him, he made his way to the loch. There he found the boat, hidden among some rushes along the bank.

So, he thought with a grim smile, his predictions had been accurate. He settled himself in the tall weeds, determined to remain awake and alert. For there was nothing Sutton enjoyed more than a good battle. His blood was already hot at the mere thought of it.

If old Lamont was out thieving, he would have to pass this way to return home. And when he did, Sutton would be here to catch him in his dark deed.

In the rain, the two figures dismounted and picked their way carefully over the mossy ground of open meadow until they came to the edge of the forest. Slipping between trees, they inched closer to the crofter's cottage, until they were so close they could hear the soft snoring from within. For several minutes they listened, then, content that the crofter and his sons had not been disturbed, moved on to the high meadow that sheltered the animals.

Weaving quickly among the clusters of sheep and cattle, they tied as many as they could. Within minutes the two were headed back across the open space, leading dozens of protesting animals.

As they ran past the cottage, a candle suddenly blazed in the darkness.

"'Twas the bleating of the sheep. It has awakened those inside," came a tense whisper.

"Aye. Run."

They continued running even when the door opened, spilling light into the darkness. A man's voice could be heard swearing impatiently.

One of the thieves stumbled and nearly fell, but at the last moment remained upright and limped on. That slight delay gave the crofter and his sons a chance to gain some ground. They could be heard directly behind, shouting orders to stop or be killed.

At a whispered command, half the animals were released. At once, sheep and cattle milled about in confusion. The crofter and his sons were shouting and swearing as they fought to make their way through the maze of dark shapes.

By the time the thieves made it to the place where their horses were tethered, their breathing was labored. One was limping badly. They vaulted onto their mounts, still keeping a grip on the lead ropes.

As they whipped their horses into a run, an arrow sang through the air, missing one of the cloaked figures by mere inches. More arrows followed as the two dropped low, hunching over their horses' backs. They sailed across an open meadow, then disappeared below a ridge. Behind them could be heard the sound of horses, running hard and fast, keeping time with their own.

Despite the lack of light, their mounts moved unerringly, passing darkened huts and cottages, keeping to the forests and high meadows. And still the horsemen trailed them, close behind.

By the time they reached the loch, their energy was flagging. But their mounts, eager to return to the stables, knowing that food and rest awaited them, strained against the ropes of animals dragging behind.

Seeing that the crofter and his sons were hot on their trail, one rider suddenly drew up sharply and released more animals in order to create more confusion, while the other rider continued ahead.

As the lone horseman reached the water's edge, a giant loomed out of the mist, sword lifted in challenge.

"Upton Lamont," roared the giant's voice. "I know what deeds you do under cover of darkness. In the name of Clan Campbell, I order you to surrender your stolen property and submit to the justice of the Highlands."

The figure reined in, dismounted and withdrew a sword, circling the giant warily.

Sutton advanced on the hooded figure and was reminded of Dillon's admonition to temper justice with mercy. His adversary was stooped and slight of stature, moving with a noticeable limp. One swipe of a sword would cut the old man into pieces.

"I do not wish to kill you," he called as he lifted his weapon. "But you must be taught that, on Campbell land, a man's property is sacred. No one has the right to help himself to what another has earned by the sweat of his—"

His voice was abruptly cut off by a dull thud. It was a sound that every Highlander knew and feared—the sound of an arrow sinking deep into flesh and bone.

As the arrow struck, Sutton felt the heat first, as though a flaming stick had been embedded in his flesh. A second arrow pierced his back, and the heat turned to pain. Hot searing pain that ripped through him, dropping him to his

knees. He tried to stand, but his body refused to obey.
With a supreme effort he got to his feet. He staggered,
managed a few steps, then stumbled before falling heavily. He was aware of two cloaked figures standing over him.

"God in heaven." The voice was hushed, breathless.
"'Twas a trap. The villains have been here ahead of us, just
waiting to catch us. Their arrows have killed this stranger."

Another voice, equally hushed, admonished, "You
cannot be certain he is dead. We must take him with us."

"They're nearly upon us. And a second band of riders
is already riding hard and fast, to cut us off from escape.
We've already lost the sheep. Must we lose our lives, as
well, for the sake of this stranger?"

The voice was soft but insistent. "We cannot leave him."

There was a sigh of impatience. "Aye, then. But we
must move quickly. There's no time for gentleness."

Sutton felt himself being dragged across grass, across
sand, and his last coherent thought was that they were even
stealing his flesh from his bones, tearing him apart limb
from limb, as he was dumped unceremoniously into the
bottom of a boat. And then he was floating, floating. And
the pain grew and grew until, at last, darkness enveloped
him, and he slipped into blessed unconsciousness.

Chapter Two

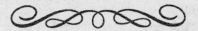

"**Y**ou linger overlong on your prayers this morrow."

Shaw looked up at the sound of Father Anselm's voice. "I had thought the chapel empty."

"So it is. The others have all gone." The old monk hesitated, reluctant to intrude on the young laird's privacy. Then, seeing the look of concern in Shaw's eyes, he decided to plunge ahead. "I think I know what troubles you, my son. It is normal to experience some doubts as the time draws near to bid farewell to home and family. But once you are at the monastery, surrounded by others who share your burning zeal to serve God, you will realize that your decision was the right one."

"My prayers this day are not about entering the priesthood, Father."

"Nay?" The monk seemed relieved. "I had feared . . . What is it that keeps you on your knees, then? Perhaps if you share your troubles, I can help you find a way through them. There are few questions about our faith that I cannot answer."

"My fears are not for my faith." Shaw paused, then gave a weak smile. "What has always troubled me and sent me to chapel to pray?"

''Ah. Sutton,'' the old priest said as understanding dawned.

''Aye. I checked his pallet this morrow. It has been three days and still he has not returned from the Lamont fortress.''

Father Anselm gave a sigh. ''There are probably dozens of lovely wenches between our two borders. And you know Sutton.''

''I do. But this time...''

''This time he does not have Dillon to answer to. With this first taste of freedom, he will no doubt feast at the banquet of life.'' Realizing what he'd just said, the old priest clapped a hand to his head and dropped to his knees beside Shaw. ''I believe I'd better join you in prayer, lad,'' he muttered. ''Lest Sutton's appetite get the better of him.''

Shaw looked up from his ledgers as a servant entered carrying lighted tapers. Because of his tutoring by the monks, and his patience with the painstaking work involved in the keeping of books, it was only natural that he had been given the duty of seeing to the account ledgers for the clan. It was a job he did willingly, to ease his eldest brother's burden. Dillon much preferred overseeing clan property to looking over dusty ledgers.

Rubbing a hand over his weary eyes, Shaw asked, ''Can the day have fled already, Dara?''

''Aye, my laird.'' The young servant added a log to the fire. ''Mistress MacCallum sent me to summon you to sup.''

''Thank you. Tell her I shall be along shortly.''

Absently rubbing at a knot of tension in the back of his neck, Shaw walked to the window and studied the lengthening shadows as dusk settled over the land. He was not one to worry. He had learned long ago to place all his cares in God's hands. Still, the nagging little feeling persisted. It was not like Sutton to stay away so long. Especially since, with Dillon gone, Mistress MacCallum lavished so much attention on the younger lairds. She had promised Sutton his favorite tarts every night. Shaw smiled. Not even the most charming wenches in the Highlands could compete with the housekeeper's sweet confections.

With a sigh he crossed the room and strode toward the great hall. While he walked along the cavernous hallways, he convinced himself that Sutton was probably already there, tucking into his first hearty meal since leaving Kinloch House. As he entered the hall he scanned the faces of those present.

"Ah. Here you are, m' laird," the old housekeeper called. "I was afraid ye were going to absent yerself, as well, and there would be no one to enjoy the fruits of my labor."

"My brother is not here, then?" His smile faltered.

"Nay, m'laird."

"Has there been any message?"

Hearing the urgency in his voice, the old woman studied a spot on her apron. "None."

Shaw took a seat at table and sipped some ale, then picked at his food. At a nearby table, Father Anselm was regaling several of the men with stories about his time spent in a distant monastery, where the monks made some of the finest spirits in the land. At some other time, Shaw would have found the tale of interest. Tonight, he paid scant attention.

"Pheasant, my laird?" asked a young servant.

He shook his head and drained his goblet.

A second servant hovered nearby. "Tarts, my laird?"

"Nay. I have had sufficient. Give my thanks to Mistress MacCallum." He pushed away from the table and took his leave.

With a little frown of concern etched between her brows, the housekeeper watched him go. She knew her young lairds well enough to sense when they were troubled. And though she doubted that anything could ever harm the virile young Sutton, she shared Shaw's concern at his prolonged absence.

Alone in his sleeping chambers, Shaw leaned a hip against the edge of the balcony and studied the darkened land below. He struggled not to give in to the worry that had tugged at the edges of his mind all day. But the thought persisted. If Sutton had engaged the enemy and won, he would have wanted to share the victory with his brother. It was their way. The two shared everything. And though Sutton may have indulged his fondness for a warm bed and a willing wench, he would never remain away from Kinloch House for so long a time.

Unless he had no choice.

Taking leave of his own room, Shaw stormed across the sitting room he shared with his brother and entered Sutton's sleeping chamber.

As they had each night since Sutton had left, servants had prepared a fire to chase away the chill, in anticipation of their laird's return. In the glow of firelight, Shaw restlessly prowled the room, pausing to touch a hand to a quiver of arrows, or trace his finger around the rim of a basin of water. Except for the precious store of religious writings that stood beside his bed, a gift from Father Anselm, his room was identical to this.

He sank down on the edge of the pallet, awash in loneliness. No one else could understand how profoundly he was affected by Sutton's absence. They were not just brothers. Their hearts, their minds, their very souls were joined in some strange, mystical way. Though others were puzzled or perplexed by their bond, they never questioned it. It was enough to know that when one was at peace, the other could rest. When one was hurt, the other shared the pain.

Shaw lay down, pulling the edge of his brother's blanket around him. He couldn't bear the thought of returning to his own room. Tonight he would sleep in Sutton's bed, in the hope that it would bring him some measure of comfort.

Shaw drew a heavy traveling cloak around his shoulders and stepped onto the balcony. Though the world still lay in darkness, the first faint ribbons of light were already touching the horizon.

During the night his sleep had been disturbed with dark, violent images. Once he had sat bolt upright at the sound of Sutton's voice calling his name. Another time he'd awakened, damp with sweat, still trembling from the vague memory of a white-hot pain that had seared his flesh.

Carrying aloft a candle, Shaw made his way to Dillon's chambers and paused in front of the massive stone fireplace. Hanging above it was their father's sword. It was said that Modric, beloved leader of the Clan Campbell, had been the fiercest warrior of any who had ever done battle in the rugged Highlands. His courage in the face of overwhelming odds was still spoken of with reverence. This sword had preserved many a Highlander's freedom. At the cost of countless lives.

Setting aside the taper, Shaw lifted down the sword, testing its weight in his hands. He touched a finger to the blade, honed to a keen edge. The precious jewels embedded in the hilt glinted in the flickering light of the candle.

He stood for long moments, head bowed, overcome with emotion.

"So. Does this mean you have come to a decision?"

Shaw turned to see Father Anselm standing in the doorway.

"Aye. I must find Sutton."

"And what if you find him dead?"

Shaw's eyes narrowed. "He is not dead. I would feel it here." He touched a hand to his heart.

"Do you realize what it is you do?"

When Shaw said nothing, the old priest walked closer. "As your confessor, I know you nearly as well as I know myself. Since your decision to serve God as a priest, you have forsaken the ways of other men. You live a chaste life. Each of your days begins and ends with prayer. And I know for a fact that you have not lifted a hand in anger or violence against any man."

Shaw remained silent.

"Yet, by taking up your father's sword, you must know that you invite hostile action that might require you to respond in kind."

"Aye." Shaw's voice trembled with emotion. "But I feel I no longer have a choice."

"A man always has choices. Think, Shaw. After all that you have sacrificed for your faith, do you wish to be a man of this world or a man above it, a man of God?" The old priest lifted both hands, as if in supplication. "Do you want another man's blood on your hands?"

Shaw stared down at the sword in his hand for long moments, seeing in his mind's eye his father, his brothers, as they prepared for battle. He studied it, weighing not just the weapon but its effect on his life. There could be no going back. If he took a life, such a deed could not be undone.

With a deep sigh, he slipped the sword into the scabbard at his waist. Balancing several knives in his palm, he selected one and tucked it into his waistband, then secured a second in his boot. Straightening, he turned to the priest.

His voice no longer wavered, but was firm and commanding. "This, then, is my choice. I will wait no longer. I leave now for Inverene."

"Alone? 'Twould be madness. At least take a column of warriors along."

"And leave our fortress and people unprotected? I cannot choose a less honorable path than Sutton chose. I go alone. God willing, I shall meet my brother returning along the way. If not, I shall confront Upton Lamont and demand an explanation. And know this, Father Anselm. My father's sword is as sacred to me as are the Church vows I hope soon to take. I will not use this weapon unwisely. I will try every other means before I will resort to the sword. But before God, I swear that I will do whatever necessary to bring my brother safely home."

With a trace of sadness the old monk nodded and lifted his hand in a blessing. "Go with God, my son."

Shaw lay flattened on a ridge, studying the scene before him. The loch was so still its surface was a mirror, reflecting the fortress steeped in shadow and the forested cliffs behind it still touched with lavender.

All along his journey Shaw had anticipated the moment when he would come upon his brother, returning in triumph. Now, having reached the end of his journey, he felt a wave of bitter disappointment. What had gone wrong? What would he find in the home of his enemy?

He pushed aside the feeling of dread and latched onto something to fill his thoughts. As he had all his life, he

carefully thought out each step of his attack. On the far
side of the fortress, the forest offered protection. The
cliffs, though steep, could be scaled. That would be the
logical means of entering Inverene. On the other hand,
anyone attempting to cross the loch would be seen from the
watchtower, unless a man waited until darkness to cover
him. But as all Scots knew, there were creatures in the
lochs. Strange, massive creatures known to devour not
only men and animals but entire boats, as well. Often the
only things that remained after an attack by these monsters were bits of debris. Thus, no sensible Scot would attempt to use the loch at night, even to invade his enemy's
stronghold. Which was why, Shaw decided, as soon as it
was dark, he would defy the monsters and swim the loch.

That done, he would make his way to the dungeons,
overpower the guards and free his brother. He would leave
it to Sutton to decide whether they would slip away under
cover of darkness to the safety of their home, or remain
and subdue these damnable Lamonts.

He backed down the hillside and sat hunched deep in his
cloak. Tearing off a hunk of bread, he satisfied his hunger and waited as darkness slowly covered the land. Then,
bundling his cloak behind the saddle, he caught up his
horse's reins and led him to the water's edge.

"How does he fare?"

Sabina looked up as her sister entered the sleeping
chamber. "No better." With her dirk she cut away the
bloodied dressing. The wound was raw, the flesh around
it red and puckered. "Help me with this poultice."

Merritt knelt and struggled to lift one muscular shoulder, then the other, as her sister applied fresh linen soaked
with herbs and aromatic spices, then wrapped Sutton's
entire torso in fresh dressings.

"You labor for naught," Merritt muttered. "I fear he has lost too much blood to recover from these wounds."

"Aye. He grows weaker each day. But I must try."

"Why? The lout challenged you with his sword. Does he not deserve to pay?"

"He has already paid, Merritt," her sister said softly. "Would you have him forfeit his life, as well?"

Her younger sister shrugged in her characteristic way. "I have more important things to do than worry about this stranger." She stood and drew on a coarse cloak.

At once Sabina got to her feet, clutching Merritt's arm. "I worry about you, alone in the night. So many things could go wrong..."

Her sister's smile was quick. "Have no fear. You know I can handle any knave who challenges me."

"Aye. But the attacks have become more frequent. And much more violent. I should be with you, in case they come in greater numbers."

"Someone must tend this wounded giant." Merritt grasped the hilt of the dagger at her waist. "Besides, the lad wasn't born who can best me." She gave her sister a quick kiss on the cheek. "See to him. I'll see to the rest."

Sabina watched with a little frown of concern as her sister strode from the chamber. Merritt had always been the impulsive one. Quick to lash out in anger, quick to tease like an imp, and quick to lavish love on her family. But she had spoken truthfully. There were few who could best her in a fair fight. Sabina's frown grew as another thought intruded. When a man was fighting for his life, he rarely fought in a fair manner. Rather, he would do whatever necessary to survive.

A low moan issued from the stranger, and instantly Sabina dropped to her knees. For the moment, her worries for her sister were forgotten. Her patient had grown more feverish. A sure sign that the wound was not clean. And the potions she had given him so far had not worked their magic.

The loch was cold, and as dark as midnight. There was no moon, but ribbons of starlight danced on the ripples created by the man and animal moving silently across the dark expanse.

On the far shore they scrambled up the embankment. Shivering, Shaw donned his dry cloak, pulling the hood over his head for warmth. He left his stallion at the bank of the loch, thankful that its jet black hide would blend into the darkness. Slipping from tree to tree, he made his way to the stables. He pulled his knife from his waistband and moved stealthily through the shelter, expecting at any moment to confront the stable master. It was necessary to silence him before he could sound an alarm to the sleeping household.

He was puzzled to note that, except for the horses, the stables were empty. Still, he checked each stall, pushing aside the hay in his search for a sleeping groom. When he had examined the last stall, he heard a footfall behind him. Cursing himself for his carelessness, he whirled. And found himself face-to-face with a cloaked figure holding a small, deadly sword.

Chapter Three

"**Y**ou grow too bold, knave." The cloaked figure advanced, brandishing the sword. The voice was a strange, breathless whisper. "Now you even attempt to steal our horses."

Shaw's temper rose a notch at the brashness of this stable boy. "I was not stealing them, lad."

"Aye. You do not steal." There was a snort of disgust, and the blade of the sword glinted in the starlight as the figure began to circle. "Just as you do not steal our cattle, our sheep."

"You speak in riddles." Shaw watched warily, waiting for an opening. Though he could easily take the lad by sheer force because of his size, Shaw had to respect the weapon in the lad's hand. Besides, he did not wish to inflict any more pain than necessary. "I am no thief."

"You are more. You are a liar and a cheat."

"I am a Campbell—"

"God in heaven. Even worse than I'd imagined. A lying, thieving Campbell." The blade slashed out, neatly slicing into Shaw's arm.

With a hiss of pain Shaw drew back, only to have the small figure advance again. He felt a wave of fury. Was he going to allow this puny lad to back him into a corner?

"I have no wish to harm you," he said as he thrusted his knife, causing the figure to hurriedly sidestep. "But I will do whatever I must to defend myself."

"If you were interested in merely defending yourself, you would not have invaded Lamont land." The blade flashed again, managing to cut away Shaw's sleeve along with a small portion of flesh.

The pain was sudden, intense, and Shaw felt his carefully controlled temper rising.

"Fool," he shouted as his hand went to the sword at his waist. "Lower your weapon or prepare to die."

"Ha! You are the one who will die, knave."

The temptation to draw his sword was great, but Shaw resisted. He could not have this stranger's death on his conscience. Instead, he lifted his knife, determined to disarm his attacker.

Shaw soon found his opponent making up in quickness what was lost in size and skill.

With grunts and sighs they thrust and parried, each managing to draw blood, yet neither willing to give an inch.

"You show a fair amount of skill, lad," Shaw taunted. "But you do not stand a chance against a Campbell."

"The Lamont was not born who could not defend his property against a lying, thieving Campbell."

As they danced forward yet again, Shaw used his superior strength to force the weapon from his opponent's hand. It fell to the straw and he pressed his advantage, driving the cloaked figure back against the stall. Pressing the point of his knife against his opponent's throat, he called, "Concede."

"I concede nothing."

"Arrogant fool." He pressed the tip of his blade until he drew blood.

On a gasp of pain, two small hands lifted in a gesture of defeat. Satisfied, Shaw lowered his knife. But as he slipped it into his waistband, he realized his miscalculation. A wink of starlight flashed on the blade of a small, deadly knife as the figure leapt at him.

"Nay." With a cry of fury he wrestled his attacker to the hay, where the two struggled for control of the knife. And although his opponent managed to inflict yet another wound, it only served to deepen his anger.

"You leave me no choice," he shouted as he knocked the knife away and pinned his attacker beneath him.

"May you be damned in hell forever," came the furious whisper. "And may your father and mother—"

"Enough." Clasping the two small hands in one of his, he dragged them over his opponent's head, then closed his other hand over the mouth that was about to emit further obscenities. "Now you will listen to me," he said through clenched teeth. His breath was coming in short bursts, and his temper was still dangerously out of control. "I did not come here to be cursed. Nor did I come to steal. I desire only an audience with Upton Lamont. You will take me to him. At once."

In sullen silence, green eyes stared defiantly at him.

He drew in several long drafts of air, then, as his breathing returned to normal, he got to his feet and bent slightly, offering his hand. One small hand reached up, as if to accept his help. And then, before he could gauge what was about to happen, he was pulled forward into the hay and the cloaked figure ducked around him and raced from the stable.

"By heaven..."

He regained his footing and began to run. The figure darted across the open space that separated the stable from the house. Tossing aside his own cloak, which was impeding his progress, Shaw began to pick up speed, until he was directly behind his opponent. With a leap, he pounced, taking the other into the dirt with him.

Though his opponent put up a brave fight, Shaw was easily able to subdue the smaller, slighter figure. As they rolled around the hard-packed earth, his big hand came into contact with a roundness, a softness beneath the cloak that could only be a—woman's breast.

His movements seemed to freeze. He knew he ought to pull his hand away. And yet, for the space of several heartbeats, he could do nothing more than feel that soft, perfectly formed mound of flesh against his palm. Despite the cold, he began to sweat. His blood ran hot. His mouth went dry. And all the while, his mind seemed to have deserted him.

"Unhand me, you lout."

He blinked. Awkwardly he pulled his hand away. At once, his opponent began to scramble free. As a last resort Shaw dragged the figure back and straddled her, effectively pinning her, until she stopped struggling and became, if not subdued, at least less defiant.

"Now," he said, when he realized she had momentarily given up the fight. "What sort of game are you playing with me? Why did you not tell me you were female?"

"I . . . find it wise to conceal that fact from my opponents."

"Conceal it! But why?"

"There are men who would take advantage of such a fact."

At some other time, with some other female, he might have felt a twinge of sympathy. But if this woman suspected he harbored even a moment's tenderness, she would surely take advantage of the situation. She had already shown herself to be a sly, clever scrapper. Besides, at this moment he was still too agitated by the struggle to be touched by her plight. Agitated, and oddly aroused. It was not because of the female, he told himself. His reaction was merely the result of the hard, physical exertion.

He stood and offered her a hand up. This time, as her small hand was engulfed in his, he braced himself, in case she decided to trick him again. However, she merely allowed herself to be helped to a standing position and began brushing the dirt and hay from her backside.

For her part, Merritt was horrified by her reaction to this lout's touch. She had long boasted to her sister that the man wasn't born who could make her blood heat or her pulse race. So why was it that she had reacted thus to this stranger? She shrugged aside such foolish questions and concentrated instead on how to escape.

"Never would I have knowingly caused pain to a woman," Shaw said softly. "Now you will explain yourself at once."

At that moment the clouds that had obscured the moon drifted across the sky, leaving them both bathed in moonlight. Shaw beheld a vision that had his jaw going slack.

Hair the color of fire tumbled free of the hood, spilling around a face that could have been carved from alabaster. The female's eyes were as green as a Highland pool. Her lips were lush and firm, and pursed into a pout.

At that precise moment she turned and tilted her head to look up at him. He heard a gasp. She grew visibly pale, and her eyes rounded in shock and horror.

"Did you not hear what I said?" he demanded. "You will explain yourself."

But she merely shrank away from his touch and cried, "Sweet Virgin, I have been possessed by a ghost."

She turned and began to run.

This time Shaw was quicker and, catching her roughly by the arm, spun her around and held her firmly when she tried to break free.

"God in heaven, help me!" she shrieked. "I am in the clutches of evil."

Shaw wondered if any woman could be this convincing if she were merely playacting.

"Please," she whimpered. "Please unhand me."

She appeared sincerely terrified. Still, he refused to be made a fool again. "Woman, you go nowhere until you explain what trick you are up to this time."

"Trick? I would never try to trick a spawn of the devil."

He only tightened his grasp and commanded, "What are you saying?"

"When last I saw you—" she struggled to get the words out over the terror that constricted her throat "—you were lying in my sister's chambers, waiting for death to claim you."

The full impact of her words had him reeling. "Sutton! God in heaven, Sutton." Not overpowered and languishing in a dungeon, but something even more unthinkable—lying near death. Suddenly all his carefully laid plans were forgotten.

Without regard to his strength he caught her by the upper arms, lifting her off her feet until her eyes were level with his. She cried out, but he seemed incapable of hearing her.

Like a madman he snarled, "Woman, you will take me to your sister's chambers at once. And if you try any tricks, I will kill you."

As she regained her footing, Merritt was too terrified to argue. Rubbing her bruised arms, she led the way.

* * *

Shaw was too distraught to form more than a few fleeting impressions as they entered the fortress and made their way up the wide wooden stairs to the second story. But he was aware that the house seemed cold and empty. There were no candles to light their way, either in sconces along the walls or in chandeliers overhead. No servants appeared. No voices rang out as their footsteps echoed through the upper hallway.

"Where is everyone?" he demanded.

"They are all abed."

"And your sister's room?"

"This one." She paused before a closed door, wondering what she would find on the other side. Surely the stranger had died, and his ghost had somehow refused to pass over to that other life.

When she lifted a hand to knock, he impatiently pushed her aside and kicked in the door, then shoved her inside ahead of him.

From her position beside the pallet, Sabina looked up in surprise at the giant who accompanied her sister. As soon as she glimpsed Shaw's face, her expression mirrored that of Merritt's, changing to shock, then horror.

"You cannot be..." She looked from the face of the stranger on the pallet to that of the giant standing before her. A giant who was brandishing a knife.

"He calls himself a Campbell," Merritt muttered, watching for a chance to relieve him of his weapon.

"Aye." Sabina recalled the words Sutton had shouted when he'd attacked. "That is what this one called himself."

"Witch, what have you done to him?" Without waiting for her response, Shaw pushed her aside and commanded, "You will both lie on the floor against that wall."

When they hesitated, he moved menacingly closer. "Now."

The two women did as they were told and watched in silence as Shaw knelt beside his brother and touched a hand to his fevered brow.

Sutton moaned and Shaw gave a shudder of relief when he realized that, though his brother's heartbeat was weak and his breathing shallow, he still clung to life. He wrapped his arms around Sutton and pressed his face to his throat, listening to the thin, feeble pulse.

He remained that way for long moments, taking comfort in the fact that his brother was alive. Frighteningly pale. Dangerously weak. But, praise heaven, alive.

At last, after taking in several deep breaths, Shaw lifted his head. "What have you given him?"

Sabina and Merritt glanced at each other, then at this stranger.

"Speak, woman. What have you done to heal him?"

"Yarrow, mixed with herbs, to stop the bleeding," Sabina said haltingly. "I have need of more herbs, but I am afraid to leave him alone while I search for them."

"That is what servants are for." Shaw gently rolled his brother to one side and stripped away the dressings. For long minutes he examined the wounds. They were the familiar deep puncture wounds made by arrows and, from the looks of them, festering. His anguish was evident in his eyes as he carefully replaced the dressings and drew the covers over Sutton's naked body.

"And for his pain?"

Sabina shook her head sadly.

"You have given him nothing to ease the pain?" He ran a hand through his hair distractedly, thinking about Mistress MacCallum's tender ministrations. There would have been balms, salves, ointments. A potion for sleep, another for fever, an opiate for pain. What sort of savages were these Lamonts?

"You will send for a servant at once."

Again he saw the look that passed between the two women before the fiery-haired one spoke. "There is but one servant, and Astra is too old to hear unless I climb the stairs and rouse her myself."

"One servant . . . ?" For the first time he took the trouble to study his surroundings. The room was a shabby relic of whatever former splendor it might have been. The floors were bare of rugs or even rushes. Except for a massive bed, which dominated one corner, the place was nearly bare of furniture. The bed hangings were tattered and threadbare. A glance at the fireplace assured him that it was not a log burning there but the legs of a settle, which had been broken up for firewood. His brother's pallet was little more than a pile of rags.

His eyes narrowed. "What about loyal soldiers?"

"None," Sabina said softly.

He turned to study her as the truth dawned. No wonder his entry had been so easily executed. "This fortress is unprotected against attack?"

"My sister and I protect it," Merritt retorted as she started toward the door.

He caught her roughly by the arm. "Nay, firebrand. I do not trust you." He turned to Sabina. "You there. You will fetch the servant."

She scrambled to her feet and, limping slightly, started toward the door.

"And remember this." Shaw drew his knife and pressed it against the pale flesh of Merritt's throat. "If you try to trick me, it will cost your sister her life."

Sabina's eyes mirrored her terror. She quickly nodded and hurried away.

Shaw fought to subdue the anger that simmered. For Sutton's sake, he must keep a cool head. But the questions that whirled in his brain were enough to make any man crazed.

"Who did this to my brother?"

"You call him your brother," Merritt replied, "but he wears your face."

"And I his. And at this moment, I feel his pain." His grasp tightened and he pressed the cold blade of the knife to her throat. "Now, by heaven, you will answer. Which of you did this thing?"

She shrugged. "It was his own doing."

"He shot arrows into his own back?" With a furious oath he tangled a fist in her hair, yanking her head back, intent upon slitting her lying throat.

But before he could draw the dagger across her delicate flesh, she managed to whisper, "Nay. I only meant that the arrows were not intended for him. But because he interfered, he unwittingly became a target."

His movements stilled. "For whom were the arrows meant?"

"For the . . . Highland Avengers."

He grew silent a moment, digesting this. His eyes suddenly narrowed in thought. "You are lying, woman."

"I speak the truth."

"Do you now? Then how did you happen upon the scene?"

When she did not immediately respond, he caught her roughly by the shoulders and turned her until she was facing him.

She could see the barely contained fury in his eyes; could feel the way his fingers dug into her flesh. His voice was low, commanding. "Answer me, woman."

Merritt had no doubt that he would kill her. But she had long ago forsworn fear of dying, rather than permit any word or deed that would besmirch her family's honor. She swallowed and said in a breathy whisper, "Do what you will with me. I will tell you no more."

"Damn you, woman." He lifted the dagger.

At that moment, the door burst open, and her dark-haired sister entered, trailed by a blanket-draped hag whose gray hair stuck out at odd angles around a face that was as colorless as porridge.

"Merritt!" cried Sabina.

"Unhand that child," cried the old woman, who, when she opened her mouth, revealed only two teeth.

"I will release her only when she tells me the truth." Shaw lifted the dagger menacingly.

"What is it you wish to know?" Sabina demanded. She had already guessed by the determined look on her sister's face that Merritt had decided to defy this stranger, even with the threat of death.

"She has told me a twisted tale of strangers who attacked my brother because they thought he was one of the band of notorious Highland Avengers."

Sabina flicked a glance at her sister, then back to the stranger. "Aye. 'Tis true."

"More falsehoods. My brother would never go to the aid of such cutthroats."

"He did not aid them. He merely became caught up in their skirmish. And when it was over, he lay mortally wounded. And my sister and I brought him here to Inverene House."

Sabina watched as the stranger considered her words, before he slowly lowered his knife.

"In the event that this woman speaks the truth," he said to Merritt, "I will spare your miserable life for now."

Seeing the spark of hope that leapt into her eyes, he hastily added, "But you will instruct your servant to do exactly as I say, or you will all die."

As he released her, Merritt rubbed the tender flesh of her upper arms, where he had left his prints, and watched him from beneath lowered lids. She would teach this lying, thieving Campbell a lesson. One he would not soon forget.

Chapter Four

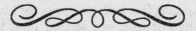

Shaw turned to the old servant. "The first thing you will do is go out into the countryside and harvest whatever herbs your mistress requires."

"In the dark of night?" The old woman's brows lifted.

"Aye. And be quick about it."

"It would be better if I could go along," Sabina protested.

"To plot your escape? Nay, woman. You will remain here."

At the finality of his statement, Sabina reluctantly recited a litany of herbs, plants and roots, while mentally fretting that she could not accompany the old woman, who had grown a bit forgetful.

"You must remember the willow bark, Astra, and bitterroot," Sabina instructed.

"And balsam," Merritt added.

The old woman merely nodded.

"You will not forget?"

"Ye will recall, my fine ladies," Astra said rather testily, "that I have forgotten more than ye will ever know about healing—"

Shaw interrupted. "Just remember, old woman, the lives of these two lie in your hands. They will remain here with me in these chambers until you return. If you should be tempted to go to a nearby village for help, or if you are not alone when you return, your mistresses will die by my hand before anyone can intervene. Is that understood?''

"Aye."

From the sullen look she shot him before taking her leave, Shaw was convinced that the old woman had indeed been planning just such a surprise for him. But, despite her barbed tongue, she seemed loyal to her two mistresses. He sensed that she would do as she'd been commanded, for their sakes. When she was gone, he indicated the bed. "You may as well rest. You are not leaving until your servant returns."

Merritt drew herself up to her full height and answered for both of them. "Do you think we would dare to close our eyes while there is a villainous Campbell watching?''

"The choice is yours," he said wearily.

"Nay, sir." Merritt touched a hand to the pain at her shoulder. "If we were given a choice, you and that savage brother of yours would be exiled from Inverene House at once."

"Hush, Merritt." Sabina placed a hand on her sister's arm. She was not eager to enrage the barbarian who had charged into her chambers wielding a sword. Besides, she had always found that more could be accomplished by being compliant than by being combative.

Her hand came away smeared with blood. "You're bleeding, Merritt," she cried. "Sit here by the fire and I will tend your wounds."

Shaw watched as the dark-haired woman efficiently washed away her sister's blood in a basin of water and dressed her wounds, using strips of linen torn from the bed hangings.

As the two women settled themselves in chairs in front of the fire, Shaw cast a longing glance at the bed. His wounds, though only minor irritations, were still bleeding. He was weary beyond belief. And he would have to keep watch throughout the night, until the servant returned. Even then, there would be no relief, for he would have to remain awake and alert and at his brother's side until Sutton was well enough to withstand the journey over treacherous terrain back to Kinloch House.

With a sigh Shaw drew a chair beside the pallet where his brother lay. Knife in hand, he sat stiffly at attention and began his vigil.

Shaw's head nodded, waking him with a start. For a moment he was completely disoriented, wondering why his body ached in so many places. Glancing down, he saw dried blood on his sleeve and tunic. His other sleeve was slashed and torn, revealing the chunk of flesh that still bled profusely.

He caught sight of his brother, lying as still as death. At once, he became alert. Reaching down, he felt the thready pulse. He glanced around. The room was in darkness, except for the faint glow of embers on the hearth. He could make out the two figures of the women, heads slumped, asleep in their chairs.

Some sound had disturbed him. Had it been the feeble shout of a child? Or the call of a night bird? Yet, as he strained, he could hear nothing more. Forcing himself to stand, he crossed the room and walked to the balcony. Below, the waters of the loch were dark and motionless. But as he watched, a sudden movement caught his eye, then disappeared. When he looked again, he could see nothing out of the ordinary.

Thinking it must be Astra returning with the herbs, he started to turn away. But a sudden flare of light rent the darkness, and as he turned back to watch, the blaze of light seemed to engulf the stables.

"God in heaven! Fire!" he shouted.

At once, both women stirred, then came up out of their chairs, running toward the door of the chamber. Shaw was ahead of them, racing down the stairs and out into the cold night air. He stopped short at the sight that greeted him. Fueled by thatch and dry timber, the fire spread with the speed of lightning. The intense heat made it impossible to get close. But even from a distance, the empty stalls were visible. Before the fire had been started, the horses had apparently been stolen.

Within minutes the roof of the stable caved in upon itself, and, fed by the flames, sent sparks shooting high into the midnight blackness. There was nothing anyone could do but stand and watch helplessly as the fire consumed the entire structure.

Shaw felt his rage growing. He needed his mount almost as much as he needed his weapons. Without a horse, he was trapped in the Lamont fortress, far from his own people.

He turned to where the two sisters stood clinging together, watching with similar looks of horror and disbelief. Their grief was palpable, as was their anger.

"So," he said, "I see firsthand the work of these Highland Avengers."

"This was not the work of the Avengers," Merritt said.

"And how would you know?"

She looked away, compressing her lips together.

"Can you think of any besides the Avengers who carry such enmity in their hearts," Shaw asked, "that they would burn your stables and steal your horses?"

Spearing a glance at her sister, Merritt replied, "The Highlands abound with men who suckled the milk of hatred from the moment of their birth."

Shaw was intrigued by her words, for he knew them to be true. He had witnessed bitterness between generations of Highlanders that seemed destined to go forever unresolved. Was that not true of their two families? The Lamonts and Campbells had been estranged since the time of their fathers.

A stooped figure emerged from the pall of smoke, carrying a basket filled with plants and roots.

"Astra," Merritt called. "Did you see who did this?"

"Aye." The old woman nodded toward the towering forest. "Horsemen, leading many horses."

"Did you know these men?" Shaw asked.

"Nay." She shook her head. "'Twas too dark to see their faces."

"But we know them to be your clansmen," Sabina added.

"And how would you know that?"

At his look, the dark-haired beauty turned away. But her fiery sister said, "It is the thieving Campbells who have always made our lives miserable. And because of them—"

"Nay, Merritt." Sabina caught her hand, adding, "There is no reason to confide in this stranger. He is one of them."

The two sisters turned away, leaving so many of his questions unanswered.

Seeing the old woman struggling beneath her burden, Shaw took the heavy basket from Astra's hands. She appeared genuinely surprised at his act of kindness. Leaning heavily on a gnarled walking stick, she trailed behind as they returned to the manor house.

*   *   *

Shaw followed the two young women to the kitchen, which showed the same signs of neglect as the rest of the house. The floor was bare of rushes. Several wooden benches lay battered and broken beside the fireplace, apparently to be used as firewood. To his amazement, he discovered that, except for a few dried fruits and vegetables, the larder was empty.

He thought of the larder at Kinloch House, filled with the carcasses of deer, boar, sheep and pigs, as well as pheasant and partridge. Anyone in the nearby villages requiring food need only ask the laird and it was given to them.

While the three women set about crushing herbs and grinding roots into paste, he made several trips outside and returned with logs and dried grasses, which he used to start a fire in the huge, blackened fireplace.

Soon the room took on a cheery note, as the warmth of the fire chased away the gloom of the predawn darkness. Astra made her way to Shaw's side, carrying a goblet.

"Ale, my lord?"

"Aye. Thank you."

It was the first nourishment he'd had in hours. He drained it in quick gulps and felt the warmth settle low in his stomach, then spread slowly through his veins, reviving him.

The old woman refilled his goblet before hobbling away.

Easing himself into a chair in front of the fire, he watched as Sabina and Merritt prepared a tea made from the bark of a willow. As the liquid bubbled, the strong earthy fragrance filled the kitchen.

He studied the two sisters, who were so different. It was not just their clothes, although Merritt's choice had his lips twitching in humor. While Sabina wore a modest gown of pale blue, to match her eyes, Merritt was dressed in the rough garb of a stableboy, with oversize breeches and boots, and a coarse hooded cloak. Sabina's hair was as black as a raven's wing; Merritt's the color of flame. Sabina stood a head shorter and had the calm demeanor of royalty. Merritt's every movement seemed charged with energy. While Sabina seemed comfortable in the kitchen, working with an economy of movement, Merritt's distaste for such lowly work was obvious in the way she sighed with impatience over each chore. Sabina seemed oblivious to everything except the herbs she was mixing. Merritt glanced up often, inquisitive green eyes studying the stranger who sat facing her.

"This will ease your brother's pain," Sabina said as she poured the strong willow tea into a goblet.

At once Shaw stood and led the women up the stairs to the chambers where his brother lay. Inside, he knelt and gently lifted Sutton's head so that the liquid could be forced between his lips. Taking the cup from Sabina, he murmured soothingly, "Drink, Sutton. We've brought you something for the pain. Drink. So that you might rest."

His brother was completely unresponsive, but with a great deal of patience, Shaw managed to force a little of the tea down his throat.

The women watched, silently marveling at the gentleness in one so strong. It was a quality they had rarely witnessed among Highland men.

"We will change his poultice now," Sabina said.

While Shaw lifted and turned him, Sabina and Merritt were able to remove the old bloody dressings and replace them with clean fresh ones. By the time they had finished, all of them felt drained from the effort.

"We must rest now," Sabina said. "For the night has been long, and we are near exhaustion."

"Aye." Shaw indicated the bed. "You may sleep there. Your servant can sleep on the floor next to your bed. I will sleep beside my brother."

The women were shocked at his suggestion, but it was Merritt who spoke for them. "You cannot keep us prisoners in our own home. We will not stay with you." She began to brush past him. "We are returning to our own rooms, to sleep until the morrow."

Catching her roughly by the arm, Shaw withdrew his sword and was rewarded with a flash of fear in her eyes.

"You will lie down." He gave her a shove, not only to add to her fear, but because the touch of her caused a strange kind of heat in his loins. A heat that was unaccustomed and unwelcome. "And you will do it quickly. My patience has reached its limit."

While Sabina and the old servant quickly retreated to the bed, Merritt lingered long enough to send him a withering look. "If I had my weapons, Campbell, you would not be so quick to give orders."

"If you had your weapons, and dared to defy me..." He dragged her close, until the heat of his breath stung her cheek. Up close she smelled of the earthy spices and herbs she had been mixing. An altogether pleasant fragrance that had him breathing it deeply into his lungs before he reminded himself how much he despised these Lamonts, who had been the cause of his brother's pain. "Woman or no, you would be dead. Now heed my orders and be quick about it."

He gritted his teeth as he shoved her away.

With her head high and her spine stiff, she marched to the bed and climbed beneath the covers. But she kept her eyes wide, continuing to watch him as he secured the room.

Barring the door from within, Shaw pulled a fur robe around himself and eased down beside his brother, taking care to place his sword in his right hand and a dirk in his left.

Though he was exhausted beyond belief, he knew he would never be able to fall asleep. Because the truth was, he was also exhilarated by the success of his quest. He had, after all, found his brother alive. Though he knew the next few days would decide Sutton's fate, Shaw was convinced that he had been brought to his brother's side during this critical time because Sutton was meant to live. Please God, he prayed fervently, Sutton had to live.

His gaze fell on the figures in the bed and his thoughts turned to the little firebrand, Merritt. She was a most annoying gnat, getting under his skin, stinging at the most unexpected times. It was obvious that, unlike her sister, Sabina, she'd had little training as a lady and much preferred the life of a warrior.

Why was she doing things that, by rights, ought to be done by her father? Where was the old villain? And where were the servants? How had Inverene House fallen into such disrepair?

So many questions. So many worries. His mind was reeling.

With the warmth of the fire at his back, and the heat of the ale in his belly, he soon gave in to the need to sleep.

Chapter Five

Merritt listened to the sounds of slow, even breathing. She knew that her sister and Astra were both sleeping soundly. But her concern was for the intruder. Was he truly asleep, or was he still watching?

She waited, biding her time. Though the Campbell had suffered only flesh wounds, they had gone unattended, causing him to lose much blood. His pain and exhaustion had been evident in his face. He would be hard-pressed to remain awake when the fire and the ale and the soft sounds of the night all conspired against him.

She was not a patient woman, but what she lacked in patience, she more than made up for in cunning. This stranger threatened the safety of her family. As always, she would do whatever necessary to protect them. And so she waited, and watched, and listened. And finally, when she could bear it no longer, she slipped silently from the bed and began to move stealthily across the room.

In the glow of the embers she could make out the glint of his sword. She would have to disarm him before slitting his throat. And she would have to move quickly, otherwise he would overpower her and gain the advantage. Her only chance lay in that brief moment of confusion when he was first jolted from sleep.

She inched closer, keeping her eye on the hand that rested atop the jeweled hilt of his sword. If she saw his fingers curl, or noticed his arm tensing, she was prepared to leap backward, out of harm's way.

His injured brother moaned in his sleep and she froze. Her heart was beating so loudly, she feared he could hear it. For long minutes she stood perfectly still, watching, listening. At last, convinced that he had not awakened, she began to move closer.

When she was beside him, she dropped to her knees and slowly, gradually, reached a hand to his sword. It did not occur to her to be afraid. Her only thought now was for the safety of her family. For their sake she would do whatever necessary.

When her fingers tightened around the hilt, she closed her eyes, envisioning what she must do. It was imperative that she lift the sword and bring it down across his throat with all the force she could muster, for she would get but one chance to slay her enemy.

Her fingers felt slick with sheen, and she offered a prayer that she would not falter as she grasped the weapon. That done, she opened her eyes. What she saw had her heart leaping to her throat.

Pale, cool cat's eyes were staring back at her.

And then, without warning, she was dragged unceremoniously to the floor and pinned beneath the furious Campbell.

"Fool," he muttered between clenched teeth. "Could you not even give me a moment's rest?"

She kicked and bit and scratched as she fought a losing battle against his considerable strength. "If I had accomplished what I set out to do, you would have had your wish. You'd have been given rest . . . for an eternity."

He grunted in pain as she raked her fingernails across his cheek. "There was no need for this, woman. I was fair with you."

To end her struggles he pressed his body firmly over hers, his thighs pinning hers, his hands grasping her flailing fists. "I could have killed you when I first encountered you in the stables, wench. But it was my intention to retrieve my brother and allow all those within these walls to dwell in peace."

She twisted her head from side to side, determined to fight him with every breath. "I will not listen to your lies," she whispered defiantly. "There has ne'er been a Campbell who did not say one thing while plotting another."

He could feel his temper getting the best of him. Clamping both her hands in one of his, he grasped her roughly by the chin, stilling her movements, forcing her to meet his eyes. "I speak the truth. My quest was a noble one."

"Noble," she rasped under her breath. The word was filled with contempt. "I find you hiding in my stable—"

His temper grew. "I was not hiding."

"And you attacked me."

"You challenged me first," he said through gritted teeth. "I had no choice but to fight."

"And now the stable has been burned to the ground and our horses stolen . . ."

He was outraged. "You cannot think that I was responsible—"

"And you continue to insist that you and your precious brother are merely innocent victims."

"Be quiet, woman. Can you not keep a civil tongue?"

"Oh, aye. You'd like that, would you? Shall I bow and scrape like old Astra, and offer you ale? And shall I say aye, my laird, and nay, my laird, and as you wish, my laird—"

"Damn you, woman!" Shaw's temper snapped. Without regard to what he was doing, he stifled her words with a hard, punishing kiss.

It had seemed the only way left to him. But the moment his mouth covered hers, he realized his mistake.

At the first touch of her lips, his blood, which moments ago had been merely heated from their struggle, was now molten lava. His breath backed up in his throat. For a moment his heart forgot to beat. Then his pulse quickened until he felt as if he'd raced clear to the top of a mountain.

In that first instant Merritt went very still, absorbing the shock. His kiss was so completely unexpected, she was caught off guard. And though her sense of independence protested, the sudden, shocking rush of heat overruled. All she could do was endure the press of his lips on hers, and the unexpected tug of desire it aroused in her, as her heartbeat began to race and her blood began to heat.

His hand fisted in her hair, and his mouth moved over hers, tasting, exploring. The body beneath his was so incredibly soft and yielding. Her lips were warm and firm. She tasted clean, fresh, like a Highland meadow kissed with early morning dew. She smelled of heather and wildflowers, exotic and primitive.

What had happened to him? Why was he indulging in pleasures he had long denied himself? And with, of all people, this free-spirited Lamont, who was not so much female as feline, resembling the mountain cats that roamed the Highlands.

Because she was prevented from fighting him, Merritt could do nothing more than endure. And by passively enduring, she found herself responding to this stranger in a way that scandalized her. Against her will, her lips opened for him as his tongue invaded the private recesses of her mouth. Her hands, still held firmly in his big palm, tensed.

Anticipating her resistance, he tightened his grasp.

Her heartbeat was so loud in her chest she could hear nothing else, except a soft sigh that escaped her lips. And though she wanted to believe it was a sigh of exasperation, she couldn't be certain it wasn't a sigh of pure pleasure.

Shaw was fully aroused. He knew he had to end this, and quickly.

He had taken his share of spills from saddles, and hard falls from trees. But he'd never been jolted with such force before. With his pulse roaring in his temples, his hand tangled in her hair, he allowed himself one last taste of her before he abruptly pulled away.

Merritt blinked, aware that the kiss had ended as shockingly as it had begun.

Both were overcome by powerful emotions that had them reeling. Shock—that a mere kiss could cause such troubling feelings. Disbelief—that they would have permitted such a scandalous act.

"Return to your bed, woman." He scrambled to his feet and strode to the fireplace, keeping his back to her.

"May you be damned in hell, Campbell." Even that epithet, hurled from between clenched teeth, gave her no satisfaction. She wanted to slap his smug, arrogant face. But she knew that might only inflame him to further indignities against her.

He heard her soft footfall as she hurriedly made her way to the bed; listened to the rustle of the bed covers as she quickly settled herself beside her sister.

As he lifted a piece of the broken chaise that was used for firewood, Shaw cursed and called himself every kind of a fool. It was the first time he could ever recall allowing his temper to get the best of him. And that temper, he realized, had led to an almost irresistible temptation.

He tossed the wood on the hot coals and watched as flames began to devour it. Wiping his hands along his tunic, he realized that they were none too steady.

The damnable woman had bewitched him. But it wouldn't happen again. It couldn't, he vowed. Because if it did, he wasn't certain he'd find the strength to resist.

The soft rosy light of morning filtered through the balcony window. Shaw sat beside his brother's pallet, watching the unsteady rise and fall of Sutton's chest as he took each labored breath. For the past hour Shaw had sat thus, willing his brother to breathe, to fight, to live.

From her position in the bed, Merritt studied the intruder, while pretending to sleep. What was it about this man that was so intriguing? He was, after all, a hated Campbell. The Campbells had been the enemy of the Lamonts for as long as she could remember. And the late-night raids, which had gone on for generations, only fueled the deep-seated hostilities. But there was something different about this vexing man, though she couldn't quite grasp it.

She closed her eyes, remembering their kiss. Her cheeks still burned at the shocking way she had responded to his kiss. Now that her sanity had returned, she felt like a traitor. A traitor and a fool. Never before had she allowed a man such intimacy. She should have fought him to the death.

"Let me go, ye savage," came Astra's voice. "I must prepare a meal before the laird awakens."

Merritt's eyes snapped open. The old servant faced the Campbell, who stood barring the door.

"The laird, is it?" Shaw asked with a trace of sarcasm. "And where was this laird last night, when his stable was burned and his horses stolen?"

"My father has given orders that he cannot be disturbed when he is sleeping," Merritt said, scrambling quickly out of bed.

"Sleeping?" Shaw shot her a suspicious look. "Or out stealing other men's cattle?"

Sabina, awakened by the argument, sat up, shoving dark hair from her eyes. "How dare you speak of our father in such a manner. He is a fair man and an honest one."

So, Shaw thought, the dark-haired one had as much fire and spirit as her sister, though she kept it hidden beneath a veil of meek humility.

He started toward the door. "Then you will not mind if I see for myself this noble paragon of virtue."

"Nay!" both sisters shouted in unison.

At once Shaw turned back to see them racing across the room. They skidded to a halt at the dark, dangerous look in his eye.

"What are you hiding?"

"We hide nothing." Merritt stiffened her spine and met his look squarely. Refusing to back down, she added tartly, "You have invaded our home and threatened our safety. You will not add to our misery by insulting our father. When he has finished his ablutions and goes below stairs to break his fast, you will have the opportunity to meet him."

"And his army along with him, I suppose?"

"We have told you the truth," Sabina said. "There are no others in Inverene House save family and old Astra. My father has no army."

"If he had," Merritt interjected, "would they not have stormed our chambers last night and rescued us, rather than force such...indignities upon us?"

She felt her flesh heat as her sister and the old servant turned to study her, and knew that she would have to deal with their questions later. She could pretend to the others that the only indignities were the loss of privacy and the domination by this intruder. For she alone must know of the more...intimate indignities she had endured.

Shaw's narrowed glance brought the full flush to her cheeks.

Having been reminded of his lapse, he felt his temper rise a notch, though he could not argue with her logic. What she said made sense. These women had no army hidden away beneath their roof. Else, they would have called upon its services last night.

"I require water and clean linens," he commanded imperiously. "And to assure that no one attempts to escape, one of you must remain with me at all times. You may decide which of you it shall be. The other will be free to accompany Astra while she goes about her chores."

Sabina turned to Merritt. "You know it is I who must see to Father, else he will fret."

"Aye. Go. I shall remain the Campbell's hostage," Merritt said with reluctant acceptance. "But you must bring me a gown and slippers. I cannot have Father see me like this."

Sabina and the old servant left the room and returned a short time later with clothes for Merritt, a basin of water and an armload of clean linen for Shaw, as well as a goblet of willow bark tea for Sutton, who remained in a deep sleep.

Ignoring his own needs, Shaw immediately knelt beside his brother, forcing the cup between his lips. For a moment Sutton stirred, coughing and choking as the hot liquid slid down his throat. But his eyes remained closed, and he seemed unaware of the one holding him.

"Sutton," Shaw whispered. "You have always been a brave warrior. Now you must fight. Do not give up. Do not leave me."

From her position beside the fire, Merritt watched in silence, feeling oddly moved by his words. It was clear that this man loved his brother deeply.

Would she not do the same for Sabina? Aye, she thought, as her hand clenched into a fist. She would move heaven and earth for the sake of any member of her family. But somehow, she had thought herself different from this savage, who was her father's enemy. Yet, watching him, she felt an unwelcome bond with this man. For she understood the love that drove him.

At last Shaw set aside the steaming liquid and settled his brother in the bedclothes. Then he walked to the basin and, removing his tunic, began to wash away the dried blood. When he was finished, he turned to Merritt, who, having draped herself in a blanket, had managed to remove the coarse clothes of a stableboy and replace them with a clean gown of pale pink while still retaining her modesty. On her feet were soft kid slippers.

The sight of her in feminine clothing was a revelation, and he had to force himself not to stare.

"I will need a dressing on this wound." His tone was sharper than he'd intended. He would do well to remember that Merritt Lamont was the enemy. "See to it, woman."

Without a word she crossed to him and tore a strip of linen. Dipping her fingers into Sabina's ointment, she smeared a small amount onto his raw flesh, and was rewarded by his sudden hiss of pain.

"Did I hurt you?" Her smile was far too sweet.

"Nay." He would not give her the satisfaction of knowing how hellishly the ointment burned.

"That is good, for I see I have missed a spot." Relishing her chance for at least a small measure of vengeance, she slathered a generous amount of ointment.

He set his teeth, determined to ignore the searing pain. "You are enjoying this, I see."

She tied the linen strip so tightly he winced. "I have always been willing, even eager, to help those less fortunate."

"Another paragon." He reached up and loosened the linen, flexing his arm to return the circulation, then allowed her to continue tying it. "No doubt you inherit such virtue from your father."

She stared into his eyes, meeting his challenging look with one of her own. "So I have been told."

As she started to turn away he caught her hand, stilling her movements. At once she was aware of his strength. With no effort he could snap the bones of her fingers like twigs. "Beware, woman. Do not try my patience."

"Nay, sir. It is you who should beware." Her eyes flashed. "You are not in your own fortress now, Campbell. You will regret the day you invaded the home of Upton Lamont."

"I already regret it." Still gripping her hand, he drew her closer, until his warm breath feathered the hair at her nape. "But I am willing to pay any price to save my brother." Cool blue-green eyes stared into hers, daring her to look away. "Even enter a den of vipers."

She was disturbed by the nearness of his naked chest, and determined to put aside such unworthy thoughts. But her gaze was caught and held by the mat of gold hair that disappeared beneath the waistband of his breeches.

"A word of warning, then." Her voice lowered to a whisper. "Take care that you do not anger this viper, or you will be forced to endure my venom."

His gaze fastened on her mouth, and a dangerous smile touched his lips. She realized, too late, what he intended. But when she tried to pull back, he dragged her into his arms.

"I think, viper, I might enjoy seeing you hiss."

Her eyes flashed. "May you be damned to eternal fire, Campbell. And your brother, as well—"

Her words were cut off with a hard, punishing kiss. This time she was prepared to do battle rather than give in. And Shaw was just as determined to dominate.

If possible, it was even more erotic to tangle with one who, though she fought like a man, was dressed in such an alluring feminine frill. The neckline was low enough to reveal a shadowed cleft between high, firm breasts. As she turned and twisted, the fabric hugged a tiny waist and flared over her softly rounded hips. Shaw found that it was an altogether pleasant diversion. One that had him quickly aroused.

The more she struggled, the tighter were the arms that held her, until, breathless, she went limp in his arms. She had intended it as a ploy, but her strategy backfired. As soon as her struggles ceased, he drew her a little away, his eyes locked on hers.

"Woman," he muttered, "you would try the patience of a saint."

"Is that what you consider yourself?"

"If the truth be known, the things I am thinking would make me the greatest of sinners." At his unexpected admission, he added, "What evil powers do you possess?"

She saw his stunned look a moment before he dragged her close and covered her mouth with his. This time, his touch, his kiss, gentled.

That was her undoing.

How could she fight hands that held her as carefully as if she were made of glass? How could she resist lips that whispered over hers like the wings of a butterfly?

She went very still, willing herself to feel nothing. But though she stood as still as a statue, she could not control the wild beating of her heart, or the breath that seemed to back up in her lungs.

Shaw pressed soft, quick kisses across her closed lids, over her cheek, along her jaw, before returning to her lips. And all the while she gave no outward sign of the turmoil that churned within.

How strong he was, she thought as his hands moved over her. And yet, for all his strength, his movements were restrained. He gave the illusion of great tenderness. How could this be? The man was a contradiction. Gentle when he should be rough. Smiling when he should be scowling. Before she could puzzle it further, he suddenly took the kiss deeper, and all her thoughts scattered.

The touch of her, the taste of her, had him mesmerized. He couldn't seem to recall why he'd been angry. Now he knew only heat and pleasure and need. As his tongue tangled with hers, the flash of desire was swift and all-consuming. Needs, so long denied, nearly swamped him. His arms tightened around her and he drew her so firmly against him he could feel her erratic heartbeat inside his own chest. Or was that his pulse, pumping so furiously?

Suddenly he was aware of a sound from the other side of the barred door. Not his pulse; someone knocking.

Astra's voice could be heard. "My lady Sabina says it is time to break your fast."

Shaw's head came up sharply. His brows drew together in a look of black rage. "Aye. Tell the lady we will come at once."

He stood very still, listening to the sound of retreating footsteps. Then, lowering his hands, he stepped back a pace. Merritt did the same.

Again, they were both forced to deal with overpowering emotions.

Shame reddened Merritt's cheeks. How could she permit her enemy such liberties? Yet, when this man held her, she seemed to lose her will to resist. His simplest touch scrambled her thoughts, leaving her floundering like a fish in a net. To cover her embarrassment, she brought her hand up in a wide arc, landing a stinging blow on his cheek.

"Damn you for that, Campbell. You will not despoil me to avenge the dark deeds of your father."

At once he caught the offending hand in a painful grasp and drew her close, until she could feel the heat of his anger. His eyes blazed. "I will do whatever I choose, Merritt Lamont. Or have you forgotten that you and your family are at the mercy of my sword?"

"I forget nothing," she spat before pulling roughly away.

Shaw stared after her, struggling with feelings of self-loathing. Why was it that this woman caused him to behave in such a manner? How could he forget, for even a moment, that she was the daughter of his father's despised enemy? She could, in fact, have been the cause of Sutton's suffering.

Perhaps she practiced witchcraft. For there was no other explanation for his strange, unexpected behavior. Women had always been his brother's weakness, and his source of pleasure. As for himself, Shaw had proudly scoffed at pleasures of the flesh. He had thought himself, because of his special calling, to be unlike other men. The woman had not been born who could tempt him. Until now.

Neither of them spoke as Shaw pulled on his tunic. Running a hand through his damp hair, he crossed the room and removed the barrier, opening the door. At once, Merritt flounced past him. But his hand shot out, slowing her movements.

He felt the quick sexual tug and immediately pulled his hand away as though burned. "You will walk beside me," he commanded.

As they descended the stairs, he took great pains to see that he did not brush against her. He could not afford the distraction.

At the rumble of a masculine voice he muttered, "I look forward to finally meeting the mysterious laird of Inverene House."

She shot him one final dark look before lifting her head in a proud, haughty manner.

Chapter Six

Merritt led the way along a dimly lit hallway. Ahead could be heard the sound of muted voices. When they reached the great hall, Shaw paused at the threshold.

Row upon row of scarred wooden tables stood empty. At one end of the room, a log burned in the fireplace. A table had been pulled close to it for warmth. At the head of the table sat a barrel-chested man hunched deep into the folds of a heavy cloak. On his left sat Sabina. On his right was a lad whose flaming hair and freckled nose made him look much like the young woman standing beside Shaw.

"You did not mention a brother," he said.

"You did not ask."

"How many more surprises shall I expect?"

She merely shot him a scathing look before striding across the room ahead of him.

"Good morrow, Father." Placing her hands on the man's shoulders, she bent and brushed an affectionate kiss on his cheek.

He covered one of her hands with his for a moment, then lifted his gaze to study Shaw. His eyes narrowed. "You would be the Campbell." He spoke the name as though it offended him.

"Aye." Shaw's reply was equally abrupt.

The man pressed his palms firmly on the table, easing himself from his chair. The strain of such effort was clearly evident on his face. But he was determined to stand and meet this intruder eye-to-eye. Sweat beaded his brow. His pupils were dilated with pain. When he was finally standing, he was nearly as tall as Shaw.

Without a word, each man took the measure of the other.

At last Upton Lamont said, "You and your brother are the first Campbells to gain entrance to my home."

Shaw kept his eyes steady on his father's old adversary. The man was indeed a menacing figure, with long red hair and bushy beard liberally sprinkled with gray. Thick, muscled shoulders wider than a longbow, and the biggest hands Shaw had ever seen, added to the impression of strength. He had no doubt how Upton Lamont had earned his title the Lawless One. Rumor had it that, in his youth, Lamont had considered himself above the law and had terrorized all who crossed him. And had amassed a fortune in the bargain.

It was Lamont's eyes that held Shaw's interest. Though they were green, like Merritt's, there was no spark of fire burning in them. Instinctively, Shaw felt that there was a sickness in the man. But whether it was a sickness of the mind or the body, he had yet to ascertain.

"I have been told that you held my daughters hostage in their chambers last night. Yet I see no army swarming about Inverene House. Why does an invader come alone?"

"I held them against their will because I feared retaliation by your army. I come in peace, to return my brother to our home. It is my only reason for being here."

Something flickered in the other man's eyes. "So, you would ask to be treated as a guest?"

"I am neither guest nor intruder. I ask no special treatment."

Again he saw an unfathomable look in the other man's eyes before Upton shifted attention away from himself by saying, "The words to be spoken between us can wait. You have yet to be introduced to my son, Edan." The name was pronounced with great tenderness.

Shaw studied a lad who looked to be about ten and two. Lively inquisitive eyes lifted to meet his.

"Edan," Shaw said, nodding his head.

"You are our first visitor in a very long time," the boy told him.

"Perhaps it is because your fortress seems inhospitable to guests. It is nearly impenetrable, what with loch, cliffs and forest."

"It did not repel you," the boy pointed out logically.

"Aye. But then, I had a compelling reason for coming here."

When Shaw returned his attention to Upton Lamont, Sabina and Merritt had helped him lower himself to a sitting position.

The older man stabbed a finger in the air. "Sit, Campbell. Though you enter my home by force, you shall partake of the Lamont hospitality."

Shaw took a seat at the opposite end of the table. At once Astra approached the laird, offering a bowl of gruel.

He shot her a contemptuous look. "What is this? Where is the meat? The fowl?"

The old servant glanced uncertainly toward Merritt before saying, "There was no time to slaughter a lamb, m'laird. Nor even time to twist the neck from a pheasant."

"Ah, well. See to it before the day has ended," he muttered, taking a generous portion of gruel before gesturing for the woman to serve their guest.

Shaw took only a very small portion, and noticed that both Sabina and Merritt did the same, leaving the remaining gruel for their little brother.

"Merritt said that the one who looks just like you lying abed is drawing his last breath." Edan's voice was as animated as his eyes.

At once Shaw felt a stab of pain and had to struggle to compose himself. His voice rang with conviction. "He is my brother, Sutton. My twin. And he will not die, lad."

"I was allowed to enter my sister's chambers and see him when he first arrived. He truly does look just like you."

"Aye." Shaw smiled. "Most cannot tell one from the other."

"Merritt said he is grievously wounded, and that the arrows that felled him came from Campbell bows."

At once Shaw's smile faded. Though he addressed the boy, his eyes narrowed on Merritt. "Your sister has much to say—to others. I have yet to hear the truth about the attack upon my brother. But the tales I have been told thus far have the ring of falsehood to them."

"Do you call me a liar?" Merritt demanded.

"I suspect that you . . . embellish the facts to suit the listener."

She shoved back her chair and sprang to her feet, reminding Shaw of a hissing, spitting cat. "No Campbell has the right to sit in my father's house and call me—"

"Merritt." Though the word was spoken hoarsely, Upton's voice had the ring of command.

At once the young woman sank down upon her chair. Shaw had to bite back his smile. Even in obedience, there was nothing docile about Merritt Lamont. Though she might not be aware of it, she used her eyes as weapons, sending him cutting looks each time she glanced his way.

"I have no reason to doubt my daughter's story." Upton Lamont pinned Shaw with a look. "'Twas dark, the hour late. Men's tempers were short. Weapons were drawn, arrows fired." He shrugged. "Such things happen when men get careless."

Shaw felt his own temper rising, something that was happening far too often since his arrival at the Lamont fortress. "Sutton is the finest warrior I know. He is never careless in battle."

"Perhaps he was merely... distracted."

At Merritt's words, Shaw turned the full force of his gaze on her. "How is it that you happened upon my brother?"

Merritt darted a look at her sister. "Sabina and I were out... searching for a lost lamb."

"After dark? While a battle was being waged?"

"The darkness seemed to come upon us quite suddenly. And, of course, we did not expect to be caught between two sides in a bloody skirmish."

"Of course." Lies. He would have to sift through a mountain of lies to find a single word of truth.

Deep in thought, Shaw tasted the gruel. Though it was thin and bland, he emptied his bowl, grateful for the nourishment that would replenish his strength. Breaking off a hunk of dried bread, he washed it down with watery ale.

"Do you return to your home this day?" Edan asked.

The others around the table, including the elderly servant, seemed uncommonly interested in Shaw's reply. Their eagerness to be rid of the intruder was obvious.

"Nay. I will not leave my brother here alone."

"But he is not alone. He has us," the boy said with the easy assurance of the young.

"Aye. But when he awakes, he will be alarmed unless he sees a familiar face. I have already decided that I will not leave here until my brother is strong enough to accompany me."

Seeing the glances exchanged between Sabina and Merritt, Shaw felt a small but satisfying sense of victory, knowing he'd managed to unsettle at least two of the Lamonts.

"So." Upton's words shattered the silence. "Though you are unwelcome in my home, you insist upon remaining."

"I will not leave without my brother."

The older man's brows drew together as he studied Shaw for long, silent minutes. The others around the table sat very still, awaiting the explosion of their father's wrath. Instead he surprised them by saying, "See that a sleeping chamber is prepared for our...guest."

"Father," Merritt objected, "he is not our guest. He forced himself upon us—"

"I need no chamber," Shaw said smoothly, ignoring her outburst. "I will stay with my brother, to see to his needs."

"That is not possible, since he lies in Sabina's chambers." Upton turned to Astra. "Prepare the room next to Merritt's chambers, since it is the largest one."

"Father, I think—" Merritt began in further protest, but her father cut her off sharply.

"As for you, Merritt, I would have you take the Campbell to the tower, where he can look down upon the land that borders ours."

"But—"

"Thank you." Shaw drained his goblet, feeling completely restored. There was nothing more invigorating than besting an opponent. And of all the Lamonts, Merritt presented the greatest challenge. It would give him a measure of satisfaction to match wits with this one. "Very well." Merritt pushed back her chair and sprang to her feet. "You will come with me, Campbell."

Shaw paused a moment to acknowledge his host. "I thank you for your hospitality, Upton Lamont." Then he spun on his heel and had to hurry to catch up with the female.

"At one time all of the land that you can see from here was ruled by my father."

Merritt and Shaw stood in the watchtower, surveying the green, verdant land below. It was a deceptively peaceful scene. Sheep grazed on hillsides. Thatched cottages were strung out beside swollen streams. Yet, Shaw knew, the countryside seethed with treachery. He could still recall in his mind's eye the scene of the Lamont stable being consumed by flame; the pall of acrid smoke that blotted out the stars.

"How is it that your father no longer lays claim to the land on the other side of the loch?"

"When a man grows old and weak, he needs sons to wield their swords in his name, else those once loyal to him may decide to turn against him and claim his riches for themselves."

"Are you saying that all your father's friends are now his enemies?"

"Nay. He still has some who are loyal to him. But most chose to look out for themselves. And when the Campbell offered them gold in return for their loyalty, they were quick to turn away from the one who once offered them protection."

Shaw was outraged. "My brother Dillon has no need to give a man gold in exchange for his loyalty. He has an army of faithful kinsmen. Furthermore, he has no desire for your father's land. There is more than enough for all."

"Liar." Merritt ground out the word between her teeth. "How else do you explain the raids on our land?"

"Raids?"

"Aye. Nightly. They steal our sheep and cattle and burn our crops and shelters."

Now he understood the empty larder. And without food, the servants would flee to another master. One who could feed and protect them.

"I know nothing of these raids, but I would venture that they are the same as those against my people. Carried out by the Highland Avengers." He studied the way the wind caught her hair, flailing it against her cheek. Without thinking he lifted a hand to brush it aside. Instantly he felt the heat and drew back.

As if sensing his attraction she snarled, "This is not the work of the Avengers. 'Tis the work of the wicked Campbells."

Clenching his hands behind his back, he turned away, studying the charred remains of the stable. "And how would you know that?"

"As if you do not know. Two years ago, a band of marauders, carrying the Campbell banner, attacked Inverene House while my father was away. They—" she swallowed, then forced herself to go on "—brutalized my mother before killing her."

He turned around to study her, feeling the sting of righteous anger. Why was it that women must always suffer so at the hands of their enemies? Men and children were mercifully killed. But women, young and old, were first humiliated, before their lives were ended.

"How did you and your sister escape the same fate?"

"Our father's man-at-arms, Kendall, along with our little brother, Edan, held the soldiers at sword point while my sister and I slipped away to find our father. By the time we returned with our father and drove off the invaders, Edan was the only survivor, though at the time, he seemed more dead than alive."

"Then he is indeed fortunate to have lived to tell of it."

Her voice nearly broke. "Aye. Fortunate. But my father has ne'er been the same since."

"In what way?"

"He . . . was gravely wounded, as well. But his body, though once strong and invincible, refused to heal. Perhaps it is because of the pain to his heart. He often lives in the past, when he and my mother were young. He refuses to accept that she is dead. And he has . . . abdicated his rule. He often thinks his old friends are still loyal, and that they are seeing to our needs. At other times, when his mind returns to us, and he questions what has happened to his home and land, we tell him that a fever sweeps the land, confining his old friends to their beds."

Shaw began to understand. "I have witnessed such things before. A man is dealt a mighty blow. One that prevents him from carrying on with his life. And so he continues in a dreamlike state, pretending that all is well. Your father does not know about the stolen horses and the burned stable?"

"Perhaps." She shook her head, and tears stung her eyes. "He seems unconcerned about it."

In that instant Shaw realized that Upton knew little about the desperate situation in which his family found themselves. He was unaware about the empty larder, the loss of servants, the disloyalty of his former friends.

Upton Lamont was laird in name only. He was so sick in mind and body and heart that the day-to-day care of his fortress had been passed to—Shaw's eyes widened at the thought—a lad of ten and two and these two females.

Having been forced to reveal the truth, Merritt blinked furiously and Shaw could see that she struggled against a display of emotion.

"You have seen enough, Campbell." Turning abruptly, she led the way down the stairs.

Shaw made his way toward Sabina's chambers, intent upon seeing his brother. As he walked, he peered into massive, high-ceilinged rooms. All were cold, lifeless. Most were cloaked in darkness, with no fire to chase away the gloom.

"As empty as a tomb." The words caused a chill along his spine.

It was difficult to imagine Kinloch House in such a state of disrepair. He was accustomed to the noisy chatter of his family home; servants, laughing, teasing as they worked; his family calling out greetings to the dozens of friends and neighbors who were always present. Even in times of crises, the big manor house teemed with the voices of soldiers loyal to their laird as well as their families, who took refuge within the walls of the fortress. At such times, they even brought their household goods and livestock, so that all would not be lost to the bands of intruders. Always there was activity, and an air of expectancy. But here, there was only silence. Neglect. And an air of quiet desperation.

Deep in thought, he passed an open doorway and saw the glimmer of firelight. Just as he was about to move on, he caught a glimpse of a menacing shadow darting across a wall. The silhouette had his heart pumping. There was no doubt that it was a sword, poised to attack.

Instinctively he reached a hand to the scabbard at his waist and retrieved his own weapon.

"Advance and be recognized," he called out in imperious tones.

His words were greeted with silence.

"Come forward at once," he commanded, "or prepare to answer to my sword."

Again there was only silence.

He strode into the room, then halted. Except for a small bed, and a table beside it, there seemed to be no furniture. No chairs were drawn up beside the fireplace. No settles. No side tables holding the usual mixture of parchment, quills and candles. The only illumination came from the fire. And in the eerie giant shadows cast by the light of the flame, the small figure huddled in the bed seemed all the more frail.

"Edan." Shaw paused at the foot of the pallet, studying the lad who lay against his pillows, brandishing a sword. "Why are you abed at this time of the day?"

"It is where I always am, except when Sabina or Merritt carry me below stairs to sup with Father."

"Carry?" But even as the word slipped from his mouth, Shaw knew, and cursed himself for his ignorance.

It should have been painfully clear from the way the lad sat so still at table, not even rising to acknowledge a guest.

Eden Lamont was a cripple.

Chapter Seven

As the realization dawned, Shaw returned his sword to the scabbard and strode around the bed until he was standing beside the lad.

"You...stay abed all day?"

"Aye."

In the strained silence that followed, Shaw cleared his throat. "Your sister told me how you fought the intruders who killed your mother. Is that when this happened to you?"

The boy nodded. "They left me for dead. But I foiled them." He suddenly brightened. "I can still lift my sword. See?"

By grasping the hilt with both hands, he managed to raise the unwieldy weapon above his head.

Shaw studied the pitifully thin arms and could see the effort such exertion cost the boy. Yet, though his hands trembled, Edan glowed with pride at his accomplishment.

"If the marauders return, I must be prepared to defend myself and my family."

"Aye. That you must." Shaw's heart went out to the lad. "You are very brave."

"Not so brave," the boy said softly. He lowered his voice, as if sharing a great secret. "I will forever see the face of the one who left me for dead. His eyes were yellow, like a forest cat's, and he had a thin, puckered scar that ran from temple to jaw. The others called him Lysander and he laughed as he cut me, again and again, with his sword. Had another not pulled him away, I believe he would have completely severed my legs."

Shaw felt a deep well of anger at the lad's words, and wondered what would drive any man to such cruelty.

"I live in fear of the night." The boy swallowed, then went on. "For he vowed that one night he will return, to finish his vile deeds for the one he serves. That is why, while the rest of the household is asleep, I remain awake and alert, my knife and sword by my side."

"What could you do, lad?"

Edan surprised Shaw by flinging aside the covers and rolling from his pallet. Once on the floor he turned and scooted backward toward the balcony, using his hands to propel himself. At the balcony he pulled himself to the railing, where he could peer into the courtyard below.

"And you remain like that all night?" Shaw asked in amazement.

"Aye. 'Tis little enough that I can do for my family."

Shaw felt a sudden shock of remembrance. "'Twas at night that your stable was burned and the horses stolen. Something woke me. I dismissed it as the cry of a night bird." He studied the lad, leaning heavily on his elbows on the ledge of the balcony. "It was you."

"Aye." Edan's eyes clouded with sadness. "But to no avail. By the time I managed to rouse you and the others, the damage had been done." He slid down the stone column supporting the balcony and began to scoot backward to his pallet. With surprising agility, he struggled under the covers. "If I had my legs, those villains would have tasted my vengeance."

He turned his face away to hide the tears that sprang to his eyes. "So you see, I take the coward's road. I am so afraid to close my eyes while night covers the land that I am forced to cower in my balcony. And even when I see invaders, my sword and knife are useless, as am I."

"I once thought of myself as you do," Shaw admitted.

"You?" The boy seemed stunned by such an admission. He turned to study the giant who stood taller even than his own father. Surely a man such as this would fear nothing.

"I also come from a family of proud warriors," Shaw said. "But early in my life I rejected the lure of battle and embraced a world of books and letters."

"Such a life would be scorned by my father. When I grow older, I must be a great warrior," Edan pronounced solemnly, "or face my father's wrath."

"Does he not know of your infirmity?"

"Aye." The boy nodded his head sadly. "But in his befuddled mind, he thinks it a minor inconvenience that will soon disappear. My sisters believe it was too great a shock for him, after the loss of our beloved mother. And so we all pretend that I am growing stronger. And since Father rarely leaves his chambers except to eat, there is little chance that he will ever see my...condition. So you see, he still expects me to take up his sword."

"There are other things, lad."

"Not to a Lamont." The boy's tone was so serious Shaw could not help but be moved. "My father has but one son. Therefore, I must be a warrior."

"I see you have given this much thought."

"Aye." Edan smiled, all guileless and innocent, and Shaw thought such a look must rival that of heaven's angels.

"Can you read?" Shaw asked suddenly.

The lad shrugged. "A little. Sabina was teaching me. But since the servants fled, she has been much too busy to spend any time on such unimportant things."

"Unimportant?" Shaw put his hands on his hips and studied the boy. "If a man is to be a leader of his people, he must be skilled in all ways. And that includes being able to read missives from his underlings, and send orders in his own hand." He paused a moment, deep in thought. The lad could not spend the rest of his life confined to this room, without benefit of challenge. "Since I am forced to remain here until my brother mends, I will undertake your tutoring."

"You can read? And write?" The boy's eyes widened.

"Aye. And so shall you."

Seeing the way the boy beamed with pleasure, Shaw gave him a measured look. "You may not be so pleased about this after we have begun. You will find me a tough task-master."

As he started across the room, Edan called, "My father has said a Lamont must be prepared for any task, no matter how impossible. When will the lessons begin?"

"On the morrow," Shaw said, pausing in the doorway. "After we have broken our fast."

He turned away, completely missing the rapturous smile that seemed to touch all the boy's features with radiance.

As he walked, Shaw's thoughts were troubled. Each hour that he was under this roof, he discovered more about these Lamonts than he cared to know. Their situation was truly desperate. And yet, though he hated to admit it about a sworn enemy, he had to admire their courage in the face of adversity.

* * *

"How does my brother fare?" Shaw stood in the doorway, watching as Sabina attempted to force liquid between Sutton's lips.

She looked up and Shaw could see that her cheeks were flushed, her hair and clothes in disarray. It was obvious that Sutton, in his fevered state, had fought against her ministrations.

She frowned. "He resists, and the fever is consuming him."

Shaw crossed the room and knelt beside her. "Forgive my brother. He is very strong, and he does not know what he is doing."

Gently lifting his brother's head, he took the goblet from her hands, muttering, "Let me try."

With extreme patience he managed to get several drops of the potion down his brother's throat. He could feel the heat of Sutton's body clear through his own clothes. Touching a hand to the fevered brow, he shuddered with alarm at the fire that raged.

"Bring me water," he commanded.

At once Sabina sent her old servant to see to his needs. A short time later, while Sabina and Merritt stoked the fire with the last of the broken furniture, Shaw sponged his brother's burning flesh.

"Treats 'im as tenderly as though he were a wee bairn," muttered Astra, watching the two men with considerable interest.

"Aye," Sabina whispered. "And can match him strength for strength."

"But of course, they are not like other mortals," the old woman added.

"And why is that?" Merritt looked up at her in surprise.

"Because they share the same face." Astra lowered her voice. "They no doubt share the same soul. Mayhap they even share the same thoughts, as well."

"What foolishness," Merritt retorted. "I do not believe you."

"Then how do you explain the arrival of this one, just as his brother lay near death?"

At a loss for any logical reason, Merritt said nothing.

"And how do you explain why the first has not yet given up his life? Do ye not deny that we expected this to be the day we put him in the ground?"

The two sisters stared at each other as the old woman continued, "Could it be that the one called Shaw, whose name means 'to share,' came here to lend his strength to his wounded brother?" She pointed a bony finger. "See how he fights for the life of the one called Sutton? I tell ye, these two are not like other mortals."

"I will listen to no more," Merritt said, flouncing away. "Next you will have them some heavenly messengers, sent on a mysterious mission from the Almighty."

But as she made her way across the room, she paused in the doorway and watched. Shaw murmured words of encouragement to his brother, before continuing to bathe his fevered flesh. He seemed aware of nothing and no one, except the one who shared his face. Often, she noted, the whispered words seemed more like a prayer.

She turned away, deep in thought. A heavenly messenger? Such nonsense. The touch of him had been real enough. And she had the bruises to prove it. Still, she thought as she made her way along the dim hallway, he had shown unusual restraint when he had kissed her. Despite the obvious heat, which he could not hide, he had resisted the temptation to take what other invaders would have considered their right. If truth be told, his resistance had been greater than her own. At the first touch of him, she had felt lost, unable to do more than endure—and enjoy.

With gritted teeth she pushed aside such an embarrassing admission. Next she would be prattling on like old Astra, bowing and scraping to the laird Campbell as though he were God's right hand. Still, as she went about her daily routine, she couldn't seem to rid herself of the nagging little thought. Shaw, of the Clan Campbell, was truly unlike any man she had ever met.

"I believe the fever has abated a little." Sabina knelt and touched a hand to Sutton's forehead.

"Aye. Your potion helped, as did the cool water. Now we will let him rest," Shaw whispered. "But as often as possible, you must force more of the willow bark tea down his throat."

"Have no fear. I will see to it." Sabina settled herself beside Sutton's pallet and took up needle and thread.

Shaw stood a moment, staring down at the scene. His brother slept as peacefully as a bairn, looking for all the world as though he would awaken at any moment and begin laughing and teasing. The woman beside him, head bent to her mending, sleek black hair shining in the firelight, resembled a portrait of the Madonna that he had long admired at the monastery. There was a sense of serenity about this woman who had assumed the care of his brother. A serenity that filled Shaw with a feeling of peace. She would not neglect Sutton. Nor would she mistreat him, even though he was her enemy. And though she appeared every bit the docile lady of the manor, there was also an air of strength and determination about her. He had the feeling that whatever task Sabina was given, it would be done.

Needing to be busy, he picked up Sutton's longbow and made his way down the stairs. Outside a misty rain fell. He studied the ashes and rubble from the stable. Already the tracks of the horses had been obliterated by the elements.

Turning away from the fortress, he entered the woods. It wasn't long until he found the tracks he'd been searching for. Moving cautiously, he soon came upon a herd of deer, sheltered deep in the forest. Fitting an arrow into the bow, he waited patiently until one of the deer separated itself from the others. But as he drew the bow, releasing the arrow, a second arrow sang through the air, landing alongside his, piercing the buck's heart. The herd scattered.

He was astonished to see Merritt step from her place of concealment and race toward the fallen animal. When she spotted the second arrow, she whirled to face him.

"What are doing here, Campbell?" she demanded.

"Apparently the same as you. I thought I would provide your father with the meat he craves."

Though she was surprised by his admission, she carefully hid her feelings behind a frown of disapproval. "There was no need. I am quite capable of seeing to my father's needs."

"I can see that. Your aim is straight and true."

She cast him a knowing glance. "See that you do not forget that, Campbell. Now begone."

"As you wish," he said, giving her a slight bow. He turned and began to walk away.

"Wait." She watched as he paused and turned. Shrugging uncomfortably, she said, "As long as you are here, mayhap you could help me carry it home."

He closed the distance between them, all the while holding back the smile that hovered at the edges of his lips. "Are you asking for a Campbell's help?"

She gritted her teeth, and foolish pride won out over common sense. "Nay. I do not seek the help of a Campbell."

"Very well." With a smile he turned away. "I will leave you to your trophy."

She bit her lip, studying the deer. Even if she fashioned a sling, there was no way she could haul an animal twice her size all the way back to the fortress. How she missed having a horse.

Though the words stuck in her throat, she managed to call to Shaw's retreating back, "I...have changed my mind."

"'Tis a woman's right, I am told." Shaw paused, but did not turn around. He couldn't. He was laughing too hard.

"I would...be grateful for your help," she managed to say through gritted teeth.

When he could compose his features, he returned to her side. "How can I refuse such a...gracious request?"

Draping the deer over his shoulders, he easily carried it back to Inverene House. Merritt trailed behind him, fuming in impotent rage.

If only she were a man, she thought for perhaps the hundredth time in her young life. She would be strong enough, and fierce enough, to restore her father's life to its former glory. No man would dare challenge her. For she knew, though she did not possess the physical attributes, that she had the heart of a warrior.

Their evening meal took on a festive air. Astra served a clear broth, skimmed from the bone and marrow. After that, they feasted on roasted venison and early spring vegetables, followed by freshly baked biscuits and fruit conserve. Each course was washed down by generous amounts of ale.

"Which of my men presented us with the deer?" Upton asked.

"Our guest provided it," Merritt said quickly.

"Nay, your daughter is too generous with her praise," Shaw protested. "It was her arrow that found its mark. The kill was hers. Merritt is an excellent marksman."

At the unexpected praise, Upton glanced from the Campbell to his daughter, noting the flush on her cheeks. After a lengthy pause he said, "Even the fire seems warmer this even. Is my mind addled, or are those fresh logs?"

"'Twas our guest," Astra said as she poured more ale into the laird's goblet. "His ax rang all the afternoon."

Merritt held her silence and sipped her ale, feeling her cheeks grow warmer at the thought of what she had witnessed. When Shaw had removed his tunic and shirt to chop wood, she had stared transfixed at the width of his shoulders, the rippling muscles of his back. Though she had often seen her father's men in various stages of undress while they worked around Inverene House, she had never before been so affected by the sight of a man's naked flesh.

"I needed something to do." Shaw lifted his goblet and drained it. "Besides, it was my way of thanking you for your hospitality." He silently blessed a childhood spent with the monks, who had insisted that study be mixed with a healthy dose of hard, physical labor in the fields. Though he knew his muscles would protest the hours of chopping, at least his body would not feel too assaulted.

"Perhaps tonight we will not be so eager to hurry off to our pallets," Upton said with a laugh. Of his guest he inquired, "You have no doubt heard about the fire that swept through the forest?"

Before Shaw could respond, Upton continued, "The forest blaze is the reason why my men have been unable to supply us with firewood, and we have been forced to burn much of our furniture to chase away the chill."

Shaw glanced around the table and saw that both Merritt and Sabina sat with heads bowed, unable to meet his eyes. How many lies had they been forced to tell, in order to spare their father's feelings?

"With logs so scarce," Upton continued, "we have been forced to retire to our beds as soon as we finish supping. But I think tonight, to celebrate our good fortune, we will remain by the fire and be entertained. Astra, fetch the minstrel."

"He . . . returned to his cottage by the loch, Father," Merritt said quickly, "until he recovers from the fever."

"Ah. What then shall we do to entertain ourselves?"

"I will play the harp," Sabina offered.

"Aye," Upton muttered as, leaning heavily upon a thick walking stick, he made his way to a seat by the fire. "Music from heaven."

Shaw carried Edan to a chair beside his father's.

As Sabina plucked the strings, Shaw found himself mentally transported to the great abbey at Edinburgh, where he had once heard a choir of novices sing like angels, accompanied by the strings of a harp. The music was indeed heavenly.

"I have missed this," Upton sighed, leaning his head back.

For long minutes they sat around the fire, allowing the strain of the day to dissolve under the gentle melodies played by the beautiful Sabina.

At last, Merritt, unable to stand so much inactivity, got to her feet. "I will fetch the board and pieces."

Edan clapped his hands in delight. "May I stay and watch, Father?"

"Of course, lad." Upton turned to Shaw. "Do you play, Campbell?"

"A little." Shaw smiled. Chess was his favorite pastime. He took great pride in his ability to outmaneuver his opponents. In fact, his family and most of his friends would no longer challenge him, because he had managed to beat them all so soundly.

When the board was in place and the carved wooden chess pieces arranged, Upton turned to his guest. "Will you play?"

"Aye. 'Twould be my pleasure."

"Good." Upton smiled as his younger daughter took her place at the other side of the board. "Merritt will play in the name of the Lamonts."

"The female?" Arching a brow, Shaw looked from his host to the fiery-haired daughter, who was watching him without expression. "I thought...I had hoped for a bit of a challenge."

Upton couldn't help laughing at the look of defiance that crept into his daughter's eyes. "Be warned, Campbell. I would be willing to wager that your words have just assured you of more challenge than you could ever dream."

Shaw turned to the lad. "Would you like to sit beside me, Edan, and learn the intricacies of the game?"

"Aye." The boy was delighted when Shaw placed him on a settle beside him.

Bowing grandly before Merritt, Shaw took his seat. "I will allow my opponent the advantage of the first move, since it may be the only one she will get."

With a look of pure venom, Merritt moved her rook.

Shaw moved his.

Their first few moves were swift, certain, each one quickly following the other. But after only half a dozen moves, both players became more cautious, as they began to acknowledge the skill of the other.

At last, after a calculated move, Merritt made a great pretense of yawning, before she called, "Astra, mayhap you could fetch a sweet tray, since this match will soon be over."

"Aye." Shaw moved his pawn to her queen. "And I shall prove that females have no understanding of the strategy necessary to win this game."

For nearly an hour more they labored over the board. The sweet tray was brought and soon emptied. Goblets were drained and refilled. Another log was added to the fire, and after a while Upton dozed in his chair, while beside him, Sabina continued to pluck the harp.

Merritt studied the board, then moved again. "The lout is determined to prove his mouth larger than his brain," she said to her little brother, who giggled.

"Now, Edan," Shaw said with obvious relish, "I will show you how to quickly surmise your opponent's strategy and take control of the game." He moved his knight.

Edan, far from tired, clapped his hands in delight, waking Upton, whose head came up sharply.

Merritt countered with her own knight.

Shaw's smile faded. Studying the board, he realized he'd made an error in judgment. When he tried to correct his mistake, Merritt winked at her little brother.

"I hope you are paying attention, Edan." Laughter warmed her words. "These same errors are made by arrogant leaders on the field of battle. They think they can confound the enemy by concentrating strength where he is weakest. A wise warrior will only show weakness in order to entice his opponent into attacking. Then, when it is too late, the opponent realizes that his enemy's weakness is really his strength." She moved her last pieces into position and looked up, meeting Shaw's eyes. "I believe you will find that you have no moves left, Campbell. I hold you prisoner."

Upton, leaning heavily on Sabina's arm, walked across the room and stared down at the chess pieces. Edan glanced from his sister to the man who sat studying each piece on the board.

"Will you yield?" she demanded.

Shaw drained his goblet, then nodded. "I confess, I am defeated." But though his words were spoken softly enough, there was a murderous look in his eyes. He was unaccustomed to being beaten, especially by a woman.

Everyone laughed and clapped and congratulated Merritt on her skills.

Shaw, in a burst of goodwill, extended his hand. "You play with great skill, my lady. I hope you will allow me to challenge you another time."

"Aye." Merritt's eyes danced with unconcealed pleasure. "Whenever you desire another lesson, I would be happy to impart some of my skill, Campbell."

"Well done, daughter. You have done your clan proud," Upton said, stifling a yawn. "And now I must bid you all good-even."

"If you will carry Edan," Merritt said softly, "Sabina and I will assist Father to his bed."

"Aye." Shaw scooped the boy into his arms and carried him up the stairs to his room. Down the hall he could hear the two young women in their father's room as they made him comfortable for the night.

"Tell me true," Edan whispered. "Did you let my sister beat you at chess?"

"Let her?" Shaw roared with laughter. "Nay, lad. I wanted badly to win. But the woman is damnably skilled.

Though I would be grateful if you did not tell her I said that."

"Said what?" Merritt's voice sounded directly behind Shaw.

He whirled. For a moment their eyes met. Then his gaze was drawn to her mouth, pursed in a little pout. He had the strangest desire to reach out and stroke a finger across her lips. The mere thought caused a rush of heat that stunned him. For a moment he could think of nothing to say. Then, forcing himself to turn away, he met Edan's questioning look. The two shared a secret smile.

"I said you showed promise. I might be willing to challenge you to another game of chess."

Behind him he could hear her little gasp of anger. Before she could say a word he called, "Good even, lad." He brushed the copper curls from the boy's forehead, then bowed in Merritt's direction.

"Good even, my lady."

"Good even, Shaw Campbell."

Biting back a grin, Shaw took his leave and made his way to Sabina's room to check on Sutton. Though his brother was still feverish, Sutton's sleep was not as deep as it had been. He tossed fitfully, occasionally moaning and mouthing words that made no sense. As much as Shaw hated seeing Sutton in such a state of pain, he realized it was a sign of healing. Until now, he had been too near death to be aware of the pain.

Outside the door, Shaw heard Sabina loudly calling good-night to her family. When she entered her chambers, Shaw said, "I leave my brother to your care, my lady."

"Aye. If he needs anything, I will minister to him through the night."

"I am grateful for your kindness."

Taking his leave, Shaw made his way along the hallway. When he entered the chambers that had been prepared for him, he undressed and sank gratefully onto his pallet. In the soft glow of the fire, he studied his surroundings. Except for the bed and a chaise pulled in front of the fireplace, there was little to distinguish it from the other sparsely furnished rooms of Inverene House. On a table were a basin and pitcher of water, along with a decanter of wine and a single crystal goblet.

Hearing movement in the room next door, he realized it was Merritt preparing for bed. The soft rustling sounds lulled him and he closed his eyes to welcome sleep. But as he began to drift, he became aware of sounds of unusual activity, after which the door to Merritt's chambers opened, then closed. Curious, he sat up and listened. Muffled footsteps hurried past his room. At once he sprang from his bed and raced to the door. Peering out, he saw a cloaked, hooded figure disappearing down the stairs.

Now what was the female up to?

Hurriedly dressing, he strapped his scabbard to his waist and grabbed up his cloak, determined to follow Merritt Lamont and learn the latest of her many secrets.

Chapter Eight

The rain had stopped, but dark clouds still obscured the moon and stars. The soaked earth was spongy beneath Shaw's feet as he followed the shadowy figure to the edge of the forest.

Once they entered the maze of trees, he could barely make out the figure in front of him. He was forced to rely on the sound of snapping twigs and crunching pine needles in order to follow.

He cursed the female's fleetness of foot. At times, he had to run to keep up with her. At other times he just barely managed to duck behind a tree before she spun around, as though sensing the presence of someone trailing her.

They walked for what seemed an hour or more, without once pausing to rest. With each step they were climbing the steep, forested cliffs that guarded the north entrance to Inverene House. Often the terrain was treacherous, with rocky outcroppings and deep gorges through which icy water tumbled. Ahead of him, the girl moved with the agility of a mountain cat, often leaping from stone to stone without regard to the dangers.

Behind her Shaw moved more slowly, determined to keep her in sight, while still remaining hidden from her view.

As she suddenly broke free of the forest, she no longer paused to cast searching looks behind, but strode purposefully ahead.

Racing across a grassy Highland meadow, she never broke stride as she passed a darkened thatched-roof cottage. She continued running until she reached a pasture. There, several dozen horses stood dozing. As Shaw watched, she pulled a length of rope from beneath her cloak and began tying the animals.

He could no longer remain a mere observer. He would not be a party to theft. "Little fool. What do you think you are doing?" Shaw demanded, coming up behind her.

She whirled, cursing like a soldier. "So, the footsteps I heard were not in my mind. You were following me. Be gone, Campbell. You do not belong here."

"Nor do you, woman." He grabbed her roughly by the arm. "Is this what the Lamonts have become? Thieves? Villains?"

"Aye." She shook off his hand and turned her back on him. "I'll steal if I must."

"I will not permit this."

"You?" She spun around, eyes blazing. "You will not permit . . . ?" She clamped her mouth shut on the curses that sprang to her lips. Instead, she challenged, "Tell me, Campbell. Is it stealing if a man is merely taking back what was stolen from him?"

He gave her question considerable thought, as his confessors often had, then replied, "Nay. That would not be stealing. 'Twould be a just deed."

"Then leave me to my . . . just deed, since the horses I steal are my own."

"I do not believe you."

"See for yourself." She tugged on the rope she held, drawing a sleek black stallion close enough to be seen in the darkness. "Is this not the steed you rode upon when you left your own land?"

"What lies...?" But even as the words escaped his lips, he recognized the horse as his. Thunderstruck, he touched a hand to the animal's smooth mane as he glanced around at the other horses milling about. "How did you know where to find these?"

"I tracked them earlier today. That is where I was coming from when I came upon the herd of deer." While she spoke she continued tying each horse, until all were secured. Then she affixed a long lead rope, before pulling herself onto the back of one of the horses.

"You had better be prepared to ride hard and fast, Campbell," she called as she nudged her horse into a gallop. "For your interference has cost me valuable time. And the thieves who helped themselves to our horses will not be pleased to give them up."

Before he could respond, she and the horses tied to the tether were sailing across the meadow.

He pulled himself onto the bare back of his steed and looked up in dismay as the light of a torch suddenly rent the blackness.

A man's voice could be heard shouting orders. In the torchlight, several figures could be seen spilling out of the little cottage.

Merritt was heading right toward them. There was no way she could change direction with so many horses thundering behind her. She would be forced to ride into the thick of an armed mob.

With his heart pounding, Shaw charged ahead.

"It is the Avengers," shouted a voice in the darkness.

"Nay," Shaw called, hoping to calm the frenzied mob. But no one could hear him above the thundering hooves and the clash of sword against sword as Merritt fought to break free.

"Hear me," Shaw cried, reining in his mount. "We are merely reclaiming what was taken from us."

"Thieves. Scalawags. You are the infamous Avengers," came a voice as the blade of a sword glinted in the torchlight.

Shaw resisted the urge to reach for his own sword. These were, after all, kinsmen. He would reason with them and set everything right.

"I am Shaw of Clan Campbell. My brother Dillon is laird."

"And I am Robert the Bruce," came a muttered reply as an arrow pierced Shaw's shoulder.

For a moment he was so stunned by the heat and pain he nearly toppled from his horse. Then, gathering all his strength, he maneuvered his mount through the sea of men until he reached Merritt's side.

She was fighting like an enraged she-bear, her blade flashing, her curses splitting the night air.

"May you be damned to hell, Campbell, for slowing me down."

Her words cut as fiercely as the blades that had been lifted against him.

When one of the men leapt onto Merritt's horse, Shaw struck out with his fist, sending the man pitching head-first to the ground beneath her horse's hooves.

She seemed not to notice as she battled furiously, her blade flashing in the reflected starlight. As she dodged the thrust of a broadsword, she grunted, "So, Campbell, you have chosen sides with your clansmen."

"Nay. But fighting never solved anything."

"Neither did cowardice. Fight, damn you. Or die a coward's death."

When another man came at her from behind, Shaw lifted his foot and drove him back with the heel of his boot. Merritt sent him a quick nod of acknowledgment, before resuming the fight.

"Behind you," she shouted, and Shaw had only a moment to turn and duck away from the brigand who had attempted to attack with a knife.

The arrow in Shaw's shoulder had turned hot pain into a raging fire. Perhaps it was the blinding pain, or the madness of the battle, but he suddenly discarded any attempt at diplomacy and, against all his years of training as a peacemaker, was forced to join in the fighting. Still, he could not bring himself to use his father's sword against these men, in the event that they were truly Campbells, as Merritt claimed. Instead, he used his wiles.

Calling on all his skill as a horseman, he urged his mount into the thick of the fray. One after another, men let out cries of fear and rage as they pitched forward from his fists and the thrusts of his knife.

"We must flee," Merritt commanded.

But as she wheeled her mount, a man's burly figure flew through the air, tackling her, dragging her to the ground. At once Shaw leapt from his mount and joined in. The others swarmed around them, over them, swords flashing, clubs flying.

Shaw waded through the bodies, frantically trying to save Merritt. But even his size and strength were no match for the frenzied mob, many of whom wielded clubs.

The first blow to Shaw's head merely staggered him. He turned, dirk lifted to attack, when a second blow dropped him to his knees.

"You do not understand. You must not harm the woman. She is under my protection. I am Shaw of Campbell. Your laird—"

"Our laird is in Edinburgh, dining with the king. And by the time he returns, he will discover he is laird no more," said the angry voice as the club was lifted and brought crashing against Shaw's skull.

Bright splinters of light danced behind his eyes. Pain, hot, searing, seemed to radiate from his brain. He felt bile rise up to his throat, threatening to choke him. And then he was falling, falling through a bottomless black hole.

Shaw felt himself being battered, and he could not find the strength to fight back. Rough hands jarred him out of his stupor each time he began to slide back into blessed oblivion.

"Nay. Leave me," he muttered, rolling to his side. But that only made the pain worse, and he moaned and tried to escape the fire that raged through him. What was causing that white-hot flame in his flesh?

"Campbell, you must wake." Merritt shook him, but his hands caught her in a viselike grip, stopping her movements.

"Be gone, witch," Shaw mumbled. "You've done enough."

"Not nearly enough," she whispered as she worked her hands free and started shaking him even harder. "You must not go back to sleep. Unless we devise a plan of escape, we will both die."

Her words worked their way through the layers of fog that shrouded his brain. He opened one eye and felt a stab of pain as he peered through the gloom at the walls of a rough shed where they were imprisoned. "You mean I am not dead yet?"

"Nay. But soon, Campbell."

He opened his other eye and looked around. "Why did they not kill us?"

"Your kinsmen are awaiting word from someone they called the Black Campbell."

"Black Campbell." He tried the name on his tongue, then slowly shook his head. "I do not know such a one."

"Nor do I. But they are awaiting orders from him. From the manner in which they spoke his name, he must be their leader."

"But if they are truly Campbells, they swear allegiance to but one Campbell." He shook his head as if to clear it. "Where are our captors?" he asked, forcing himself to sit up. At once the room spun around and he thought he might be sick.

"They are in the cottage. From the sounds of them, they are celebrating our capture with great quantities of ale."

He strained, and could hear loud voices and laughter. "Why are we not tied?"

"Two of their company stand outside the door of this shed, to see that we do not escape. Besides, since you never even drew your sword, they have branded you a coward who needs naught but a guard."

He touched a hand to the arrow that protruded from his shoulder and gave a sudden hiss of pain. "Remove this."

"Nay. I have already examined it, hoping I could pull it out. It is embedded far too deep. To remove it is to risk bleeding to death. We will have to leave it where it is until we return to Inverene House."

The pain had him gritting his teeth, but he forced himself to stand. Staggering to the door of the shed, he peered between the cracks and studied the scene. A torch sputtered, illuminating a small circle of the darkness. Two Highlanders stood guard. Both held swords at the ready. It was plain that they were taking no chances that their prisoners could escape.

"You must find a way to get them inside," Shaw whispered.

"But how?"

He touched a hand to the swollen mass at the base of his skull. He couldn't seem to make his brain work. "We must think of something." Suddenly he said, "I know. Tell them I am dying."

He stretched out on the earthen floor, and the groan that escaped his lips was not an act.

Merritt mulled that over, then shook her head. "Nay. These men care not whether we live or die. But there may be a way..."

He could tell by the tone of her voice that she had already thought of something. "What are you planning?"

She glanced at Shaw. Instead of answering him she asked, "Are you certain you can overpower them?"

"Aye."

"You will not faint, Campbell?" Her tone was smugly superior.

He clenched his teeth. "If you bring them in, I shall see they do not leave. Now tell me what you plan."

"These men will surely resent having to stay out here and guard us when the others are warm and snug by the fire, enjoying a tankard of ale."

"Aye. So what is it you plan?"

"I plan to invite them to come in out of the cold."

Shaw braced himself as Merritt walked to the door of the shed. The searing pain nearly blinded him, but he knew he must remain alert, for he would have but one chance to overcome these brutes. Grasping a rock in one hand, and a handful of sand in the other, he watched and waited.

Opening the door, Merritt tossed aside her heavy cloak to reveal a torn, bloody shirt that exposed more of her bosom than it covered, and a pair of men's breeches that molded her hips and thighs like a second skin.

In the blink of an eye she transformed herself from young innocent to seductress as she cooed, "I am cold. And lonely. I need a man to warm me."

Too late, Shaw realized what she really planned to do. But to stop her now was to court death for both of them. All he could do was watch in stunned silence.

In the light of the torch, the guards' jaws dropped as she placed her hands on her hips in an enticing manner and beckoned them closer.

"What of your own man?" one of them asked.

"He is not my man. He was merely an addle-brained peasant oaf in need of coin, who agreed to accompany me. Besides, I think he is dead."

In response, Shaw muttered an obscenity beneath his breath. "An oaf, am I? You will pay for that, wench."

"Hush," she cautioned. "Have you never playacted?"

"Nay. But apparently you have had much practice."

She turned away from his censure and shot a brilliant smile at the two guards.

"It is a trick," one of them cautioned.

"Trick or no," the other muttered, "she is a comely wench. You can remain here and stand watch. I intend to pleasure myself."

While the one guard remained aloof, the other crossed the distance between them and tried to draw her into his arms. But Merritt was too quick for him, ducking just out of reach inside the shed.

The guard swore and stepped closer. "Hold, wench," he said, snaking out a hand to stop her.

She allowed herself to be caught, then, in full view of the other guard, allowed the man to gather her into his arms. The second guard, jealous of what he was missing, stepped closer. Out of the corner of her eye Merritt watched him, knowing he would not be able to resist the temptation for long.

"Mmm," she muttered aloud. "You are so strong. I have always had a weakness for strong men."

From his position on the floor Shaw's fury rose like bile to his throat. The thought of the brute's hands on one as young and unsullied as Merritt had his blood boiling.

"And I have always enjoyed a warm, willing wench," the guard said, as he covered her mouth with his.

Merritt nearly gagged as his foul breath mingled with hers. It took all of her willpower to keep from pulling away and scrubbing her mouth with the back of her hand.

When he lifted his head, the second guard crossed the distance in quick strides to stand beside them, awaiting his turn.

Forcing a laugh to her lips, Merritt tucked a hand beneath each man's arm and led them into the shelter. After the torchlight, their eyes needed a moment to adjust to the dim interior of the shed.

That was all the time Shaw needed. Rising up, he tossed sand in the first guard's eyes, blinding him. He brought the rock against the second guard's temple, sending him sprawling. While the first guard was still rubbing his eyes, Merritt dropped her cloak over him, then began pummeling him with her fists. As he struggled to free himself, Shaw gave him a resounding blow that had him joining his friend in the dirt.

"Come," Shaw said, removing his father's sword from the villain's scabbard. "Someone may have heard the scuffle. We must flee."

But as they ran from the shed, she veered away from him and raced off across the meadow.

"What are you doing?" he demanded.

"I will not leave without my rightful property," she cried. "Else all of this would have been in vain."

While he watched in consternation, she secured the horses once more, then pulled herself onto a mare's back. When she reached Shaw's side, she freed his stallion.

As he mounted, the door to the cottage opened, spilling light from the fireplace into the night. Several men stumbled out, laughing and talking, swilling ale.

Merritt swore under her breath. "Once again, it seems, Campbell, you have managed to slow me down just enough to get caught in a trap. If I did not know better, I would think it was deliberate."

At that moment the men looked up and realized that, in the darkness, the horses were heading toward them and the prisoners were escaping. Struggling to remove their swords from their scabbards, and clumsily fitting arrows to bows, they began shouting for the others.

"There is no time to waste," Merritt called. "Ride, Campbell. Or prepare to meet your Maker."

Chapter Nine

Dozens of knives and arrows whistled over their heads as their steeds raced across the meadow.

Shaw, bent low over his horse's neck, was forced to endure torturous pain with every jarring movement as he whipped the animal into a gallop.

Ahead of him, he saw Merritt suddenly stiffen, then slump low over her horse's back. Racing to her side, he saw the arrow that pierced the flesh of her upper arm. He caught her in his arms just as she was about to fall to the ground, and was amazed to see that she still held the rope attached to the horses. Despite her pain, the lass kept her wits about her. Taking the rope from her hands, he wrapped it around his wrist.

"Is it embedded deeply?" he demanded. "Are there other wounds?"

"Nay. Hush." With just a slight hiss of pain she tore the offensive arrow from her flesh and discarded it. "It is not serious. It just caught me unaware. I never get hurt," she said, still reeling more from the surprise of it than from the pain.

Though he was amazed at her callous disregard for her own safety, he shouted, "Hold fast to me, then, for we dare not slow down yet."

She wrapped her arms around him, and he urged his horse into a gallop. As she clung to him, her fingertips encountered a warm, sticky mass. His tunic was soaked with his own blood. And his wounds, unlike hers, were dangerously deep.

"Can you continue to ride?"

He gave a nod of his head and spurred his horse faster.

Behind him, the men cursed and swore as they tried to follow on foot. But without their horses, they were soon forced to drop back. When Shaw and Merritt were out of range of the arrows, he allowed his horse to lessen its frantic pace.

Once they reached the forest, he slowed his steed to a walk. The other horses, accustomed to the rugged Highland terrain, picked their way easily over rocks and boulders.

Shaw set his teeth against the blinding pain and prayed that he could remain conscious until he reached Inverene House. But with every mile, his determination faded. Perhaps it would be best if he could just die now. Death would be preferable to the pain he was enduring.

"Hold on, Campbell," came Merritt's voice from a long way off.

He opened his eyes and saw that he was slumped over her, nearly crushing her with his weight. Why then did her voice seem so far away? He knew his strength was ebbing, and struggled to remain awake and alert.

"We are almost home," she whispered.

"Home." He savored the word, seeing in his mind's eye plump Mistress MacCallum, hovering like a mother hen, while the servants scurried about seeing to his every comfort.

He wanted desperately to lie down. With his arms firmly around Merritt, he lowered his head until his lips were pressed to the little hollow between her neck and shoulder. Despite his pain, a not altogether unpleasant sensation welled up inside him.

"If I must die, then at least I will do so with a smile," he muttered.

The words, spoken against Merritt's sensitive flesh, sent chills racing along her spine. "You will not die, Campbell. I will not let you. For I would like the pleasure of killing you myself."

"Then do it now." He set his teeth against the pain. "I must lie down, else I will plunge headlong from my mount."

"We cannot stop," came Merritt's voice, low, soothing, warming him despite the chill of the night. "See. There." She pointed, and he roused himself enough to look up.

"The towers of Inverene House," she cried excitedly.

"Aye." He felt a moment's frustration. Not Kinloch House. Not home. But at least it was sanctuary. He could put a stop to this painful jarring. He could rest. He forced himself to sit up straighter.

The horses, sensing home, broke into a run. From sheer strength of will, Shaw managed to hold on until his mount came to a sudden halt.

As he began to slide to the ground, Shaw felt a hand beneath his elbow.

Merritt's voice was close beside him. "Just a few steps, Campbell, and then a few steps more, and we will be warm and safe."

"Warm and safe," he echoed, forcing himself to put one foot in front of the other.

And then the door was opened, and he was being propelled up the stairs to his chambers. He saw the pallet where he'd been lying...was it only hours ago? He was eased down upon the bed. Someone tugged off his boots, and he felt his shirt and tunic being cut away.

Voices drifted in and out of his consciousness.

"... told you it was too dangerous."

"'Twould not have been, had the lout not followed me."

"... must remove the arrow, else it will fester."

"Aye ... lodged in the bone."

"He was most brave." Merritt's voice came to him, soft, almost dreamy, and he felt her hands upon him, or thought he did. "I do not know how he managed to sit on his horse with such a wound." Then her words sounded close to his ear, and her tone returned to its usual brisk command. "Bite down on this, Campbell."

Something thick and leathery was placed between his teeth. A terrible, searing pain seemed to go on and on, until he thought his whole body had been put to the torch. And then, just when he could bear it no longer, he slipped away. And the pain was no more.

"How does he fare?" Astra entered the chambers and was surprised to find Merritt lying beside Shaw's pallet, too weary to return to her own room.

The lass had not changed from her breeches and boots. Her torn, bloody shirt bore testimony to her night's ordeal.

"He sleeps."

"The arrow?" Astra asked, pointing to the clean dressing on Merritt's arm.

"A minor wound, which will cause some pain for a few days, but no lingering effects. The Campbell, on the other hand ..."

"His wound is clean," Astra whispered. "But it will cause him considerable pain. He will be forced to endure

great discomfort. Sabina has sent her potions and ointments, as well as willow bark tea. Shall I see to him?"

"Nay. You have done enough." Merritt took them from
the old servant's hands. "It will be up to you to see to Father and Edan on the morrow."

"Aye. I'll see to them. But ye must get some rest now,"
Astra scolded. "Else ye will be the next one to be ailing."

"You know better than that, old woman. I have ne'er
been ill a day in my life."

"Too stubborn, y'er mother used to say." The servant
limped away, closing the door of the chambers.

Merritt knelt beside Shaw and applied ointment to his
wounds, then, pillowing his head in her lap, she held a
goblet of willow bark tea to his lips.

As the first few drops of hot liquid trickled down his
throat, he began to cough and sputter.

"Woman, on top of everything else, would you poison
me?"

She was so delighted to see him awake she could barely
disguise her joy. But at once she sharpened her tone. "Aye.
The temptation is strong. However, this is merely a healing brew."

"Healing brew or witches' brew?"

She laughed. "'Tis the same one you've been forcing
down your brother's throat."

"No wonder he resists. It is foul tasting indeed."

She placed the goblet between his lips again, forcing him
to swallow several more sips before he shoved her hand
aside.

"You must be feeling much improved," she commented, "since the strength has returned to your grip."

"Aye. And you'd best remember that if you try to ply
me with willow bark tea again."

She set aside the goblet and pressed a hand to either side of his face. Her tone softened. "You were gravely wounded, Campbell. You must sleep."

He closed his eyes a moment, savoring the gentleness of her touch. "I nearly went mad back there."

"Aye. The pain must have been unbearable."

"Nay. It was not that." He opened his eyes and stared up at her. "It was because of the way those two brigands dared to touch you."

For the space of several heartbeats their gazes locked. She wanted to make light of the incident, but the look he gave her was so powerful, so keen, she swallowed and said, "I can take care of myself, Campbell."

"Aye. So you can, firebrand. But if those louts had harmed you, I would have killed them. Even if it had cost me my last breath."

At the intensity of his words, her throat felt unusually dry. Shifting his head from her lap, she rolled aside and scrambled to her feet. Peering down at him she muttered roughly, "Go to sleep now, and stop wasting precious energy with such foolish words."

But his eyes were already closed. His breathing was slow and rhythmic.

It was pain that woke Shaw. Pain that seemed to radiate to every part of his body. His skull felt as if it had been crushed. His shoulder throbbed, shooting spasms along his arms, his hands, even his fingers, which he clenched and unclenched as he tried to control the pain. He glanced down and realized that he was naked. A length of linen covering had been tossed over his lower torso for modesty.

He rolled to one side in an effort to find some small measure of comfort, and discovered, to his surprise, that Merritt lay sleeping beside him.

She was still wearing the garb of a stableboy that she had worn for her nighttime escapade—mud-spattered boots and breeches and torn, bloody shirt.

The sight of all that blood had his heart pounding as he remembered the stricken look on her face when she'd been hit by an arrow. She'd been surprised, and stunned. But even at that, she hadn't been the least bit overwhelmed.

A tender smile touched his lips. Firebrand. The name suited her. Awake, she was always charging about, filled with restless energy. And, as she'd proved again and again, she was fearless in the face of danger.

In sleep she seemed so much younger, so much more innocent. He studied the gradual rise and fall of her chest, and his gaze was drawn to the darkened cleft between her breasts, clearly visible beneath the tattered garment. At once he felt a rush of heat and forced his gaze upward, to the pale column of throat, where a pulse thrummed steadily. He could still recall the feel of her flesh as he'd buried his lips there, struggling to hold on. It had been the touch of her, the feel of that warm, vital flesh, that had infused him with the strength to resist giving up.

She sighed in her sleep, and his gaze flew to her lips, pursed in a little pout. Surely God had created those full, sensual lips for but one purpose. The thought of kissing her had his pulse racing, and he lifted his gaze to her small, upturned nose. Sweet heaven, how she could lift that nose in the air and look down at him as though he were an errant child.

He studied the shadows cast upon her cheeks by her lowered lashes. The sudden shocking urge to press a kiss to each eyelid had him wondering about his sanity. How was it that the mere sight of this female had him forgetting all about his pain?

The woman was a contradiction. Those small hands had been made for embroidering fine linen or lifting a crystal goblet to her lips. They had not been made to wield a sword or grasp the reins as she scampered about the countryside like a thief in the night.

He studied the untidy spill of fiery curls and reminded himself of her equally fiery temper. Merritt Lamont was not a particularly pleasant person to be around. She found fault with everything he did. It was plain that she resented his intrusion into her life. And she certainly didn't need his help. Last night, she had made that abundantly clear.

His gaze was drawn again to her eyes, and he was startled to find her studying him from beneath a fringe of lashes.

"So, Campbell, you are awake. Are you in much pain?"

"Aye." He turned his head away, uncomfortable at having been caught staring at her.

At once she sat up, shoving the tangles from her eyes. Leaning over him she murmured, "What can I do? Shall I prepare a potion?"

"Nay," he said, a little too quickly. The unpleasant taste of willow bark tea was still on his tongue. "But perhaps you could . . . knead the stiffness in my shoulders."

"Roll over," she commanded.

He did as he was told, and she straddled him. A sigh of pleasure escaped him as her strong fingers began massaging the muscles of his back and shoulders.

"Does this ease your pain?" she whispered.

"Mmm. Aye." He closed his eyes and gave himself up to her ministrations. He couldn't recall having ever felt anything so soothing as this touch of her fingertips on his flesh.

"Does this hurt?" she asked, lightly skimming the area around his wound.

"Nay. It feels good."

Merritt worked in silence, kneading his flesh, all the while marveling at the difference between his body and her own. Broad of shoulders and narrow of waist. Skin bronzed from the sun. Sculpted ridges of sinew and muscles that rippled beneath her fingertips.

Why this strange tingle at the touch of him? Was it because she had begun to imagine those strong arms holding her? Those big hands moving over her? How could she permit such foolishness? Had she not fought him each time he'd tried to kiss her? Aye. And she must continue to resist. For he was, after all, not only a mere man, but a Campbell, as well.

He lay so still, she thought he might have slipped back into sleep. Her movements slowed, her touch gentled. Perhaps she had misjudged the Campbell. Though he resisted using his sword, he had behaved in a most heroic manner last night. Without him, she wondered whether or not she would have managed to escape the angry mob.

"You have the touch of an angel." Shaw surprised her by rolling over and catching her hands in his.

At once she tried to pull away, but was held fast.

"Release me, you oaf."

"An oaf, am I?" In the blink of an eye his arms came around her, roughly dragging her close, until her breasts were flattened against his chest. The thrill that shot through him was as unsettling as an arrow. "Last night, while you tended my wounds, I heard you sing my praises."

She struggled to show none of the acute discomfort she was experiencing. The press of her body against his caused a rush of heat that left her shaken. "The pain must have affected your mind. Never would I heap praise upon a Campbell."

He bit back the smile that sprang to his lips. "And did I imagine the gentleness of your touch just now, my lady? Or the softness that I detected in your eyes?"

"You did indeed, lout." She shot him a scathing look, hoping to cover the fire that blazed within as his hands began a lazy exploration of her back.

His words were warm with unspoken laughter. "I thought you a better liar than that, firebrand."

As she tried to pull away, his hand cupped the back of her head, and his lips met hers. "Am I imagining this kiss, as well?" he murmured as his mouth claimed hers.

For one brief moment, time was suspended. All thought scattered. Even their hearts forgot to beat as they came together in a fiery embrace. Merritt's arms slid around his waist and her hands clung to warm, bare flesh. Shaw's hands tangled in her hair, pressing, kneading her scalp, as his lips moved over hers. There was hunger in their kiss. And need. A need so deep, so compelling, they moaned as they took the kiss deeper and clung to each other as if clinging to life itself.

Merritt was stunned by her response. At least before, when he'd kissed her, she had managed some show of resistance. But this time, she was lost. Lost in a kiss so filled with hunger and desperate need that she could no more resist than she could hold back the day.

"My lady," came Astra's voice from the hallway.

At once Merritt's head came up sharply. For a moment she seemed utterly confused.

"I have brought clean dressings for m'laird Campbell's wounds," the servant called.

As the door moved inward, Merritt gathered her wits about her and scrambled to her feet.

The elderly servant paused. She saw the confusion on Merritt's face as she rearranged her clothing. The flush of guilt on her face was unmistakable. Astra glanced from her mistress, who avoided her eyes, to Shaw, who lay upon his pallet. He had modestly drawn a linen covering over himself.

"There are clean clothes for both of ye and a pitcher of hot mulled wine," she said, placing a pile of linen upon a table.

"Thank you, Astra," Shaw said, and the servant heard the warmth of a smile in his voice as he sat up. "Would you say the mulled wine has healing powers?"

"Aye."

"Then, since it is far more tolerable than willow bark tea, I shall have some at once."

The servant filled a goblet and handed it to him. He drank deeply.

"Shall I stay and help ye dress the laird Campbell's wounds?" Astra's sharp eyes burned into her young mistress's, and she was rewarded by a deeper flush on cheeks already heated.

"There is no need." Merritt's tone was abrupt, to cover her embarrassment. It galled her to think how easily she had succumbed to the Campbell's charm. And how easily the old servant could read her confusion. "I can manage, Astra. See to my father and brother."

"Aye." Without another word, the old woman left the room, closing the door behind her.

As soon as the door closed, Merritt poised for attack.

"Do not look so smug, Campbell. Mine was a momentary lapse. But it will not happen again. And there will be no further talk of what happened here. Praise heaven it can remain our secret. There are no servants in Inverene House to carry tales about your prowess."

"I know not what you mean," he muttered, sipping his wine.

His lack of remorse only made her own temper rise. "Does it not bother you that we were nearly caught in a...most awkward position?"

"Not a whit," he responded.

She gritted her teeth and swallowed back the oath that sprang to her lips. "I wish to wash and dress," she said stiffly. "I would be grateful if you would turn your back until I am decent."

Rolling to one side, Shaw got cautiously to his feet, draping the linen around him for modesty. For a moment the room started to spin and he was forced to hold on to the edge of a table for support. As his surroundings slowly came into focus, he made his way to the far side of the room, where he poured himself another goblet of wine before striding to the fireplace. For long minutes he stared moodily into the flames.

Hearing a splash of water, he turned for a glimpse of the female. She refused to look at him. But though his glance took in the slender hips encased in snug-fitting breeches, and the spill of fiery tangles, it was the bloodstained shirt that caught his eye. Though he couldn't explain why, the sight of her blood made him angry. Angry and determined.

Setting aside his goblet, he stirred the hot coals and added another log. As fire licked along the bark, he came to a decision. He would have to remain alert. Alert and watchful. And if the female should try to slip away again for one of her nighttime visits to a neighbor, he would follow. Not to interfere, of course. Just to make certain that the bounty was indeed Lamont property. And to see that she came to no harm.

It was obvious that this lass took far too many dangerous risks for the sake of her family. The fact that she
seemed completely unconcerned about the Highland
Avengers bothered him. He was becoming convinced that
she knew their identity. Why else would she defend them
at every turn? Most probably they were lads from the village, and she was determined to keep them from facing
retribution by the Campbells. But whether or not she knew
who they were, she was behaving in a most foolhardy
manner, traipsing about the countryside without benefit of
armed companions.

While he resided in Inverene House, it would be up to
him to save the little firebrand from herself.

Chapter Ten

"Sit," Merritt commanded when she had finished her morning ablutions. "I will change your dressings before you wash."

Shaw sat in the chair she indicated, and was achingly aware of his discomfort as he was once more forced to endure the touch of her fingers upon his flesh. But this time, her touch was far from gentle. As if to prove that their kiss had indeed been but a momentary lapse, she refused to meet his eyes as she roughly tore away the bloody linens and smeared liberal amounts of stinging ointment over his wounds.

Though he made not a sound of protest, Merritt was rewarded with a clenching of his fists. At least, she thought, this Campbell was human. All too human, if that kiss be any proof.

That kiss.

She had to struggle to keep her gaze from straying across his hair-roughened chest, his powerful hands, which rested tensely along the arms of the chair. She was far too aware of him. Aware in a way she resented. He had come unbidden into her home and into her life. He would not invade her heart, as well.

When she had secured fresh linen dressings, she turned away. "Astra has provided you with clothes." She pointed to the breeches, shirt and tunic atop the table.

"What happened to my own clothes?"

"We had to cut them off. They were beyond saving. We tossed them in the fire."

He walked to the basin and began to wash. Seeing his half-naked limbs, and feeling again the unsettling flutter in the pit of her stomach, Merritt glanced away with a feeling of self-loathing. She must learn to steel herself against any further entanglements.

When he dried himself, Shaw pulled on the clothes and made a sound of disgust.

Across the room, Merritt looked up, noting the droplets of water in his hair, which made him look strangely appealing. "What is wrong, Campbell?"

Shaw winced as he glanced down at himself. "This tunic bears the Lamont crest. If the men of Kinloch House were to see me in such as this, I would be the object of much ridicule."

For the first time since Astra had left, he caught the hint of humor in Merritt's eyes. "Mayhap you would prefer to walk around as naked as the day you were born."

"'Twould be preferable to the Lamont crest upon my person."

"Then consider what you would be forcing the rest of us to endure," she lied. The truth was, she found him far too easy to look upon. But she would never give him the satisfaction of knowing such a thing.

She saw him suddenly flinch as he lifted his sword and attempted to place it in his scabbard. His wounds were still raw and his pain was evident.

Taking pity on him, she crossed to him and took the sword from his hand. As she secured it in his scabbard, her hands brushed his waist and she felt an unexpected jolt. Glancing up, she was scorched by the heat of his gaze narrowed on her.

Needing to fill the awkward silence, she muttered, "You should have used your sword last night, Campbell." She strode to the door of her chamber to escape the nearness of him. "But I thank you for coming to my rescue."

"You are most welcome, my lady."

"But I still say 'twas your fault that we nearly lost our lives." She paused at the door and turned, lifting her head defiantly. "And I will thank you not to interfere again."

"Aye. I'll remember." He held the door, then took her arm as she started toward the stairs.

The flutter in her stomach, she assured herself, was merely hunger. It had nothing to do with the touch of this . . . Campbell.

She was grateful when he left her at the top of the stairway to check on his brother.

Shaw knocked on Sabina's door and waited until she bade him to enter.

"How does Sutton fare this morrow?"

"I am puzzled. Though he shows little change, his sleep was restless. During the darkest hours of the night he seemed in much distress. But now he sleeps peacefully. In fact," she added, "I thought I saw him smiling a short time ago."

Shaw wasn't at all surprised. Considering how much pain he had endured during the night, it was to be expected that his twin would share his suffering. And the smile . . . He thought about the brief, shocking kiss he'd shared with Merritt. Aye. That would no doubt please his worldly-wise brother.

"Has he taken any of your potions?"

"Very little. He still...resists." She was grateful for the long billowing sleeves that hid the fresh bruises on her wrists.

Now that he had tasted the bitter brew, Shaw understood his brother's continued reluctance, though he regretted that the lass had to bear the brunt of Sutton's wrath. "Astra provided me with hot mulled wine, which she claims has healing powers. Mayhap we should try a little of that instead of the willow bark tea."

Sabina nodded and filled a goblet, which she handed to Shaw. At once he knelt and cradled his brother's head, tipping the cup to his lips. Sutton took several long drinks before clamping his mouth shut on any more. Both Sabina and Shaw were overjoyed.

"That is the most nourishment he has taken," Sabina said.

"Then we will thank Astra for the favor." Shaw smoothed the covers over his brother before getting to his feet. Staring down at the steady rise and fall of Sutton's chest, he felt his hopes rise. Though his twin was a long way from recovering, he was no longer at death's door. And each day saw his strength grow.

"How did you sleep, Father?" Sabina asked solicitously as they gathered around the table to break their fast.

"Badly." Upton glowered as Astra offered him a bowl of gruel. "I heard much commotion. Whispering. Footsteps up and down the hall. Doors closing. Is there no one who will direct the servants in the proper way to fulfill their duties?"

Sabina shot a glance at Merritt, who looked away. "I will see that the servants retire early tonight, Father," Sabina said softly.

"See that they do. A warrior needs his rest. Is that not so, Campbell?"

Shaw nodded. "Aye, sir."

"You do not look rested, Campbell. Is that blood oozing through your tunic?"

Shaw glanced down at the dark stain that had worked its way through the dressing. "A minor wound. A... tree branch that snagged my flesh when I was trailing the herd of deer."

"Tree branch. Ha. Such a wound is unworthy of mention," Upton scoffed. "When I was your age, I was engaging my enemy daily. My body bears the scars of a score of encounters with arrow, dirk and sword. But not one of my enemies ever bested me."

"Tell us again about your battles, Father," Edan coaxed.

"Which tale would please you, lad?"

"The time you stood alone against an entire army of invaders."

"Aye." The gruel was forgotten as Upton said, "'Twas in the days before Rob and his armies. 'Twas even before the Highlanders had banded together to repel invaders. In those days, we were nothing but a wandering ragtag band of young fools, always hungry, always cold, and always ready to do battle against anyone who lifted a sword against us." He glanced around at his son and daughters. "Living in this fine house, surrounded by servants to do your bidding, you would not know about such things. But then, times were very hard. Not at all as they are now, what with all the luxuries you enjoy."

Shaw saw Merritt and Sabina exchange glances, then lower their heads as their father continued.

"The invaders were young savages, newly arrived on our shores from some heathen land. They had left a bloody trail of death and destruction. When we caught up with them, we sent our women and children to hide in the forest while we engaged them in battle."

"Tell us about the battle, Father," Edan urged. His eyes were animated, and it was easy to see that he imagined himself that same brave young warrior.

"Our weapons were crude. A few swords. Dirks carved from stone and animal bone. Tree limbs used as clubs. But we stood together, back to back, determined to repel the barbarians."

"And you were the tallest, and the strongest, and the bravest," Edan said, clapping his hands.

"Aye. That I was, lad. The leader. The one the others looked up to. And I led them well. 'Twas my sword that inflicted the most pain. My voice that called out words of encouragement to the others. My skill that brought the savages to their knees, until the Highland meadow ran red with their blood."

"And then what, Father?" Edan's food was forgotten now in the excitement of the tale.

"Then we were rid of the invaders," Upton said fiercely. "And the others no longer needed me." His voice lowered. His gaze focused on his big hands, palms resting upward atop the scarred table. "The others were content to become soft and lazy. To till the soil and raise their bairns. But what about me? Did they give a care about me? What is a warrior to do when the battles end?"

"The battles never end," Merritt said.

"Aye." Upton lifted his gaze to his daughter. The smile returned to his lips. "We are two of a kind, you and I, lass. We'll never be content to grow soft and lazy and settle in to raise our bairns. There will always be another battle, another challenge."

Throughout Upton's narrative, Shaw held his silence, watching first the father, then the children. It was obvious that they had heard the tale many times before. And though Edan seemed pleased by his father's story, he sensed an underlying sadness in Sabina and Merritt.

Upton's eyes lit with pleasure when Astra returned bearing a tray heaped with steaming mounds of freshly sliced venison. "Now this is how a warrior should ever break his fast," Upton said as he filled his trencher and began to eat.

Shaw sipped his ale and forced himself to eat, knowing that the food would renew his strength. But while he ate, he thought about the story he had just heard. There had been similar tales in his own boyhood. But the hero had always been Modric of the Clan Campbell. And the villain had always been the man who was now seated across the table from him.

As if reading his mind, Upton said, "You are quiet this morrow, Campbell. How does your brother fare?"

"He grows stronger. Though he is not yet awake, I believe he has passed through a veil. I no longer fear for his life."

"Has he spoken?" Merritt asked sharply.

Shaw turned to study her. Was that a tremor of fear in her voice?

His eyes narrowed. "Why does that concern you?"

She shrugged and turned away, avoiding his probing look. "It is of no concern to me, Campbell. Except that the sooner he recovers, the sooner you can be on your way back to your people."

"I hope it is not too soon," Edan said as he filled his plate a second time. "For Shaw has promised to tutor me in my letters."

The others looked up in surprise.

"You read, Campbell?" Merritt asked.

"Aye. My brothers and I were raised in the monastery of Saint Collum after our parents were killed," he responded. "The monks taught us to read and write, as well as how to till the soil."

"I'll wager they didn't teach you how to wield a sword," Upton said with a scornful laugh.

"Nay. They are men of God, not of war. But the Highlander does not live who does not know how to fight. Though I must admit," he said with a rueful smile, "that my brothers are more skilled in that area than I."

"And why is that? Were you sickly as a lad?" Edan asked.

"Nay. But I have no love for war."

"No love for..." Merritt looked at him as though he were mad. "Does your blood not run hot when you lift your sword? Do you not feel a sudden thrill when you race your mount across a Highland meadow and charge into a murderous mob?"

Shaw threw back his head and roared. It was a full, rich sound that had the others smiling. "Nay, lass. But I feel certain my brothers have experienced such as you have just described. For nothing fills them with fire like the thought of battle. As for me, I will fight my battles on the chessboard, and be inspired by the lofty words inscribed in a book."

Hearing mention of reading, Edan asked eagerly, "Can we begin our lesson soon?"

"Aye, lad." Shaw drained his goblet, pleased that his pupil was so impatient to learn. "As soon as you have finished your meal, the lessons will begin."

* * *

"You will form your letters upon this parchment, that I may see how far you have advanced in your education," Shaw said, handing Edan a quill and scroll.

He had carried the lad to a dusty, neglected room in the east wing of the keep. There, seated in a chair beside the window, the lad took great pains to form each letter.

While he worked, Shaw set a roaring fire in the fireplace, then moved around the room, tearing down heavy draperies and opening dirt-streaked casements to allow the fresh air and morning sun to stream in. Soon, despite the dust motes and cobwebs, the room took on a cheery air.

Several hours later Merritt found them, heads bent over a book. Edan's sweet young voice could be heard reading haltingly, while Shaw nodded encouragement.

"In the year of our Lord, 1295, Upton of the Clan Lamont in Argyll took for his bride Brinda, daughter of Galen of the Clan MacArthur in Argyll. Brinda did present her laird husband with three bairns. Sabina, Merritt and Edan."

Seeing Merritt, Shaw dropped a hand on Edan's arm. "That's enough for now, lad. We have company."

"What did you bring us?" Edan asked, eyeing the tray in Merritt's hands.

"Tea and biscuits, with clotted cream and fresh preserves. Astra said this will keep you until our midday meal."

"I have not seen food such as this for a year or more," the boy cried in delight.

"Aye. 'Twould seem that Astra has been inspired by the fresh meat and logs provided by your tutor."

While Edan happily buttered a biscuit and popped it into his mouth, Shaw watched as Merritt slowly circled the room.

"I'm glad you chose this room. 'Twas once my mother's sitting chamber," Merritt said softly. "There were lovely tapestries upon the walls, and the chairs and settles were covered with her finest embroidery. There was always a cheery fire blazing on the hearth, and we children would play while she and the servants spun wool. We often took our midday meal in here, then fell asleep on the rug before the fire."

"Did you sup here, as well?"

"Nay. At night we would sup in the great hall with Father and his soldiers. There they would tell of their battles, and a scribe would write every tale in the family book." She nodded toward the heavy manuscript that rested beside Edan. "That is the book of our lives."

"The lad has been well taught," Shaw admitted. "You and your sister have done a fine job." He saw the color that crept into her cheeks and was oddly pleased that it was his praise that put it there. "In just a few short lessons he should be able to read anything."

"Then I will be able to read about Father's battles," Edan said with enthusiasm.

"What is more, Edan, you will be able to chronicle the rest of your family's history, from the death of your mother to the present time," Shaw told him.

Merritt's smile fled. "From the looks of it, he may well be inscribing the end of our family history."

"Nonsense." Shaw lifted the heavy book and replaced it on the shelf where it had been residing for so many years. Wiping the dust on his breeches, he turned to Edan. "We will end your lesson for today. But each day, after we break our fast, we will continue, until you learn all the letters, and you can read every page in this book."

"Aye." The boy's eyes sparkled with undisguised pleasure. "Where do you go now?"

Shaw cast a mysterious smile in Merritt's direction. "Since your horses have reappeared, I think it is time to build a pen to hold them."

She clapped her hands in delight. "Truly?"

"Aye. You would not want them to run away again, would you?"

She watched as he popped a biscuit into his mouth before striding from the room. When she caught her little brother observing her closely, she turned away. "Enjoy your treat," she commanded, "before I carry you above stairs to your pallet."

"Why must I go to my room?" the lad demanded.

She stared at him. "Because you always do. You said your chamber is the only place where you feel safe, with your sword and knife by your side."

"Well, I have changed my mind," he said firmly. "I think I would prefer to sit outside in the sunshine and watch Shaw work."

Merritt laughed, a clear, crystal sound, as she bent and lifted her brother in her arms. Though she would not admit it to him, the same thought had occurred to her. There was no place she would rather be than watching the Campbell take on a task she had expected to have to do herself.

Chapter Eleven

"Fool! You allowed my hated enemy to escape. Again you have failed me."

Deep in the forest, the two men faced each other in the small hut. The leader's eyes blazed with fury.

The peasant recoiled as though lashed. "Y'er enemy is cunning, m'laird. Furthermore, my men are leery of retaliation, for they know the reputation of y'er enemy's clan."

"I'll accept no more of your whining. You will finish what was begun, or answer to my sword. Is that clear?"

"Aye, m'laird."

"And if any man questions my authority, he must die. Now go and see to what I have commanded."

The peasant hurried away, eager to escape the wrath of the evil Black Campbell.

"Without a stable, how will you keep the horses from bolting?" Edan called from his position beneath a gnarled old tree.

"You shall have to watch and see," Shaw replied.

Sunlight sparkled on the loch and filtered through the trees as he bent to his task. It was a glorious afternoon. The perfume of evergreen and wildflowers wafted on the breeze. Birds chirped overhead.

After chopping saplings, Shaw cut notches in a ring of trees, then fitted the saplings into the notches. The work was hard, and he soon shed his tunic and shirt.

Edan stared in fascination at the muscled giant who seemed never to tire as he grappled with trees and heavy limbs. "I see now what you are doing," he called. "It is a circle."

"Aye. A closed circle that will keep the horses from roaming."

"But what if the invaders return?" Merritt asked from her perch in a branch of the tree. "What is to stop them from stealing our horses again?"

"The same thought has occurred to me. If I must, I am prepared to sleep out here." Shading the sun from his eyes, Shaw glanced at the lass. She had no idea of the pretty picture she presented, with her hair blowing in the breeze, her cheeks bright with color. From beneath her billowing petticoats he glimpsed a length of shapely ankle. Always before, his natural inclination would have been to turn away from such a distraction. But here in this raw, primitive fortress, something was happening to him. Something he neither understood nor tried to fathom. He merely enjoyed the view and even seemed not to mind the way his blood heated at the sight of her.

"We could lay some traps, to catch them unawares," Edan called suddenly.

Shaw's attention shifted. "What sort of traps?"

"Father once spoke of setting traps to catch his enemies," the boy explained. "Ofttimes they were nothing more than deep pits, covered by leaves and branches."

Shaw stared at the lad in amazement, then burst into laughter. "By heaven, the tutor has much to learn from his pupil. That is precisely what we shall do, Edan. I will begin digging the pit at once."

"I will help." Merritt slid to the ground and picked up a shovel.

"Nay." Shaw caught her hand in his, stilling her movements.

"You may be strong, lass, but I'll not have your hands raw and bloody from turning the soil."

Merritt's throat went dry. Why did the touch of this man always cause such unsettling feelings? For the merest whisper of time she thought about standing still, just so, to allow herself the luxury of his touch. But out of the corner of her eye she could see her little brother watching her closely and knew that her high color gave her away. She took a step back, forcing him to break contact.

"You can fetch branches and leaves," Shaw said, "while I dig."

Merritt reluctantly scampered off to the woods, returning a short time later dragging branches and tree limbs. Again and again she made the trip from the woods and back, until the ground beside the animal pen was littered with enough greenery to cover several pits.

By the time evening shadows grew long, she and Edan could no longer see the top of Shaw's head as he labored in the deep hole. And when nighttime fell and Astra summoned them to sup, Shaw crawled from the hole with the aid of a rope tied to a tree. Together he and Merritt covered the hole, then carefully examined the fruit of their long afternoon of labor. With the branches and leaves in place, there was no trace of the yawning chasm that lay in wait for anyone attempting to make off with the horses.

"We will all sleep better this night, my lady," Shaw said as he pulled on his shirt and tunic, "because of the cleverness of this fine young lad."

With ease he lifted Edan in his arms and settled him high upon his shoulders. The boy clung to Shaw's head and let out a whoop of joy.

As they made their way inside, Merritt saw the flush that colored her brother's cheeks, and marveled that a single word of praise from this Campbell could make the lad so happy.

"Venison again," Upton complained as Astra served their meal. "I had hoped for mutton."

"M'laird should be grateful—" the old woman began, but a look from Sabina cut her off in midsentence.

"I told Astra to cook the rest of the deer before any sheep were slaughtered, Father." Sabina filled his goblet with ale.

"A wise decision," he muttered as he savored fresh spring vegetables. "Even the laird should be above wasting heaven's bounty."

Noting the sad look on Merritt's face, Shaw sensed that she was grieving for the sheep that had been stolen. Again he marveled at the secrets she and the others had managed to keep from their father.

"And to atone for having no mutton, Father, Astra has baked her spirit-soaked cake, laden with currants and bits of fruit." Edan's voice was tinged with excitement.

"And how would you know that?" Merritt asked. "Did you peek in the kitchen?"

The boy laughed. "Astra whispered her secret, for she knows it is my favorite."

"And mine." Upton turned to Shaw and his smile dissolved into a frown of annoyance. "A sound of ax against wood assaulted my ears this day. Would you know anything about that, Campbell?"

"He was assisting the men in cutting more logs," Merritt put in quickly.

"That is work that is best left to the servants. I would think a Campbell warrior could put his strength to better use by engaging in a few battles with the local villains. Besides, splitting logs ought to be work considered too demeaning for the grand and glorious Campbells." Upton seemed about to pontificate further on his favorite subject when Astra entered the great hall carrying her cake sliced into large portions. At once Upton's mood lightened. "Brinda knows that this is my favorite confection. That must be why she baked it for me."

Everyone around the table visibly tensed. Though the mere mention of his wife always seemed to soothe Upton Lamont, it pained his children to see how his mind tricked him into believing she was still with them.

"'Twas probably what made me choose her for my bride," Upton muttered as he polished off his portion and waited for Astra to serve him another. "At my first bite, I thought I'd tasted heaven."

He glanced up, fixing his older daughter with a look. "Has your mother taught you the secret of her cake yet?"

"Nay, Father. But . . . soon," Sabina said haltingly.

"It is one of woman's finest weapons," he said sharply. "What man can refuse to take as his bride a female who can bake such as this?" He studied the dark-haired girl over the rim of his goblet. "Ofttimes I neglect to notice that you are growing up, Sabina. A pretty thing, is she not, Campbell?"

"Aye." Shaw ducked his head after glancing at the lass, whose cheeks had turned crimson under her father's scrutiny.

"Soon," Upton said fiercely, "I will arrange a marriage between you and the son of one of our Highland lairds. Any clan would be willing, nay eager, to lay claim to such, since, along with a fine dowry, I will give my pledge of protection." He peered at Sabina, who kept her gaze averted. "There are probably those who will even go to war for the hand of a daughter of Lamont of Argyll, for there is not a better match to be made in all of Scotland."

Their father's glance slid to Merritt, who, unlike her sister, held her head high and met his look squarely. "And what am I to do with you, lass? You have neither your mother's comely looks nor your sister's sweet disposition."

"As you have so often said, I am my father's daughter."

"So it would seem." Upton scowled. "How the gods mock me. They send me a fine, brave son whose courage cost him his legs. . . ."

At that, Edan pushed aside his cake and sat with head bowed and eyes downcast.

"Cast aside your fears, lad. Soon enough your strength will return and you shall walk."

He turned to Merritt. "Aye. And the gods send me a daughter whose spirit outshines any man's and who refuses to behave like a female."

Merritt's spine seemed to stiffen even more. Her father glowered at the lass, who refused to back down even in the face of his wrath. "You have resisted all attempts to learn the maidenly arts. I fear even a dowry of regal proportions and an army of swords pledged to the clan of your betrothed will bring no offers for your hand."

"It's just as well, Father," she said with a sigh. "I'll not be bargained for like a brood mare."

"A brood mare!" His temper blazed. "It was no brood mare I saw when I looked into your mother's eyes. Nor was it—"

"More cake?" Astra asked, sliding yet another portion in front of him.

Distracted, Upton's voice trailed off and he sighed with pleasure as he filled his mouth. At once, his temper was forgotten.

Merritt patted her brother's hand and whispered something that caused him to put aside the pain inflicted by his father's carelessly spoken words. Soon the lad was eating again, though his smile faltered from time to time.

Shaw studied the people seated around the table. They were certainly not what he'd expected to find at Inverene House. The fierce warrior, Upton, seemed nothing more than a shell of a man, his mind dwelling in the past while his body slowly failed him. Yet, despite his often unkind words, his family continued to honor and respect him, and there were times when Shaw saw remnants of the man he must have been. Upton's three children were decidedly distinct. Sabina had the manner and bearing of a queen. Merritt burned as brightly as a wildfire. And Edan had the quick mind of a scholar. But what was most appealing to Shaw was the way they all worked together for the common good. If a fire was needed, they would provide it, even if it meant sacrificing opulent furniture. If a stolen flock needed retrieving, they would see to it, no matter how dangerous to life and limb.

"What of you, Campbell?" Merritt asked. "You have eaten little. Do you not care for Astra's confection?"

Shaw pulled himself back from his thoughts. "The food is fine. My compliments, Astra."

The old servant acknowledged his kind words with a nod of her head as she circled the table, refilling goblets. Soon Upton pushed away from the table, and the others followed suit. When the older man made his way to a chair in front of the fire, Shaw lifted Edan in his arms and placed him on a nearby settle, while Sabina made ready to play her harp.

Merritt glanced at Shaw. "Would you care for another lesson on the board?"

He saw her sly smile and couldn't help returning it. "I would welcome the chance to best you, my lady. But I have spent little enough time with my brother this day. If you will excuse me, I would go to him now."

"When you have finished with him, I will be here to challenge you, Campbell," Merritt called to his retreating back.

He smiled at the haughty tone. A challenge. Aye. She was that.

Sabina's nearly bare chambers were softened by the glow of a fire burning on the grate. From below stairs could be heard the music of the harp, and Sabina's voice lifted in song.

Inside the room all was silent, save for the occasional hissing of the log on the hearth, and the slow ragged breathing of the figure on the pallet.

Shaw knelt beside the bed and studied the beloved face of his brother. Sutton's chin was now covered by a shaggy growth of golden beard. Dark circles rimmed his closed eyes. His skin was pale and chalky, stretched tautly across high, firm cheekbones.

A moan escaped Sutton's lips. Instantly Shaw touched a hand to the pulse at his throat and was relieved by the steady rhythm he detected.

"You grow stronger, Sutton. Soon, I know, you shall rid yourself of this demon that holds you in its grip. Then shall you rise from your pallet of pain and become once more the brave, strong, impulsive warrior whose courage inspires men and whose clever wit charms women."

He continued in the same soothing tone, "I miss you, Sutton. I feel lost without the sound of your taunts and teasing laughter." Shaw knew he was saying these things more to comfort himself than his sleeping brother, but now that he had begun, he couldn't seem to stop himself. There was so much in his heart that he needed to say. So much love. So much concern for this once strong, virile man who now lay as helpless as a wee bairn.

"My life is meaningless without you. It is as though I am only half-alive. A part of my heart slumbers, while the rest of it struggles to continue beating. Throughout the day, while I work at mundane chores, my thoughts are of you. Even at night, my sleep is disturbed with troubling images. I feel your pain, Sutton. I share your discomfort. Come back to me."

As a shadow crossed the threshold, Shaw looked up to see Astra's stooped figure silhouetted in the doorway. She wore the troubled look of one who was frozen in fear and seemed poised to flee at any moment.

"Enter," he called.

He saw the way she hesitated before obeying. Obviously she had overheard much of what he'd confided to his brother, and the old servant had decided that he was a fool or a madman. It mattered not to Shaw, and he offered no explanation. Let others think what they would. He cared only that his brother would awaken, and they could leave this sad, troubled family and their problems far behind and get on with their own lives.

As Astra crossed the room she muttered, "My lady Sabina ordered me to fetch some hot mulled wine."

"Thank you. It is the only thing my brother seems willing to swallow." He took the goblet from her hands and, cradling Sutton's head in his lap, began to force the liquid between his lips.

Sutton managed several swallows before he turned his head aside, refusing any more.

Shaw handed the drink over to the servant. "Set it aside, Astra. Mayhap he will take some more before I leave him."

The old servant did as she was told, all the while keeping a close watch on the two of them. Shaw struggled not to laugh, though some demon inside him tempted him to begin ranting and raving like a man possessed. It took all his willpower to resist. He had no doubt the old woman would flee the house as though the devil himself were after her, and would most probably never allow herself to return.

She'd convinced herself that he and his twin were some sort of evil spirits. So be it. He would not attempt to disabuse her of her thoughts.

He returned his attention to his brother, wiping the dampness from Sutton's fevered brow, smoothing the covers up to his chest, all the while crooning words meant to soothe.

"It seems strange to see you lying so motionless. You've always been the impatient one, whether facing foe on the field of battle or plying your charms on the lasses. You used to accuse me of spending precious time abed that could be better used honing my skills with broadsword and mallet."

A haunted smile touched his lips. "Ah, my brother, the time we wasted on foolish rivalry. Remember how Dillon used to box our ears whenever the fighting got out of hand? How wise he was, knowing that we would instinctively put aside our differences to stand together against anyone who threatened us. And how we would fight him." Laughter warmed his words. "We would come at him with our fists, only to find ourselves suddenly sprawled on our backs, bruised and bloody. He tossed aside our jabs like a stallion fending off errant colts.''

Across the room, old Astra huddled before the fire, watching and listening. In all her years, she had never before met a man like this Campbell. There was unusual gentleness beneath all that strength. A goodness that he kept hidden beneath a mask of danger. Humility beneath a guise of arrogance. And above all, love shining through all his words and actions. Love for this brother who had his face.

Putting aside her fear, she picked up the goblet and approached Shaw. ''Mayhap ye could force a few more drops down his throat,'' she said softly.

Surprised, Shaw looked up. Holding out his hand, he said, ''Aye. Thank you, Astra. You may go now and see to the others.''

The old woman needed no coaxing. Shaw watched as she made her way from the room, then lifted his brother's head and bent to the task of forcing liquid to Sutton's lips.

''God in heaven!''

At his muttered exclamation, the old servant hastily retraced her steps and found him, head bent, hand paused in midair.

Sutton's lids had suddenly opened. Blue-green eyes were peering into Shaw's with a mixture of curiosity and confusion.

Chapter Twelve

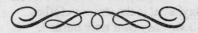

"Praise God, you have awakened."

"And why would I not?" Sutton winced, then gingerly touched a hand to his temple. "How much ale did I drink? My head is on fire."

"I've no doubt of that, after the wounds you suffered. But it was not ale, my brother, that put you down. 'Twas the dirks and arrows that found your back."

"Dirks? Arrows?" Sutton closed his eyes a moment, obviously dazed and troubled. When he opened them he glanced around the bleak, barren room and asked, "What is this place? I know it not."

"Inverene House."

Sutton stiffened. "The fortress of our enemy?"

"Aye."

"Are we their prisoners, then?"

"Nay." Shaw shook his head quickly, to calm the alarm he could read in his brother's eyes. "Do you recall leaving Kinloch House to confront Upton Lamont?"

Sutton nodded, but it was plain that he could barely recall anything.

"When you did not return after several days, I came searching for you, and found you here, near death's door."

"Ah. And did you slay the cursed Lamonts?"

"I merely overpowered them, and ordered them to see well to your care or they would answer to me."

"You!" Humor danced in Sutton's eyes as he looked up at his gentle brother. His gaze moved from the familiar, beloved face to the unfamiliar tunic, bearing the Lamont crest, and to the jeweled hilt at his waist, something he had never seen before upon his brother's person. "You look different. Mayhap it is the strange clothes."

Shaw flushed. "My own were burned."

"Is that our father's sword in your scabbard?"

"It is. Though I have not as yet had to use it."

"You overpowered the Lamont army without a weapon?"

Shaw sighed. There was so much to explain. "I will tell you everything in time. But first, you must give me the names of those who attacked you, so that I may keep my vow to avenge this foul deed."

Sutton passed a hand over his eyes. "I recall a hooded figure. Mayhap…whispered voices. I know not. My brain seems befuddled."

"'Tis but a momentary lapse," Shaw said softly. "It will come back to you in time. And when it does, I will seek out those who did this, and they will pay dearly. For now, it is enough to know that you have returned to the land of the living. Rest now, my brother, and conserve your strength for the days to come."

Sutton needed no encouragement to close his eyes. These few moments had left him too weary to do otherwise.

"You will be here when I awake?"

"You know I will, Sutton. I have vowed to remain until you and I can leave this place together."

"Together." The word was a whispered sigh.

Shaw knelt beside the pallet, watching the steady rise and fall of his brother's chest. He had never known anything to give him such pleasure. His joy at his brother's awakening filled him with renewed energy.

Sutton had passed through the darkness and had emerged into the light. And though there would still be pain and discomfort ahead, the worst was over. He would rise up to fight another day.

For long minutes Shaw remained on his knees as the monks had taught him, giving praise and glory to God for this generous gift of his brother's life.

At last he roused himself and made his way down the stairs. He paused in the doorway of the great hall. It was obvious that Upton and his son had retired for the night. Only the two lasses remained.

Sabina and Merritt sat close together, huddled before the fire, heads bent, voices lowered to a whisper. When they caught sight of him, their words abruptly ceased. Both women watched warily as he entered the room and crossed to them.

"Astra has told us of your brother's miraculous recovery," Sabina said.

"Aye. Praise heaven."

"So, Campbell," Merritt called, "what curious tale has your brother given you regarding his wounds?"

Shaw fixed his gaze on her, to gauge her reaction. "I bade him to conserve his energy. On the morrow, if he feels stronger, we will talk at length. Then he will tell me everything."

He was rewarded with a flush that crept over her cheeks, and a lowering of her gaze. It would give him the greatest satisfaction to uncover her lies. But for now, he must forgo revenge and think only about what was good for Sutton.

"Instruct Astra that my brother will need broth to regain his strength."

"We ate the last of the meat," Merritt reminded him.

"Then I shall go out and slay a deer." He headed toward the door.

"Now? Tonight?" Merritt's tone was incredulous.

Something in her voice caused Shaw to pause. She was not merely questioning his actions. She seemed truly dismayed.

He turned to study her. "Why should it trouble you if I go out into the night?"

"There is no reason." She shrugged uncomfortably beneath his gaze.

"So, little firebrand, I take it you've planned another nightly raid, and I have just unraveled your well-laid plans."

"You've done nothing of the sort. Do you think I need your approval, Campbell, to do as I please?"

In swift strides he crossed to her and caught her roughly by the arm, holding her firmly when she tried to pull away.

His voice was low with controlled anger. "Aye, my lady. Mark me well. Though I allow you much freedom, I am your captor. You and your family are my captives. While I am under your roof, you will obtain my approval before you enter or leave Inverene House."

"And if I do not, what will you do?" She tossed her head, eyes blazing. Her words burned with sarcasm. "You cannot even lift your sword against those who attack you. What will you do to one errant woman?"

His voice was deadly calm, the only outward sign of just how much self-control he exerted when dealing with her. "If you dare to cross me, you will find out. I promise you, my punishment will be swift. And suitable to your deed. The choice is yours, my lady." He released her and turned away.

Merritt rubbed her bruised arm. There was something compelling about this man. Though he was slow to anger, and he had made it clear that his sword would be a last resort, she had no doubt that he was as good as his word. Still, she refused to be cowed by a Campbell.

"One more thing," Shaw said, directing his words to Sabina. "My brother's pallet is little more than rags. He needs fresh bed linens."

"And will our wealthy captor provide them, as well?" Merritt asked contemptuously.

He refused to look at her, but his eyes narrowed as he muttered, "If need be."

"There is no need," Sabina said quickly, hoping to keep peace between these two. "It will be done."

He nodded in satisfaction. "I will return shortly. See that there is a fire blazing and a kettle simmering."

Both Merritt and Sabina breathed an audible sigh of relief when the imposing young giant strode from the room.

Shaw knelt beside the banks of the swiftly running stream and drank deeply. The tracks of the herd he'd been following had taken him much farther from Inverene House than he'd intended. It would probably be dawn before he made it back.

Glancing up, he peered through the tall spires of the forest to the sliver of half-moon that glowed in the night sky.

After the work he'd put in this day, he ought to be exhausted and ready to sleep like a bairn. But the truth was, he felt oddly exhilarated by the thrill of the hunt. Now that Sutton was mending, he felt that no task would be too great. If he had to move a mountain or level a forest to return his brother to the fullness of his life, it would be done.

Getting to his feet, he caught the reins of his mount and began leading him down the steep incline. Flung across the horse's back was the biggest stag Shaw had ever killed. Tied to the saddle was a brace of pheasant.

He smiled as he picked his way among rocks and trees. Upton Lamont would be a happy man when old Astra prepared all this food. But he hadn't done this for the Lamonts, he told himself sternly; he'd done it for Sutton. The Lamonts meant nothing to him. Sutton, on the other hand, meant the world to him.

Now that his brother had come back from the brink, he would do everything in his power to help him regain his strength. Then they would be done with these cursed Lamonts forever.

His horse nickered softly and drew back on the reins. Shaw saw that the horse's ears had flattened, and its eyes were wide with fright.

Lifting his head, he strained to see through the darkness, but the density of forest blotted out all but a fragment of moonlight.

Again the horse pulled back and a faint sound reached Shaw's ears. A dog barked. And then there was another sound. A voice. A woman's voice. Calling. Coaxing. But as the sound grew nearer, Shaw recognized it, and fought back a wave of absolute, raw fury.

Merritt's voice. The female was somewhere out here, accompanied by a hound. After he had gone to such pains to warn her, she had deliberately disobeyed him and had gone out into the night.

The dog's barking increased, as did the sound of her voice. But there was another sound. Crying perhaps, or the call of a flock of night birds.

And then, as dozens of dark shapes spilled over the hill and began the steep descent toward him, Shaw realized what he had heard. Sheep. It was the bleating of sheep. The damnable female had gone off on another of her night raids. And this time, she'd helped herself to someone's sheep.

He only prayed there weren't a dozen armed men close on her heels. But even as the thought took shape in his mind, he heard the distant thundering of hoofbeats. And the angry murmur of men's voices heading his way.

Merritt took no notice of the pain in her arm where an arrow had grazed her flesh. She had boldly tossed aside the bloody arrow and struggled to ignore the warm sticky mass that now soaked the sleeve of her shirt.

She seemed unaware of the tree branches that snagged her hair, and the cold night wind whistling past her face, as her horse sped along behind the flock of sheep. Though tiny currents of fear occasionally intruded, she nudged them aside, determined to see her task to its successful conclusion. She was halfway home, and no one, by heaven, was going to stand in the way of her success. And now that she had reached the shelter of the forest, she had an even greater chance of outrunning the men who followed. This forest was, after all, her home. From her earliest days she had roamed these wooded hills. She knew every fell, every glade, every rock.

The hound, trained to herd, yapped at the heels of errant animals and kept the flock from scattering. Though they moved at a fast clip, they remained a tight, contained group.

As they came up over a rise, Merritt watched with satisfaction as the hound nipped at the heels of the leader of the flock, turning it in the direction of Inverene House. The rest of the sheep followed, moving across the darkened hillside in undulating waves.

As she urged her mount forward, a darkened figure stepped from a stand of trees. Her heart leapt to her throat. At once she pulled her sword from its scabbard and advanced, prepared to do battle.

"So, firebrand, I see you cannot keep your word for even one night."

"You!" Relief flooded through her, and for a moment she felt a rush of heat at the sight of the Campbell. "I'd been prepared to fight for my life."

"You may yet have to do that, judging by the sound of those curses."

"Ha. Those oafs will never find their way through this forest."

"It takes but one oaf, lass, to run you through with his sword. And it would seem his deed would be justified, since you are stealing his sheep."

"They are Lamont sheep," she cried.

"Oh. Aye. And once again, you are merely the innocent victim retrieving that which is rightfully yours."

"'Tis true."

"Can you prove that?"

She gave a little hiss of impatience. "Why must you always demand proof of my righteousness?"

"Because that is the law."

"And a Campbell would never break the law," she muttered sarcastically.

"Tell me," Shaw demanded. "How can you prove that the sheep are yours?"

"See that hound?" she asked.

When he turned to where she pointed, she said, "The thieving Campbells stole not only our flock, but its guardian, as well. Old Kale has been with us since Edan was a bairn. If it weren't for Kale, the flock would have been scattered and hopelessly lost."

Shaw couldn't argue with her logic. Every Highlander knew that a hound trained to herd sheep was loyal even unto death. And the dog was heading directly toward Inverene House.

"But why tonight, when I forbade you to leave?"

That question would be more difficult, she knew. But she would try to hold her patience in check. "To understand, you must know that it breaks my heart to see my family going hungry while thieves grow sleek and fat off their ill-gotten goods."

Her words, spoken from the heart, touched him deeply.

"When I located Kale in a meadow far from here," she went on, "I knew I'd found our flock. I've been waiting for my chance to retrieve them. And this night was perfect, with the threat of rain and little moonlight to give me away. If I did not take the chance tonight, who knows when the opportunity might come again?"

"And so you disobeyed me."

At his words her chin lifted in that haughty way he'd come to recognize. "Aye. I chose not to obey you, Campbell. You are not my master."

"Woman..." As he stepped closer and caught her arm, he heard her hiss of pain at the same instant that he felt the warmth of her blood.

Peering closer, he saw the dark stain that soaked her sleeve and smeared the front of her tunic. "God in heaven. You are wounded."

"It is but a badly aimed arrow from one of the thieves."

"And what if his aim had been better?" His tone roughened to hide the tender feelings that surfaced. "You could have been lying dead somewhere in a field, and no one would be the wiser. On the morrow, your family would mourn your loss without even knowing where to look for you."

"Sabina would know. I told her before I left."

"Then why could you not confide in me, as well?"

"Have you forgotten? You forbade me to leave Inverene House."

"I forget nothing, woman. But if you knew you were going on a dangerous mission, you should have taken me along."

"You!" She gave a laugh of contempt. "You are not even man enough to draw a sword and—"

At that moment a shadow passed over them, and they both thought it was the clouds passing over the moon. But as Shaw glanced upward, he caught sight of the darkened outline of a mountain cat crouched on the limb of a tree overhead, about to spring.

"Hush, lass. Do not move."

She tossed her head. "How dare you give orders—"

There was no time to argue. In one quick movement, Shaw dragged her roughly from the saddle and withdrew his dirk from his waist. Glancing up, Merritt gave a cry of alarm.

"God in heaven, my weapon." She fumbled with her sword, but her movements were too slow.

Everything seemed to happen in the blink of an eye.

As the animal sprang, Shaw pushed Merritt out of the way, leaving himself the only target. With an economy of movement he tossed his knife with deadly accuracy.

The cat continued downward, landing directly on top of Shaw. Merritt watched in shock and horror as man and animal fell to the ground in a tangled, bloody heap. For long moments the two exploded into snarls and grunts of pain. And then an eerie silence settled over them. When at last Shaw crawled out from beneath the dead cat, Merritt felt her heart begin to beat once more.

"Forgive me, Campbell. I did not know—"

They both looked up as the sound of men and horses drew nearer.

"You must go," Shaw commanded. "See to your flock."

She hesitated. "Nay. I will not leave you."

"Have you not learned your lesson yet, firebrand?" He bent and withdrew his blood-drenched knife from the animal's hide, wiping it in the grass before sheathing it. "Do not argue with me. Just go."

"But what about you, Campbell?"

His gaze was drawn to the blood seeping down her arm. For some strange reason, it filled him with quiet rage. He understood her better now. This was a deadly game she played. And all for the sake of her beloved family.

"I am learning that there are other predators in this forest. I will deal with them the same way I dealt with this one."

She noted a subtle change in his tone. When he brought his gaze to hers, she saw the hint of something dark and dangerous.

Impatiently he lifted her into the saddle, then slapped the horse's rump, sending the animal into a run. When she looked back over her shoulder, Shaw had already blended quietly into the shadows.

Shaw rejoiced when a light rain began to fall, for he knew that the sound of the raindrops on the canopy of leaves overhead would drown out the sound of the flock's bleating.

From his place of concealment in the thick branches of a tall tree, he counted nearly a dozen horsemen. They had fanned out in every direction, in the hopes of detecting their lost sheep.

Occasionally he would hear snatches of their conversations, or muttered curses as they fought their way through tangled vines and brambles.

"'Tis the accursed Avengers, I tell you," came a voice from the darkness.

"Aye. When the Black Campbell finishes with them, they will be the dead avengers," replied another.

Above them, Shaw remained perfectly still, his mind racing. He would have to learn the identity of this Black Campbell, and soon, for the man besmirched the good name of all Campbells. But for now, he must eliminate the threat of these men.

He did not worry about taking on a dozen armed men. But he would do it on his terms. First he must separate some from the others, to make the odds more to his liking.

When the horsemen moved away, he slipped to the ground and moved stealthily into the shadows. Scooping up as many big stones as he could carry, he perched on the lip of a ravine and tossed them over the edge. As they rolled downward, they snagged more loose stones, until they became a small avalanche.

At once two horsemen paused, listened, then turned in the direction of the sound.

"They are this way," one of them called.

"Aye. I hear them." The other urged his mount into a gallop after him.

In the darkness, neither of them saw what lay ahead. It wasn't until their mounts had plunged over the abyss that they realized what they'd done. For several moments their curses and cries broke the stillness. Then there was only silence.

When a cluster of horsemen raced up to see what had happened, Shaw moved on, darting from tree to tree. Suddenly he came upon a lone rider. Picking up a tree limb, he wielded it like a club. With a grunt of pain the man fell to the ground. Shaw dragged him into the underbrush and emerged moments later wearing the man's cloak. Catching up the horse's reins, Shaw pulled himself into the saddle and rode up to three men, who stood huddled in the shelter of a gnarled evergreen. The rain beat faster now, and they shivered in their cloaks.

"We are wasting time here," one of the riders called.

"Nay," another argued. "A flock of this size cannot simply disappear."

"I see them," Shaw shouted, whipping his horse into a run.

At once the others followed suit.

Satisfied that all three were following, Shaw led them deep into the woods, then managed to turn so that they were heading in the opposite direction from Inverene House. He knew that, with the light from the stars blotted from their view by trees and clouds, these men would soon be hopelessly lost.

He slid from the saddle and drew his mount beneath an outcropping of rock. When the others passed by, he waited, then returned to where the last of their number still lingered. They had built a fire and were huddled around it for warmth, passing a flagon of ale from man to man.

Keeping to the shadows, Shaw surveyed them with a grim smile of satisfaction. Their number was now far more manageable.

"Where have the other louts gone?" one of the men muttered.

"Mayhap they have returned to their cottages."

"Mayhap they found some local wenches to take them in and keep them warm and dry."

Someone laughed. "We may not be dry, but we can enjoy the same pleasure right here."

Shaw froze as he caught sight of one of the men, clearly illuminated by the flames. The man stood taller than the others. In his hand was a vicious-looking broadsword. In the light of the fire his yellow eyes gleamed like a cat's. A thin, puckered scar ran from his temple to his jaw. It was the man Edan had described so vividly.

The man turned, revealing something lying on the ground directly behind him. For a moment Shaw thought it nothing more than a discarded cloak. But as he watched, the cloak moved, and he realized it concealed a familiar figure. A figure that had his heart stopping.

The man bent and dragged the cloaked figure to its feet, knocking aside the hood, revealing a mass of fiery tangles. It was obvious that her hands and feet were firmly bound.

"Now, wench, ye'll tell us where ye've taken our sheep, or I'll cut out y'er tongue so ye'll never be able to speak again. But before I do, I'll see that the lads and I find a good use for you."

The others roared with laughter.

As he watched, Shaw felt as if all the breath had been knocked from his lungs.

Once again Merritt had defied him. And was now being held captive by a brute who would take great pleasure in inflicting pain.

Chapter Thirteen

Shaw's mind worked frantically.

If he were Sutton, he would simply charge ahead, using his exceptional skill with sword and dirk to rain blows on his enemy and rescue the lass. But he was not his brother. Though he had received the same training with weapons as Sutton, he'd had little chance to put it to practical use. While Dillon and Sutton had gone off to war, he had remained behind, to pray for their safe return. His skill with a sword had never been tested on the field of battle.

It was not fear for his own life that held him back. His life mattered not. But for Merritt's sake, he could not afford to fail. If he blundered into their midst and became a prisoner, as well, he would only add to the lass's misery.

He was reminded of his love of the game of chess. He had always been adept at planning strategy. Mayhap... Nay, his mind seemed to have gone numb.

Oaf, Merritt called him. Aye, in times of peril, he was little better than an oaf. He would need more than prayers now, he thought glumly. Think, oaf. Think.

Suddenly, a plan began to take shape.

Quickly doffing his hood, he pressed his hands into the mud at his feet and smeared it over his face and into his hair, until it stood out around his head in stiff tufts. Tying his cloak haphazardly around his waist to conceal his sword, he streaked his shirt and tunic with more dirt. Then, pasting a silly smile on his lips and feigning an awkward, uneasy gait, he stepped into the circle of firelight.

"Hold," a short, stocky man shouted, aiming the tip of his sword at Shaw's chest.

"Ye would like me ta hold y'er sword, m'laird?" Like a simpleton he held out his muddy hands toward the weapon.

The men standing around the fire, their spirits lifted by the ale they'd consumed, burst into raucous laughter.

Merritt's head came up sharply, and she peered at Shaw with utter disbelief.

"Begone, you addle-brained lout," cried the leader.

"Please, m'laird," Shaw cried in an odd, high-pitched whine. "I beg a bite to eat."

"A beggar," said a thin, wiry peasant whose front teeth were missing. "Let him stay, Lysander. We can have sport with him. 'Twill pass the time."

"I have a better way to pass the time." The leader drew Merritt close and pressed the flagon to her lips. Most of it spilled down the front of her cloak, but enough passed her lips to cause her to choke and gag, bringing another round of laughter from the others.

To draw attention away from her Shaw called, "Please, m'laird. I'll do anyt'ing for a drop of spirits."

"Grovel on your hands and knees like a dog," the stocky man ordered.

At once, Shaw fell to his knees in the mud while the others gathered around, chortling. Out of the corner of his eye he saw that the leader, though still holding Merritt firmly in his grasp, had turned his attention to the circle of men.

"If he is hungry," one of the others called, "why does he not eat the dirt?"

They began calling and taunting. "Eat the dirt, simpleton."

To the amusement of all, Shaw scooped up a handful of mud and shoved it into his mouth. While the others drew closer and continued their laughter, the stocky man took the flat of his broadsword and brought it down across Shaw's back. The force of the blow flattened Shaw into the mud, and he sprawled there, facedown, while the others roared with laughter.

"Let him stay and be our court jester," the toothless one jeered.

"Aye, Lysander," called another. "You will be our king, and the fool will amuse you."

The leader seemed to consider for a moment, enjoying his position of authority, then sat down on a rock and dragged Merritt to her knees in the dirt at his feet. "All right, buffoon. Amuse me. But take care. If you do not make me laugh, I will have my sport by allowing my cohorts here to carve you up in little pieces."

"May I have a sip o' ale first, m'laird?" Shaw cackled. "To wash ta mud from ma mouth?"

"I'll not waste fine ale on the likes of you. Now quickly, amuse me, lest I tire of this sport."

"Aye, m'laird. Thank ye, m'laird." Shaw bobbed up and down like a cowardly imbecile and picked up several rocks. After testing their weight for a moment, he proceeded to juggle them with a fair amount of expertise, all the while blessing the old monk, Father Zachariah, who had taught him this trick when he was but a mere lad.

Though the other men clapped and shouted for more, the leader seemed bored. "Enough. Any dolt can juggle a few stones. Beware, jester. You have yet to make me laugh."

Shaw thought about aiming the stones at Lysander's head, but Merritt's situation was still too precarious.

Setting aside the stones, Shaw positioned himself in front of the fire and lifted his hands. Pointing to a huge boulder, he called, "If ye will watch, ye will see great winged birds and terrible beasties."

At once he began moving his hands and fingers, creating shadow pictures that were amazingly like birds and animals. Soon these simple peasants were caught up in the moment and forgot everything as they tried to identify each image.

While he manipulated his fingers, Shaw glanced at the leader. Even Lysander had momentarily forgotten the woman.

Across the fire, Merritt's eyes met Shaw's. He darted a look at the forest, and she nodded her understanding.

Shaw relaxed a little as he said, "This one ye will all recognize." Turning his fist, he created the image of a shapely maiden. Then, by using his fingers, he made her walk.

The peasants hooted and cheered, and Shaw did it again and again until he could sense their growing dissatisfaction.

"Enough," Lysander called. "I would prefer...the real woman to mere pictures."

While the others stared in surprise at his sudden shift of mood, he dragged Merritt up by the front of her cloak and pressed his mouth to hers. With her hands and feet bound, she was helpless to fight him.

"I intend to have this wench first," Lysander announced. "When I've tired of her, the rest of you can fight over what's left." With that he tore her cloak from her.

Seeing that she was dressed in the garb of a stableboy, he arched a brow. "Wait. What is this?"

The others gasped in surprise at her strange manner of dress.

Despite her fears, Merritt tossed her head and faced him, eyes blazing.

"Now," Lysander said, his look turning from surprise to understanding, "why would a female go about the countryside at night dressed in such as this?"

He glanced around. The others had fallen silent.

"I will tell you why. The female is up to no good. Could it be that she offers assistance to the hated Highland Avengers?"

While the others murmured agreement, he grasped her roughly by the arm and said, "Speak, wench. Why are you out on this dark night in such clothes?"

She held her silence.

Lysander's hand swung out, landing across Merritt's face with such force her head snapped to one side. "Tell me, woman, and quickly, before I lose my patience."

As he watched her, Shaw's heart fell. He'd seen that look too often to think she would bend to this man's wishes. Even in the face of brutality and certain death, Shaw knew that the defiant Merritt Lamont would never answer the question.

"Very well. You have sealed your fate." Lysander took a knife from the waistband of his breeches and lifted it to the neck of her shirt. In one quick motion he slit the cloth. The remnants gaped open, revealing the swell of high, firm breasts, barely covered by a pale chemise.

"A comely wench," one of the men shouted. "Hurry, Lysander, and take your pleasure. For when ye've finished with her, I'll surely take a turn."

With his hands digging into the soft flesh of her upper arms, the leader dragged her close and pressed his mouth over hers.

"Wait," Shaw said boldly. He searched his mind for something, anything, that would serve as a distraction.

Lysander lifted his head and cast a hateful look at him.

"I have yet to make ye laugh, m'laird," Shaw added in his shrill tone. "But I know this will do it, if ye will but spare the lass for a moment."

"Nay, fool. I have had enough of your tricks."

"Please, m'laird. I would do anyt'ing, anyt'ing," he emphasized, "for a drop of spirits."

"Then you can stay and help us kill the woman when we've finished with her." Lysander's yellow eyes glittered with hatred. "For the wench must learn that no one defies me. And then, fool, when it is your turn to die, we will grant your wish and give you a drop of spirits before we slit your ugly throat."

"One trick, then, m'laird, before I must die," Shaw cackled.

With his awkward gait Shaw made his way to Merritt. Keeping his silly grin in place, he bowed grandly, saying, "Ta lasses of my village ofttimes ride me like a proud steed."

With that he lifted her onto his shoulders and began to stumble around the fire.

"A proud steed indeed," the toothless man called. "More like a hobbled goat, if you ask me."

Everyone, including the leader, burst into laughter. But his smile faded when Shaw began limping in circles, faster and faster.

"Put her down, you oaf, before you fall and break both your necks. Not that I mind her death, mind you. But I want her alive until I've had my pleasure with her."

"Aye, m'laird."

With that, Shaw dropped to his knees, depositing Merritt gently in the grass, some distance from Lysander. As they disentangled, Shaw managed to slip into her hand a small knife that he'd kept hidden at his waist.

"Run, lass," he whispered, "and never look back."

Merritt stared mutely up at him. Before she could utter a word, Lysander shouted, "Enough! Fetch the woman back to me, fool. I have already grown tired of your tricks."

"Aye, m'laird."

Keeping his back to the others, Shaw waited until he was certain that Merritt had cut her bonds and could make good her escape.

Up until this very moment, he'd hoped and prayed that he would find some other means of settling this. But now, there was no other choice. He must resort to the sword, even though it meant taking a life.

Clutching the jeweled hilt, he felt the heat that surely must have warmed his father's hand in this same manner. Unsheathing his sword, he tossed his cloak aside and turned to the stunned peasants.

"Now, lads." His voice returned to its own deep timbre. "'Tis your turn to amuse me."

Merritt lay in the grass a moment, struggling to rub some feeling back into her numb ankles and wrists. But with the return of feeling came a surge of pain, for the vines used to bind her hands and feet had been tied so tightly they had actually cut to the bone.

At first she could only crawl through the grass. When she could manage to stand, she made her way haltingly to a line of trees a short distance from the clearing. Her head swam from a blow to the skull administered by Lysander when he'd caught her in the forest. And the earlier arrow wound to her arm was bleeding afresh.

Leaning wearily against the trunk of a tree, she sank slowly to the ground and closed her eyes against the sickness that rose up inside. Impossible. She was never ill.

She thought about the Campbell's fierce command to run and never look back. Though every ounce of her being shouted for her to obey, her perverse nature forced her to remain and stand her ground.

Was he not, this moment, fighting for his life? Aye, his life and hers. How could she turn her back on such nobility? Especially from a Campbell?

She forced herself to stand and bite down on the pain. Let no man ever say that a Lamont walked away from a fight. Especially one involving a cowardly Campbell.

Her fingers curled tightly around the hilt of the knife Shaw had given her. The brute named Lysander would pay. With that thought firmly in mind, she staggered into the fray.

Riding on a crest of fury, Shaw disposed of the first swordsman with ease. Surely he was a peasant lad who had seen little battle in his young life, for he was slow and clumsy.

Within a few strokes the toothless man had been beaten, as well. As he fell, mortally wounded, he called to his comrades for help, thus signaling to Shaw that they were coming up behind him. He quickly turned and faced two more opponents, who, though they struggled mightily, could not best him. He returned lunge for lunge, thrust for thrust, until he'd managed to disarm both men. But as they begged for their lives, their voices were suddenly stilled. Shaw saw that each man had taken a knife to the chest.

He whirled. And found himself face-to-face with Lysander and the stocky man who had beaten him with his broadsword.

"You would kill your own men?" Shaw asked incredulously.

"Aye," Lysander replied. "Any man who would beg for his measly life has no right to it."

"And who are you to decide that?"

Lysander's lips curled in a feral snarl. "I am their leader. I am the one who answers to the Black Campbell. And I am the one who will see you floating facedown in the mud, fool."

He lunged and Shaw deftly sidestepped. When Lysander lunged a second time, the stocky man came at Shaw from the opposite side. Though Shaw managed to fend off their thrusts, they could see that he was tiring, and they increased the frenzy of their attack, thrusting, parrying, inflicting dozens of minor wounds until Shaw's tunic and shirt were smeared with his own blood.

Shaw, too, managed to inflict wounds upon them. But when the stocky man made a move to run, Lysander's voice stopped him.

"No man runs from a fight and lives to tell about it. You will stay and see this through."

"I am wounded," the man cried.

"Aye. But you are not dead yet."

The man reluctantly returned to the battle, only to have his arm slashed viciously by Shaw's sword tip.

"Kill him," the man shrieked in pain, "before he renders us helpless."

"See," Lysander shouted. "Already he tires. He cannot continue fighting both of us."

Without a word Shaw drove the other man back against the trunk of a tree and pressed his sword to his throat.

"Spare me," the man begged.

No sooner were the words out of his mouth than he slumped forward, a knife in his heart.

Shaw whirled to find Lysander facing him.

"Now, fool," the leader of the pack of thieves cried, "I will show you how you may join those others."

The two danced around the fire, blades flashing, each managing to inflict wounds upon the other, but neither able to disarm the other.

"You are losing blood," Lysander taunted. "Soon enough you will be too weak to hold your sword."

"Do not worry yourself about me," Shaw replied. "When you are flattened beneath the heel of my boot, I will still be standing."

"You wield your sword like a gentleman," Lysander said. "But I know how to fight like a viper."

"Aye. An apt description." Shaw's blade slashed through flesh, drawing a river of blood. "Soon you will be crawling on your belly like a viper."

Lysander gave a cry of pain and lunged, determined to bring this duel to a conclusion.

As Shaw stepped back, his foot caught in the twisted vines of a gnarled old tree and he went sprawling backward. At once Lysander's face was lit with a cruel smile of triumph.

"Prepare to die," he cried as he lifted his sword.

As he lunged, he suddenly seemed to stiffen, and the smile was wiped from his lips. A look of surprise was followed by a grimace of pain as he reached a hand to the hilt of a knife buried in his shoulder. With one quick motion he pulled the blade free. At once blood spilled from the wound.

When he looked up, Shaw had retrieved his sword and was struggling to his feet.

With a shriek of pain Lysander bolted and fled into the forest, taking for himself the refuge he had refused his men.

Shaw turned to see who had saved his life. At the edge of the clearing, Merritt stood perfectly still.

"I thought I told you to flee," he shouted.

Her mouth opened, as if to issue a sharp retort. But though her lips moved, no words came out. Instead, while Shaw watched in shock and horror, she sank to her knees in the grass.

Chapter Fourteen

"God in heaven, lass." In quick strides Shaw was kneeling beside Merritt.

She was deathly pale, propped up on one elbow in the grass, determined not to give in to the need to lie down. Blood streamed from the wound in her arm, to mingle with the blood that oozed from the torn flesh of her wrists.

He felt a sudden wave of fury at the sight of her looking so shattered. Instead of the tenderness he'd shown his wounded brother, he flew into an unreasonable rage.

"I ordered you to flee!"

"Aye. But you know how I dislike being ordered about."

"You defied me!" He felt his anger deepen. "I did not risk life and limb to have you remain here and be killed."

"No one asked you to. Lest you forget, Campbell, this is not your battle. I am quite capable of taking care of myself."

"Aye. And look at you. Your flesh bloody and broken. Your clothes torn from you. And your head..." He touched a hand to the swollen lump at the base of her skull and heard her catch her breath at the pain.

"Your poor, battered head..." At once he gathered her into his arms. It was not, he reasoned, because he had an overwhelming desire to hold her and assure himself that she was truly alive. He merely wanted to keep her from falling.

As his arms came around her, she offered no resistance. Just this once, she told herself, she would allow herself to be weak. In fact, she was grateful for his strength, for her own was quickly failing.

"Am I so terrible to look at, Campbell?" she muttered against his throat.

A rush of feelings surged through him. Anger. Dismay. Followed by a surge of tenderness. Incredible tenderness.

He swallowed loudly. "Aye. It fair tears my heart out to look at you."

She pushed a little away to stare up at him. "You do not look much better. I do not know what looks worse. The mud or the blood."

He grinned. "We are a fine pair. A sword-wielding, knife-tossing firebrand and the oaf whose life she saved."

"Aye. Do not forget 'twas I who saved your miserable life."

Suddenly she found herself weeping for no good reason. Tears flooded her eyes and ran in little rivers down her cheeks. Her body shook with sobs, and Shaw's arms tightened around her.

With all her remaining strength she lifted a hand to his mud-streaked cheek. "My fearless, heroic oaf. I have ne'er seen such courage."

He lifted her hand to his lips and pressed a kiss to the bloodstained palm. "It does not take courage to wield a sword, my lady."

"Nay. I do not mean the sword. Though you were truly splendid when you wielded it." Her tears fell faster as she whispered between shudders, "It took such courage to play the fool. My heart nearly broke as I watched you, for I

knew that you were allowing yourself to be . . . humiliated
for . . . my sake.''

"Shh. Hush now. You must rest," he murmured. "You
are overwrought.''

"I will ne'er forget this, Campbell. Ne'er," she cried
with such vehemence it shook her entire body.

He gathered her against his chest and held her while the
tears ran their course. And when at last she had grown
quiet, and her breathing grew soft and steady, he looked
down at her and realized that she had slipped into unconsciousness.

Merritt awoke in a cocoon of warmth. For long minutes she lay unmoving, savoring the heat of morning sunshine against her face. Her lids fluttered open and she
peered around.

She was wrapped in Shaw's cloak on a bed of furs and
fragrant evergreen boughs. Nearby a stag roasted over a
fire. The wonderful aroma perfumed the forest. Overhead a chorus of birds entertained, flitting from tree to
tree, filling the air with song.

Memories of the previous night came flooding back and
Merritt felt her cheeks flame. She could recall being lifted
in strong arms and deposited gently in a warm, soft pallet. She had a vague recollection of murmured words and
whispered endearments, and the gentlest hands she had
ever known removing her blood-soaked garments, while
leaving her chemise, and her dignity, intact.

She remembered something else. A warm body lying
beside her, and muscled arms cradling her all through the
night, and a voice, low, deep, crooning to her as if she were
a wee bairn.

Hearing the splash of water, she turned her head. On the
banks of a nearby stream she saw Shaw pull on his shirt

and tunic and run a hand through his hair before turning toward her.

When he saw that she was awake, he hurried to her side. "Good morrow, my lady. How do you feel?"

She knew her face was flaming, but she hoped he would blame it on the sunshine. "As though I had been through a war. How do I look?"

"Much better. There is color to your cheeks now. Last night, your pallor had me concerned."

She smiled up at him. "You look better, too, Campbell, without all that mud and blood." In fact, he looked like a magnificent golden warrior, with droplets of water still glistening in his hair and his broad shoulders straining the seams of his linen shirt. "I see you washed your garments."

"And yours." He pointed to a low-hanging bush near the stream, blooming with shirt and breeches and tunic.

"Astra would be proud of you."

"Aye. As would the housekeeper of Kinloch House, Mistress MacCallum."

"Has she taken care of you since you were a lad?"

Shaw handed her a hollowed-out gourd filled with water and settled himself beside her, leaning his back against the trunk of a tree. "My parents were killed when I was but a few years old. After that I went to live at the monastery of Saint Collum. There, every lad had to see to his own needs. There were no women to wash or cook or clean for us."

"I'm sorry," she mumbled, thinking about her own carefree childhood.

"Do not be, lass. Though it was far from idyllic, it could have been so much worse, had not old Father Anselm taken us in. We were safe and warm and well fed, and educated by the finest scholars in all of Scotland."

"But was there no one to soothe away the hurts, or comfort you when your young world fell apart?"

He stretched out his long legs beside her, and she found herself staring at his muscled thigh as he crossed one foot over the other.

"Sutton and I always had each other," he said simply. "We always felt we needed no other."

"How strange it would be to have another share your face. Astra thinks—" She suddenly stopped, appalled at what she was about to reveal. "Forgive me, Campbell."

He chuckled, and she was aware of how pleasant was the sound of his laughter. "You may tell me, lass, for I've probably heard it said before. Most people fear twins. They think we are the spawn of the devil."

She stared at the gourd in her hands, afraid to meet his eyes. "Astra thinks that you and your brother possess but one soul."

"Ah. And she fears that it is an evil soul, does she?"

"I think, perhaps, in the beginning, she believed that. But I am certain by now she realizes that there is goodness in you."

"Careful," he cautioned, though the word was warmed by a smile, "or the next thing you know, you may be saying nice things about a Campbell."

"Aye. I'll be careful." She handed back the gourd and started to sit up. At once her head swam, and a low moan escaped her lips.

Shaw caught her by the shoulders to steady her. His eyes were troubled. "You must take things very slow and easy today, lass, until your strength returns."

"But I must get home."

"Not today," he said firmly, as he lay her back against the pallet. "Today you will eat and sleep. And tomorrow, if you are feeling stronger, we will return to Inverene House. Now sleep, and I will see to our food.''

She thought about arguing, but she had not the strength. Instead she closed her eyes and listened to the sound of Shaw's footsteps as he moved around their encampment. Within minutes she had returned to her dreams.

''Have you had enough to eat, my lady?''

Merritt sighed. ''More than enough. If you keep plying me with food, Campbell, I shall soon be as plump as a stuffed goose.''

''You must eat if you are to regain your strength.''

''Aye. So you keep telling me.'' Content, she leaned her head back against the fur robes that Shaw had folded beneath her head for her comfort.

''You do not fear for the sheep?'' he asked.

''Nay. Kale would never rest until he returned them to their home. Knowing that, the thieves had kept him penned up, else he would have begun the trek home a fortnight ago. Once I knew the flock was safe in his care, I returned to the forest, intending to lend a hand to whatever you had planned.''

''Until Lysander caught you.''

''The lout managed to land a lucky blow,'' she muttered, touching a hand to her head.

Shaw wisely said nothing, knowing the lass thought herself a better warrior than most men. If truth be told, she was.

Starlight filtered through the branches of trees and a ribbon of moonlight trailed a path of gold along the ground, casting their campsite in an ethereal glow.

She sighed. '''Tis peaceful here.''

Shaw nodded and stretched his feet toward the fire.

"It is difficult to believe that there are those who use this place to rob and kill."

"Put such thoughts from your mind, my lady."

"Aye. I know it does no good to dwell upon what is past. But when I think about what almost happened..." She shivered and he immediately drew his cloak around her, allowing his hand to linger overlong at her shoulder.

After a moment he reluctantly moved his hand away and sat back.

"Last night, Lysander suggested that you might be out in the darkness assisting the Highland Avengers." Shaw chose his words carefully. "I do not suggest that such a villain could be correct. But...you have often defended them to me. Could he be close to the truth?"

Her tone rang with righteous indignation. "I spoke the truth, Campbell. I was merely taking back what was mine."

"And you did not see these Avengers on your quest?"

She shook her head firmly. "I did not." She shot him a sideways glance. "Now I have an important question for you."

He arched a brow.

"How did you learn to make those shadow pictures?" she asked.

"These?" He lifted his hands to the light of the fire and the image of a flying bird appeared on the rock face.

"Aye." She watched, amazed, as he made the bird fly away, then return.

"It was something Sutton and I did at night to amuse ourselves. There was little time for play in the monastery."

"Could you teach me?"

"It is simple enough. Here." He caught her hands in his and lifted them to the firelight. Bending two fingers down, he left the other two up, so that they resembled the antlers of a stag. Forming her other hand into four legs, he showed her how to put the two together to form a complete animal.

As the creature began to move across the face of the rock, she laughed in delight.

"More," she cried happily. "I want to do more."

It was so good to hear her laugh. She had become a lass again, young and carefree. "This, then, is a tortoise," he told her as he brought her thumb through her closed fist.

"Indeed." She wiggled it, then turned to him excitedly. "Oh, Campbell. I want to learn more. When we return, we will entertain Edan. Oh, how he will enjoy it. Teach me another."

He taught her a hare, a fish swimming, a horse and rider. And with each lesson, she became more animated. She moved her hands and fingers as he instructed, turning to him in triumph with each success. She looked up at him, eyes shining, cheeks flushed, and in that instant he knew that he had never seen anyone so fresh, so vital, so beautiful in his life. And never had he felt more stimulated, or more alive. It was as though he'd been asleep for all these years and had suddenly been awakened to all the awe and wonder and beauty around him.

"Is there more, Campbell?" She turned to him, brows delicately arched, lips parted.

"Aye." He reached a hand to a wisp of hair that drifted across her cheek. He hadn't meant anything by the gesture. It had been a purely reflexive action. But now that he'd touched her, he couldn't seem to stop. He moved his finger along her cheek, reveling in the softness of her skin. His tone softened. "So much more, my lady, that I could teach you. That we could learn ... together."

He saw the way her eyes went wide. "Nay. You mustn't, Campbell."

"Aye, my lady. I know 'tis wrong. But I must at least hold you." He drew her into his arms with exquisite tenderness and moved his hands across her shoulders, down her sides, along her back.

With each movement, her resolve wavered, as shivers of pure delight pulsed through her.

"When I saw that madman threatening you," he murmured against her temple, "I lost all sense of purpose except to set you free." He closed his eyes a moment against the pain in his heart. "I knew that nothing else in life would ever matter again if I failed you."

Her objections were forgotten. Even as she brought her hands up between them to push him away, her limbs betrayed her. Her arms encircled his waist and she drew him close with a sigh. "I have never been so overwhelmed with feeling as I was when I beheld you offering your life for mine. My heart...my heart was filled to overflowing with feelings...."

"Shh," he whispered against her lips. "It is over, lass. And now...I can wait no longer, for I've needed to do this for a very, very long time."

It seemed the most natural thing in the world to kiss her. But once his lips touched hers, need swept through him, startling him with its intensity.

Her mouth moved under his, eager, avid. She kissed him with a hunger that matched his. She clung to him, eager to taste, to feel. To give.

He kissed her until they were both breathless. With teeth and tongue and lips, seducing, possessing. And still he could not stop. He wanted to fill himself with her, to give and take and give until they were both sated.

And wonder of wonders, she kissed him back. And returned passion for passion. It was more than he could have ever hoped for.

The night had become so quiet that she could hear the roar of her heartbeat in her temples. The fire had grown dangerously hot, until she longed to rid herself of all her garments and lie, naked and cool, beside this man.

Somewhere on a distant treetop, a night bird cried and its mate replied. A hound bayed to the moon. A forest creature stepped into the circle of firelight, then disappeared in a rustle of leaves. But the man and woman who clung to each other were so lost in the wonders of their newly discovered passion, they were aware of none of these things.

When Shaw moved his hands along her back, she could feel his touch over every inch of her body. Her breasts tingled with unexpected need. Her thighs pressed to his, sending liquid fire surging through her veins.

He tore his mouth from hers and pressed it to the soft, sensitive hollow of her throat. When she moaned softly and moved in his arms, he became even more aroused and pressed moist kisses down her neck and across her shoulder.

His fingers paused at the ribbons that laced her chemise. God in heaven, what was happening to him? He wanted her. Desperately. He struggled to hold on to some sense of sanity. But he could feel himself slipping over the edge. He wanted to feel her, warm and moist and willing. The need for her was so great, he thought he must take her. Or go mad.

"I want you." His words were an impassioned plea whispered inside her mouth. "Say only that you want this, too, and let me taste paradise."

"I . . . cannot think."

She struggled to remember why she should object, but her mind refused to cooperate. All she could think of was the way he tasted, dark and mysterious, and the way she felt in his arms, safe and warm and...cherished.

Cherished? By a Campbell? Had she gone daft? Was not this man her father's sworn enemy?

"Nay, wait," she cried.

As quickly as the words were spoken, they were swept away on a tide of madness, as his hands and lips worked their magic. He took the kiss deeper, and she experienced a hunger unlike anything she'd ever known. A hunger that only this man could feed.

Aye. Cherished. Loved.

Shaw thrilled to the eagerness with which she returned his kisses. But even as he did, he thought of her muttered exclamation, raised in protest. What had come over him that he would ignore a lady's plea? Even her cry of resistance hadn't been able to cool his ardor but had driven him further into insanity. Was he a man of honor, or was he no better than the men he'd fought?

Calling on all his willpower, he lifted his head and drew a little away. Framing her face with his hands, he tenderly brushed her swollen lips with his thumbs.

For several moments he took in deep drafts of air to clear his mind. When he could trust his voice he said, "Forgive me, my lady. 'Twas but a moment of madness. Rest now. I'll walk the perimeter tonight, to assure our safety."

She blinked and watched as he got to his feet and strode away. Within minutes he blended into the shadows of the forest.

Madness? Was that all this was to him? She pressed a hand to her eyes. And she, like a fool, had thought it love.

For more than an hour she lay on her pallet and listened to the rustle of leaves and the sound of his footsteps as he kept watch.

It shamed her to admit that, had it not been for the Campbell's strength of will, she would have spent the night in his arms. And in his bed.

Chapter Fifteen

Curtains of mist danced low over the water. Dawn light streaked the eastern sky. Distant ribbons of pale pink and mauve heralded another perfect spring morning.

Deep in thought, Shaw leaned his back against the trunk of a tree and watched as Merritt slept. His brow was furrowed, his mind greatly troubled.

What had nearly happened between them last night had left him badly shaken. The lass was an innocent. And he... He experienced a wave of revulsion. He had thought himself a man of God, but his experience last night had taught him that all his years of prayer and discipline had not prepared him for temptation in the form of Merritt Lamont.

So what was he to do about it? He allowed his gaze to move over the lass, indulging himself for a moment in the breathtaking sight of her. The ribbons of her chemise hung loose, revealing a shadowed cleft between high, firm breasts. Even in repose, there was a sense of energy, of vitality about her. Perhaps it was the way she sighed in her sleep and shifted positions in a most seductive manner. A tangle of red curls kissed one cheek and she brushed them away with a sweep of her hand before burrowing deeper into her nest of fur.

He forced himself to turn away from the tempting sight of her. As he walked to the stream, he resolved that what had nearly happened last night must never be allowed again. If he were truly a man of honor, he was obliged to leave the lass as he'd found her—unsullied, unharmed and unfettered by guilt.

As for himself, he must remember always the path he had chosen. A commitment awaited him when he returned to Kinloch House. A commitment that did not leave room for the feelings he'd experienced in the arms of this woman.

Stripping off his clothes, he strode into the frigid waters and swam until the bone-chilling cold forced him back to shore.

Merritt lay very still, listening to the soft morning sounds. Overhead a pair of doves cooed. Nearby a fox gave its shrill cry. An answering bark echoed in the distance.

Slowly, tentatively, she sat up and waited for the images before her to come into focus. As her vision cleared, she saw Shaw striding toward her, looking very much like a bonny, golden-haired giant.

"How do you feel this morrow?" He dropped to his knees beside her and instinctively reached out a hand to steady her.

As one, they felt the jolt. Merritt stiffened and looked away, avoiding his eyes. Cursing his lapse, Shaw pulled his hand away as if burned.

"I am fine. Much stronger," she added for emphasis.

He got to his feet, towering over her. "Do you feel strong enough to ride?"

"Aye." She looked up at him and shielded the sun with her hand. "I dare not tarry longer. My family will be worried."

He was forced to offer her a hand up. Keeping his cloak wrapped firmly around her for modesty, she accepted his help and was lifted to her feet.

He was watching her so closely she felt her cheeks grow warm. "You are certain you are up to riding, my lady?"

She nodded, afraid to trust her voice. He was close. Too close. And the memory of last night was still too vivid.

"You will want to wash yourself in the stream before we begin our journey."

"Aye. If my father were to see all this blood, he would ne'er let me out of his sight again."

Perhaps it would be the best thing for her, Shaw thought. Aloud he said, "While you wash, I will prepare some food."

She walked to the stream, then followed the banks until she came to a tangle of vine and brush. Knowing they would serve as cover, she undressed and stepped into the water. The morning sun had warmed it only slightly, and she was soon shivering as she hurriedly washed the blood and grime away. Within minutes she strode from the stream, grateful to pull on dry, sun-warmed clothes.

As soon as she approached the fire, Shaw thrust a flagon of warm ale into her hands and draped a fur robe around her shoulders.

"Drink, my lady. It will chase away the chill of your bath."

"Thank you." She drank, savoring the warmth that flowed through her veins.

He helped her to sit, then handed her a joint of roasted venison, before taking another for himself. They ate in companionable silence.

"Now that I am rested and recovered, I am most eager to see my family," Merritt admitted.

"And they will be relieved to see you. Especially Edan. By now the lad will have no doubt driven himself half-mad with fears over your absence."

"Aye. And poor Sabina has had to cope alone with Edan, and father, and your brother."

At the mention of Sutton, Shaw felt a pang of guilt. Not once since all this had occurred had he given a single thought to his brother's recovery. This woman had so bewitched him, she had managed to drive all other thoughts from his mind.

Needing an outlet for his uneasy thoughts, he snuffed out the fire and set about dismantling their camp. When all was in readiness, he saddled his horse.

"If you are ready," Shaw said, extending a hand.

"Aye." She placed her hand in his and was helped to her feet. With his arm around her waist, he walked with her to his horse. After pulling himself into the saddle, he lifted her easily in his arms.

"You will tell me when you grow weary." His muffled words, whispered against her temple, had her head spinning.

"I will tell you." The truth was, she would never grow weary of being held in his arms, so close to his heart.

If she could, she thought as the horse began following along the banks of the swollen river, she would remain just like this, safe and secure within his embrace, forever. She had no way of knowing that the man who held her harbored the same thoughts.

Thunder rumbled in the distance. The sun had long ago taken cover behind a bank of dark, roiling clouds. The air had grown heavy with the threat of an impending storm.

Shaw could sense Merritt's flagging energy. Though she put on a brave face, he could see the effort this journey cost her. Her lids grew heavy. Several times her head bobbed as she struggled to stay awake and alert. Her wounds, though healing, were taking their toll.

"Are we close?"

"Aye, my lady. Soon you will be home."

"Home." For a moment her lips were touched with a smile. Then her eyes closed once more.

A short time later he whispered, "I believe there is something you would like to see, my lady."

Breaking free of the forest, the horse moved out at a swift pace, taking the steep cliffs with breathtaking speed. Below them lay the imposing sight of the Lamont fortress. To one side, horses milled about in the makeshift enclosure Shaw had put together. On the other side, spread out on a rolling meadow between the keep and the chapel, a flock of sheep grazed peacefully under the watchful eye of the hound.

At that beautiful sight, all Merritt's weariness vanished. Her eyes shone with happiness.

"Inverene House," she breathed.

"Aye, my lady. You are indeed home."

He heard her little laugh of delight as the horse broke into a run.

In the courtyard Shaw slid from the saddle and gathered Merritt into his arms. Even before they reached the door it was thrown open and Astra rushed forward.

At once, Shaw set Merritt on her feet and took a step back, breaking contact.

"What have ye done wi' my lady?" the old woman demanded.

"I am fine, Astra." With a reassuring smile, Merritt caught the old woman's hand.

"Truly, child?"

"Aye."

Eagerly she and Shaw swept past the servant and strode inside.

"The laird is supping in the great hall," Astra called as she closed the door and followed along behind.

When they paused in the doorway, Astra cried, "M'laird, look who has returned safely to us."

At once three heads came up sharply, and Upton, Sabina and Edan broke into wide smiles and shouts of glee at the sight of Merritt.

"We had thought you dead," Sabina cried as she jumped up to greet her sister with a warm embrace.

"I told her you were not," Edan put in quickly. "I knew you would return."

"As you can see, I am not dead." Though she walked more slowly than was her custom, Merritt crossed the room and hugged each one of them before taking her place beside Sabina.

"The lady needs sustenance, Astra." There was a trace of impatience in Shaw's tone, though he tried to soften it. The journey had taken its toll on his nerves, as well. It had been a hellish torture to hold Merritt in his arms all those long miles, knowing that, when they returned to Inverene House, they must put aside forever what had transpired between them in the forest. And for both their sakes, they must never touch each other with tenderness again. For to do so was to tempt fate.

And so he had held her, mile after endless mile, wondering what it would have been like to give in to the passion that had burned between them, though he knew that even indulging in such thoughts was wrong.

"It has been a long, tedious journey," he added, to mask his discomfort.

At once the servant hobbled away and returned with a platter of steaming lamb and two goblets of hot mulled wine. Without thinking of himself, Shaw pressed a goblet into Merritt's hands, "Drink, lass. It will revive you."

She did as he bade, feeling the heat slowly return, chasing away the weariness. While she drank, Shaw broke off a hunk of meat, then passed the trencher to her and said, "Now you must eat, else the wine will go to your head."

Suddenly she felt ravenous. Without a word she ate, feeling her energy quickly restored.

During this entire time, her family watched in silence. Now they could hold back their questions no longer.

"Tell us," Sabina demanded. "Where have you been? And what happened to you?"

"I went out in search of..." Merritt paused and glanced at her father, who was watching her intently. "Those stray lambs I told you about. I found them in the forest, and was returning them to the flock, when I was caught by a group of thieves."

"I warned you that you were courting danger," Sabina said with a cry of alarm. "But you never listen."

"What was I to do? Someone had to go after the lambs—"

"How did you escape the thieves?" Edan broke in. "Were they very strong and very wicked?"

"They were indeed. The Campbell rescued me." Merritt chanced a shy look at the man who had taken his place at the far end of the table.

"The Campbell?" Edan seemed extraordinarily pleased that his tutor, who until now had seemed only interested in books, should display a taste for battle.

"Truly?" Sabina's brows arched in surprise.

Even Upton turned to study him with new respect.

Shaw emptied his goblet, feeling the warmth of the wine revive him. Sitting back, he surveyed the Lamonts, who suddenly seemed to be talking at once.

All except Upton, who was studying his daughter through narrowed eyes. When, a short time later, Shaw excused himself, saying he wished to see how his brother fared, Upton watched him with equal interest.

He noted that the Campbell paused beside his daughter and asked if she could manage the stairs by herself.

But he did not touch her.

With absolutely no inflection in her voice, she assured him she could manage just fine.

But she did not look at him.

The voices of his children washed over him as they demanded every little detail of Merritt's adventure. But Upton was no longer listening. Instead, he was seeing, in his mind's eye, the way he and his beloved Brinda had behaved when they had first realized the deep feelings each had for the other. Timid, shy, overwhelmed by emotions too strong to handle, they had hoped that by convincing others that such feelings were not real, they could convince themselves, as well.

Aye, he thought, young love was a strange and wondrous thing. And, as he recalled, a force unlike anything else in the world.

Renewed by food and drink, Shaw took the stairs two at a time in his eagerness to see his brother. He paused in the doorway to Sabina's chambers and noted the low-burning fire. He would have to chop more logs on the morrow or the lass would be forced to burn her furniture once more just to keep from freezing in this cold, drafty wing of the fortress.

He had convinced himself, from what Sabina had told him below stairs, that Sutton would be lying helplessly upon his pallet of rags. Instead, he caught sight of his brother leaning his back against a pile of fur throws, sipping from a goblet.

Sutton looked up. "So, you have returned to us." His eyes danced with unconcealed joy.

"Aye. I had thought to be gone but a short time in pursuit of a deer. Instead, I was delayed." Shaw decided that his tale of adventure would wait for a more opportune moment. Right now, he cared only how his brother was feeling. "You look much stronger than when I last saw you."

"I am determined to regain my strength as quickly as possible. After all, I must, if I am to survive these Lamonts," he said with a frown.

Shaw knelt beside him and touched a hand to his shoulder. "What are you saying? Have you been mistreated?"

"Mistreated? Aye. And abused. The woman attempted to force foul-tasting poisons down my throat, and 'twas by sheer strength alone that I managed to thwart her."

Shaw bit back his smile. "It is not poison. It is willow bark tea, thought to have some healing powers. They tried to make me drink it, as well. But these people are not hoping to harm you, my brother. They are merely following my orders to see to your needs."

"I tell you, Shaw, it is fortunate that you were able to overpower these Lamonts, or I would already be lying dead in their lair. The woman is a hag, determined to kill me while I sleep."

Shaw chuckled. "I know old Astra is frightening to look upon, but her heart is good. She is a loyal servant who is forced to see to far too many duties for one old woman, though she is a bit brusque."

"Brusque? Nay, she is more than that. She is cruel. I tell you, Shaw, the woman enjoys inflicting pain. She pummels me while I sleep. She applies salves and ointments that turn my flesh to fire. But she is learning that I am not like other men she may have tortured. I am a Campbell, and she will not succeed in her evil deeds as long as I have a single breath left in me."

"I will talk with her," Shaw said softly, soothingly.

He had never before seen his brother in such a state. He intended to get to the bottom of this and learn just what Astra had done to make Sutton so agitated.

Sutton's frown deepened. He nodded toward the doorway. "Then you may talk to the wench now. For here she is, ready to inflict her latest torment upon me."

Shaw turned, then froze.

The woman poised in the doorway to do battle with his brother was not old Astra. It was Sabina.

Chapter Sixteen

Beautiful, gentle Sabina. Dressed in a gown the color of heather, her dark hair pulled back with matching ribbons. Holding a silver tray, she stood uncertainly in the doorway, staring beyond Shaw to where his brother lay scowling at her.

"I...brought a bit of food," she said hesitantly. To Shaw she added, "I thought, since you were here, you might wish to help your brother sup."

"That is most kind of you." Shaw took the tray from her hands and placed it on a table.

Lifting the lid, he sniffed at a tureen of clear broth before handing it to Sutton. "It smells heavenly. This will restore you, my brother."

Sutton glowered at the woman over the rim of his bowl. "How do I know it does not contain poison?"

"Had I but thought of that," Sabina said tartly, "'twould have lightened my chores considerably. Mayhap on the morrow, I will lace your gruel with poison. At least then I will no longer have to listen to your litany of complaints."

Shaw lifted a brow in surprise. Was this the same mild-mannered Madonna who had sat beside his brother's pallet, going without sleep, ministering to his every need? When had she turned into this dour shrew?

"Aye. A bit of thin gruel. A sip of watered broth. And foul swill that is not even fit for swine," Sutton muttered. "If you do not poison me, you will starve me."

Shaw swiveled his head to study his brother. Had his injuries completely altered his personality? Was this churl the same charming rogue who had never met a wench he did not wish to bed?

Whatever had happened between these two while he was gone?

"I assure you, Sutton," he said calmly, reasonably, taking several sips of broth to ease his brother's mind, "the lass wants only to see you get well." He handed the tureen back to his brother, then turned to the lass. "Is that not so, Sabina?"

"Aye." Her eyes flashed. "The sooner the better. For then, we will be rid of this lout, and our lives can be returned to us."

"Take your miserable life and welcome to it," Sutton mumbled between sips of broth. "Look at this place. Have you e'er seen a more wretched hovel? The wench's bed linens are in tatters. The settle is broken. There are no rushes upon the floors, no tapestries upon the walls. And look at my embarrassing excuse for a pallet."

Shaw did look. First at Sabina's cheeks, glowing scarlet with shame and anger. And then at the pallet. He saw at once that the rags had been replaced with clean linens and several soft fur throws. The lass was as good as her word.

"Such insults are unworthy of you, Sutton. I see nothing wrong with your pallet." The tone of Shaw's voice betrayed his growing impatience with his brother. "Now what is this about ointments that turn your flesh to fire?"

Sutton set aside his tureen with a clatter. "The female enjoys inflicting pain upon my person. I believe she has deliberately added to her salves the leaves of nettles and plants that cause my skin to burn."

Again Shaw turned to Sabina. "What say you, lass?"

"Your brother's wounds were unclean and festering. Without my special ointments and salves, he would even now be writhing in a bed of pain. Instead, because the potions cleansed the wounds, he is healing well enough to find fault with everything."

"Roll over," Shaw commanded.

When Sutton did as he was told, Shaw knelt and examined the wounds. "It is as the lass says. They show no sign of the infection I had seen earlier. Thanks to her diligence, they are healing, brother."

He motioned to Sabina. "Come, lass. Apply your medicine and I will attend you."

She handed him several strips of fresh linen, then knelt beside Sutton and began to apply the ointments. As she did, her patient sucked in his breath, then began emitting a string of savage oaths.

Beside her, Shaw grinned, remembering how the salves had burned when Merritt had applied them to his wounds. But such obscenities in front of a gently bred lady like Sabina were unwarranted.

"You owe the lady an apology. You are as sulky as a hound who intruded his nose in a beehive. This must be another sign that you are healing," Shaw commented as he helped Sabina wrap his brother in fresh linen.

Sutton offered no such apology. Instead, when they had finished and managed to roll him over, he was still muttering a few choice words.

While he was complaining, his gaze fell upon Sabina's hands as she gathered up the soiled linen. For a moment his eyes widened. At once his hand shot out, catching her roughly by the wrist.

She was surprised by the strength in one who had been so severely wounded. Though she tried to pull away, he held her fast.

"Release the lady at once," Shaw cried. "Why do you assault her?"

His brother ignored him. His gaze was fixed on the purple bruises that encircled Sabina's wrists. "How did you come by these?"

For a moment she held her silence, refusing to meet his eyes.

His voice deepened. "Tell me. Now, woman. Before I completely lose my temper."

She lifted her chin, meeting his gaze firmly. "You inflicted them."

"I?"

She nodded. "Each night, as you fought me in your sleep."

"But..." He thought of all the battles he had fought lately. Or thought he'd fought. Had they all been in his mind?

He swallowed and tried to rekindle his anger, which had suddenly faded. "If I was such a brute, why did you continue to minister to me?"

"Because your brother ordered it. Because I reasoned that the sooner you regained your strength, the sooner we would be rid of the uninvited Campbells." Her voice lowered to almost a whisper. "And because, though you were too much of a fool to admit it, you needed me, and would have died without my care."

She yanked her hand away and scrambled to her feet. In a flounce of skirts, she rushed from the room.

When she was gone, the two brothers stared at each other in silence.

It was Shaw who finally spoke. "My journey has left me weary beyond belief. I believe I will sleep now. But on the morrow I will return before I go below stairs to break my fast. There is much I would ask you about the attack that brought you here."

"Aye. If only I could remember. But, alas, it is gone from my mind."

"Perhaps in time you will recall."

The two brothers clasped hands and exchanged identical measured looks. Neither of them spoke of what had just transpired.

When he was alone, Sutton stared morosely into the flames of the fire and struggled to ignore lingering feelings of shame and guilt. Could it be that his fevered mind had played tricks on him? And that he had, in his agitated state, inflicted pain upon an innocent lass?

He closed his eyes and rolled to one side, moaning softly. God in heaven, how the female must hate him. But no more than he hated himself at this moment.

Shaw was awake and outside before dawn. While the others were still asleep he slaughtered several sheep and delivered them to a grateful Astra in the kitchen. Then, removing his tunic and shirt, he set about the task of chopping wood for the many fireplaces. As he labored, he marveled that Merritt and Sabina had managed alone for so long. How it must have pained them to be forced to burn their family's furniture and tapestries in order to provide heat for their father and brother.

It had been obvious that they had been near starvation when he'd arrived. He felt a wave of fresh anger at the thieves who had made off with their horses and flocks. It was a wonder this family had survived.

As he mopped his brow he studied the fallow fields, the aging, unkempt outbuildings, with sagging roofs and crumbling walls. At one time, Upton Lamont, laird of Inverene, had been the most feared and respected warrior in all the Highlands. Now he resembled his buildings. He was a shell of the man he'd once been, lying abed, reliving in his mind the achievements of his youth.

Since the brutal attack upon their fortress, none of the Lamonts were as they had been. Upton crippled in mind, his son, Edan, crippled in body. The servants run off, the lasses, no longer pampered and cared for, left to fend for themselves. And all because of this mysterious Black Campbell.

Who hated Lamont enough to do this evil deed? As ax bit into wood, Shaw pondered the question. If even half the rumors about Upton Lamont were true, he had made a score of enemies in his younger days. Any one of them might have waited until the perfect moment to seek revenge.

Another puzzle. The identities of the Highland Avengers. If they did not steal for the Black Campbell, then for whom? He thought of the poor villagers who had remained loyal to Upton Lamont. Could some of the village lads have decided to seek vengeance against this Black Campbell? It seemed the most likely explanation. That could also be the reason why Sabina and Merritt were so determined to defend the Highland Avengers. They would die rather than betray anyone loyal to their father.

By the time he had chopped enough wood to feed the fires for another day, Shaw's body was already protesting the brutal exertion. As he made his way to the great hall, staggering under the logs in his arms, he came to a decision. He would find help, even if it meant going out into the nearby villages and soliciting workers. Since he was pledged to remain here until Sutton was strong enough to return home, he may as well spend the hours constructively. Besides, it would help keep his mind off a certain lass whose image had kept him awake most of the night, even creeping into his dreams to tease and taunt him.

"Ah, 'tis good to smell mutton cooking in these kitchens again," old Astra sighed as Shaw entered with an armload of logs.

"Aye. I have worked up a mighty appetite." He stacked up the wood and tossed another log in the fireplace.

"There was a time when we would have three or four sheep roasting, as well as a plump pig and a dozen or more pheasants. And that was just for one meal," the old woman added proudly.

"How many servants were in your charge?" Shaw leaned a hip against the table and watched her gnarled old hands as she kneaded dough.

"A score or more for the kitchens and scullery. Another score worked above stairs, assisting the lady Brinda and her lasses. Oh, 'twas a fine, lavish keep, where royalty hunted wi' the laird and dined and danced into the wee hours. I used to think there was no finer place to be than Inverene House." Her voice lowered. "And then the laird lost his wife in a bloody attack and himself grew... weak... and everything changed."

"Where did the other servants go?"

"Some packed up their families and left to seek a better life. Some accepted the protection of the Campbells and are now their servants. Most remained in the village, though they knew they were doomed to a life of hardship without the protection of the laird. They are fair game for every thief and villain."

Shaw picked up a lump of raw dough and popped it into his mouth, much the way he always had in the kitchen at Kinloch House. "So they would no doubt band together to fight off any invaders."

"Aye."

"Unless those invaders were the Highland Avengers."

"The Avengers have ne'er harmed the villagers. In fact, they have protected them against the black-hearted villains."

Shaw smiled to himself. It was as he'd suspected. "Have you kept in contact with the villagers?"

She gave him a crooked smile. "Most of them are kin. Nieces, nephews, cousins and the like."

Shaw reached for a second lump of dough and was rewarded with a rap on his knuckles from her wooden spoon. With a sly grin he said, "I would like to meet them, Astra. Would you accompany me to the village later today?"

She eyed him warily, then surprised him by slicing off a thick slab of freshly roasted mutton and handing it to him. "Here. Ye've done the work of three men, while the others are still abed."

"You wouldn't want to add a biscuit or two, would you?" he asked as he devoured the meat in a few quick bites.

She spread honey on several biscuits and watched them disappear into his mouth just as quickly.

"Now begone wi' ye," she said. "The others will be down soon to break their fast. I've work to get done . . . if I'm to accompany ye to the village later."

Shaw brushed a kiss over her cheek, then hurried outside for another load of logs.

In the kitchen, old Astra stood very still, a dreamy smile on her face, a hand pressed to her cheek.

Shaw knocked on the door to Sabina's chambers. When she opened it, he entered carrying an armload of wood.

Sutton's eyes blinked, and his vision seemed unusually clear for one who should have been sound asleep. "Is that you, brother?"

"Aye." Shaw knelt by the fireplace and tossed a log on the embers. Soon he had coaxed a roaring fire, and the chilly room began to take on a warm glow.

Across the room, Sabina's cheeks sparkled from a fresh scrubbing, and she wore a clean gown of rose velvet, with matching ribbons in her hair.

"Why are you doing the work of a servant?" Sutton asked.

Shaw wished he could spare Sabina's tender feelings. But he had decided that, now that his brother was mending, it was time for honesty.

"There are no servants at Inverene House." Shaw picked up the silver bowl of gruel that lay warming beside the fire. "My lady, if you wish to go below stairs to break your fast, I will remain here and assist my brother with his meal."

Before she could respond, Sutton, appearing thunderstruck, shouted, "No servants!" Then, as his gaze swept the room, it made perfect sense. "So that is why the lady's bed linens are in tatters. And why I often seemed to awaken in a place that reminded me of a dungeon."

Across the room Sabina looked stricken at his description of her home.

At once Shaw said, "You should know that the Lamonts have been under siege."

At the mention of battle, Sutton's interest was instantly piqued. Here was something he could understand.

"Who attacks the Lawless One?" he asked as he dug into the gruel with obvious relish.

Sabina flushed at the use of her father's hated nickname. Her tone became defensive. "Upton Lamont is no longer known as the Lawless One. That title more aptly applies to your kinsmen."

Sutton set the bowl of gruel aside with a clatter. "Are you accusing the Campbells of breaking the law?"

"Aye. Thieves have stolen our horses and sheep and cattle. They have driven away our servants, defeated our army."

"I've heard of these thieves. The Highland Avengers. You cannot accuse these men of being Campbells."

"You think not?" Her hands balled into fists at her sides. "With my own eyes I saw the men who killed my mother and left my little brother for dead. These men boasted that they swore their allegiance to one called the Black Campbell."

From his pallet Sutton looked from Sabina to Shaw, then back again. "I have ne'er heard of this Black Campbell."

"Nor have I," Shaw said softly, "until recently. But in the forest, the thieves who captured Merritt made that same boast."

For a moment Sutton was silent, digesting all that he'd heard. "Then there is an outlaw among our kinsmen who blackens the name of every Campbell."

"Aye." Shaw met his brother's look, and the two were gripped by the same thought.

Somewhere in this Highland wilderness was a dangerous traitor who must be brought to justice.

Chapter Seventeen

Upton Lamont sat in his chair in front of the fireplace. The mutton in his belly, the fire at his feet, had him feeling content and replete. He studied his younger daughter, who sat, head bent over needle and thread, attempting to repair her brother's torn tunic. Her impatience with the task was evident in her face. Her lips were pursed in a little pout. Her eyes resembled storm clouds. Each time she pricked her finger, she emitted a hiss of anger.

"Where is your Campbell, lass?"

Merritt's head came up sharply. "He is not my Campbell."

"Aye." Her father swallowed back the chuckle that threatened. How she reminded him of himself when he was young and tempestuous. "Where is the Campbell?"

She shrugged. "He and Astra went to the village."

"For what purpose?"

She couldn't hide the edge to her voice. "He did not choose to share his reason with me." In fact, he had barely spoken to her this morrow. Ever since their return from the forest, he had ignored her, choosing instead to spend all his time either in the kitchens with Astra or in Sabina's chambers with his brother.

Father and daughter looked up at the sound of approaching horses. At once Merritt retrieved the sword that hung over the mantel. As she turned, the door was thrown open and Shaw strode inside, followed by Astra and a dozen or more men, women and youths.

Merritt's eyes flashed dangerously. "What is the reason for this invasion, Campbell?"

"It is no invasion, my lady." Shaw stepped aside so that she could see the familiar faces of the peasants from the nearby village.

In her presence, the men snatched their caps from their heads and the women lowered their heads, in deference to the lady of the manor.

"These people are loyal to the laird of Inverene House." Shaw saw the surprise in Merritt's eyes before she composed herself. "They wish to serve him."

Upton, spotting an elderly man leaning upon a walking stick, called, "Colbert, is that you? Has the fever left, then?"

The man hobbled closer and smiled. Shaw had already warned the peasants that the laird had been confined to his pallet by a mysterious fever sweeping through the Highlands.

"Aye, m'laird. So it would seem."

Upton seemed slightly amused at the old man's words, and Shaw began to wonder. Had the laird of Inverene known all along that the stories of a fever had been pure fabrication? Did the villagers know the truth about the laird, as well?

"I was afraid to return to Inverene House," Colbert said, "for I'd heard stories that it was under siege from Campbells. But the lad here assures me that ye are still laird, and that ye desire my services."

"Aye, Colbert." Upton sat up straighter, knowing the servants were milling about, peering at him with great curiosity. It wouldn't do to have them see any weakness in their laird. "I desire the services of all of you."

The other peasants broke into wide, eager smiles.

Upton looked into the crowd and called, "Dulcie. Is that you, lass? Why, look at you. You've grown from a child to a woman."

"Aye, m'laird," said an apple-cheeked young woman, whose little son and daughter peered from behind her skirts.

To Shaw, Upton said, "Dulcie is Astra's niece. I watched her grow up here at Inverene House. Why, she knows every nook and cranny of this old place. And hid herself in quite a few, as I recall."

"I am a wife now, with two small bairns," the girl said with pride. She drew a tall, strapping peasant forward. "This is my husband, Adair. He is strong and eager to work."

"Then you are welcome in Inverene House," Upton said. "As are all of you," he called to the others. "For there is much to be done."

His words caught Shaw by surprise, and he found himself wondering again just how much Upton had surmised. Could it be that the elder Lamont had not been fooled by his daughters' attempts to shield him from the truth?

"Ye've wasted enough of the laird's time," Astra called impatiently. "Ye will all follow me to the kitchens, and I will tell ye y'er duties."

The old servant was suddenly in her glory now that she had a household staff to direct once more.

As the peasants filed from the great hall Astra said to Shaw, "I will take the women and assign them their tasks, if ye will show the men what needs to be done."

"Aye, Astra."

Shaw led the men outside. In no time they had been divided into groups. Several brawny young lads, with Adair in charge, headed toward the forest with axes over their shoulders. In no time the air rang with the sound of trees falling and logs being chopped.

Two lads were assigned to the flock of sheep, while a large group of men began the difficult task of filling in the pit and rebuilding the stable that had been burned, in addition to repairing the other outbuildings.

Dusk was falling when Shaw finally made his way to the house and walked down the hallway. Fresh rushes had been strewn on the floor, giving off their clean, earthy fragrance. The wood shone with beeswax, and a score of candles glowed in sconces along the walls. Before Shaw could enter the great hall, Merritt stepped through the doorway and caught his arm, pulling him aside.

"Do you know what you have done?" she demanded.

"Done?" Puzzled, Shaw struggled with the urge to gather her into his arms and crush her petulant mouth under his. Each time she came near him, the temptation was the same, and he experienced a wave of heat that left him weak with need.

"You have brought half the village to Inverene House to work."

"Aye. And even that number will stagger under the load of work that needs to be done."

"You must keep your voice low," she commanded, "lest my father hear. Already he is in the great hall, awaiting a feast." Under her breath she whispered furiously, "How shall we reward the loyalty of this army of workers, Campbell? We have barely enough food for ourselves. And we cannot promise them protection from invaders."

"You are wrong, my lady. With new workers, you will soon have enough food to feed the entire village. Why just today, Adair and his men managed to bring down a stag and three does while they worked in the forest. As for payment, you now have a flock of sheep, many of which will soon lamb. I regret that I was forced to promise many of the villagers a payment in lambs as a reward."

"You promised our lambs? And how will we build our flock if we are forced to give away all our newborns?"

"I promised them only those lambs in excess of the current number in the flock. So, though you will lose some lambs, your own flock will double."

"And what about protection?" she demanded. "How can all these people be kept safe from invaders?"

"I made them another promise," he whispered. "That the swords of Inverene House would be raised in protection of all."

"The swords of Inverene House?" she asked incredulously.

"Aye, my lady."

"And whose swords might they be?"

"Mine and yours," he said with a grin. "And that is more than they had before."

She thought it over, then reluctantly nodded. "I think, Campbell," she muttered as she walked by his side into the great hall, "that you are far too generous with your promises."

"You must admit," he said in an aside, "that your day has been far easier than those in the recent past." He looked around at the gleaming wood and the table groaning under the weight of so much food. Instead of a hollow, empty room, the great hall was filled with a dozen or more villagers and their families seated at the tables, their voices raised in a symphony of conversation. "And the rewards far greater."

Merritt watched as Astra directed a serving wench who carried a tray filled with steaming venison and placed it in front of Upton for his approval. "Aye. My mouth waters thinking about the rewards."

"Then come. Let us indulge ourselves, for the long days of fasting are over."

As they took their places at table, Sabina came flouncing into the room, her usually composed face twisted into a mask of anger. Though she tried to hide them, tears glittered on her lashes.

"What is wrong? What has happened?" Merritt asked.

"'Tis the wounded boar in my chambers."

Hearing her, Shaw came around the table and caught her hand, searching for fresh bruises. "Has my brother harmed you, my lady?"

"Nay." She looked down, ashamed of her outburst. "He is not a cruel man. But his brusque manner and harsh demeanor try my patience."

"I beg your forgiveness," Shaw said softly. "Sutton is a warrior, more accustomed to the field of battle than to enforced idleness. He has ne'er spent this much time in a pallet since he was a bairn."

"Aye, a bairn. He behaves like a spoiled bairn," Sabina muttered. "He moans, and complains, and finds fault with all that I do."

"If you will be patient another day or more, I will find a way to gently remove my brother from your chambers, my lady, and have him brought to mine."

Instead of the relief Shaw expected, Sabina looked alarmed. "Nay. You must not."

Both Shaw and Merritt stared at her in surprise.

"'Twould...open all his wounds and cause bleeding afresh.'" Sabina glanced at her sister for support. "I do not wish to prolong his agony, even though he is an evil-tongued Campbell, for that would only mean that he would have to remain here at Inverene even longer. Nay," she insisted, tossing her head for emphasis, "we must not remove him from his place of repose until he is completely recovered."

"Then you must assign one of the servants the task of seeing to his needs," Shaw said. "That will free you of the burden."

"It is no burden," Sabina said, reaching a trembling hand toward a goblet of ale. "I do not mind caring for your brother. Truly I do not."

Shaw felt his respect for the lady Sabina deepen. Without regard to her own comfort, she was pledged to see his brother safely healed.

Merritt, on the other hand, studied her sister with a curious look. Sabina had always been the thoughtful, compassionate one. But she had protested the removal of her patient so vehemently. Too vehemently. Was she, perhaps, feeling something other than compassion for the handsome warrior who slept in her chambers? Had the quick-tempered lout stirred something else in her sister's heart? Why else would she insist upon caring for him, when she could just as easily assign the task to a servant?

All Merritt's questions were quickly chased away by the food and warmth and merriment in the great hall. From the blazing fires at either end of the huge room to the food and wine and voices raised in laughter, Merritt felt an overflow of joy mingled with relief. Could it be that the days of hunger and hardship were finally over? Could all the looting and burning and killing become a thing of the past?

She lifted a goblet of wine to her lips and drank deeply. Oh, if only it could be so. She would gladly put all of those troubles behind her forever.

Candles sputtered in pools of wax as Shaw made his way along the upper hall to Sabina's chambers. Below stairs the servants had cleared away the remains of their sumptuous meal, and Sabina had entertained with music from the lute, while Upton, feeling stronger than he had in years, had engaged his younger daughter in a rousing game of chess.

Now the sounds had faded as the servants made their way to their pallets. Only the Lamonts remained below. Shaw had left them to their privacy, to quietly talk over the events of the day among themselves.

He opened the door and paused on the threshold, his gaze on the figure in the mounds of fur.

A servant had assured him that his brother had taken nourishment, emptying a bowl of clear broth, as well as several bites of fish, before giving in to exhaustion. Still, despite his own weariness, Shaw needed to see for himself that Sutton was comfortable. The dreamy smile on his lips was a sure sign that he suffered no pain.

As he knelt beside his brother, the smile deepened. Sutton stirred. When he saw Shaw, his smile vanished.

"I thought . . . Where is the woman?"

Shaw touched a hand to his brother's brow and was relieved to feel no fever. "She remains below stairs with her family. How do you fare?"

"I weary of this weakness that holds me in its grip. I am a warrior, my brother. I have no use for weakness."

Shaw smiled. This he could understand. "I know it is vexing. But think of this as a battle. And each day you must fight it, day by painful day, until your strength returns and you are once again the invincible warrior you once were."

"If that were the only battle I had to fight, I could manage."

"What other battle is there?"

"There is also the woman."

"Sabina? I do not understand."

Sutton drew his brother close and whispered, "I must lie here night after night and watch as she undresses in the dark and slips into her bed. And in the morn I must feign sleep while she goes about her ablutions. But I have seen her as she washes herself and dresses for the day. She is the most perfect female I have ever beheld."

Shaw started to smile but his brother's hand tightened on his arm. "'Twould be easy for one such as you to resist such temptation. Women have ne'er been your weakness. But for me it is a taste of the fires of hell to be forced to watch and feel and desire, and be unable to move."

"Aye." Shaw patted his hand and got to his feet. "I see now why you vent your frustrations in her presence. But if you could speak more softly to the woman, I would be grateful. For you have been the cause of her tears. And such things upset . . . other members of her family."

"I care not for the feelings of these Lamonts. Nor do I care for the woman. She is merely some sort of evil spirit, sent here to test my strength of will."

"And what is that supposed to mean?"

Sutton passed a hand over his eyes in a gesture of weariness. "I know not. I know only that sometimes, when I look at her, I see an angel of mercy. But it is the fever. And when I truly awaken from this illness, I will see her as she is. A hag. A Lamont. The daughter of our father's enemy."

"The Lamonts are not what we thought them to be."

"What are you saying?"

Shaw merely sighed and said gently, "You must sleep now, for I see that your mind is still befuddled."

"Aye. Befuddled by the—"

At that moment Sabina entered in a swirl of skirts, looking flushed and breathless. "Forgive this late hour. I brought you hot mulled wine to help you sleep."

"You see, brother?" Sutton muttered.

"Remember what I asked of you. Speak softly," Shaw said under his breath.

Sabina knelt beside Sutton's pallet and lifted his head slightly, holding the goblet to his lips. As she did, her dark hair swirled forward, whispering over his naked chest.

He drank deeply, before saying, "Thank you, my lady. That was most kind."

She seemed surprised and flustered by his unexpected gratitude.

"You are most welcome. I hope the night passes without pain."

"Sleep now, my brother," Shaw called. "Good even, my lady."

He realized at once that neither of them seemed to hear him. With a last glance at them, he closed the door and made his way to his own chambers.

Inside, as he stripped off his clothes, he thought about his brother's words. *'Twould be easy for one such as you.... Women have ne'er been your weakness.* If only he could unburden himself to his twin. But he had no right. Sutton had troubles enough of his own.

His musings were suddenly interrupted as the door opened and Merritt swept in. Her eyes were glowing, her smile radiant.

"My father bested me tonight on the board."

He tossed aside his shirt and turned to her with a smile. "Why does losing to your father make you happy?"

"Do you not see?" She danced closer and clasped her hands together. "His mind has come back to him. For so long now he could not concentrate on the chess pieces. But tonight he not only played, but he won."

"Ah. I do see. And I am glad, my lady."

"It is because of you," she said, her voice lowering. "Because of the food you provided, and the logs for the fire, and the servants. He has found a reason for coming back to us from that other, more pleasant place where he dwelled for so long in his mind."

She suddenly became aware of his hair-roughened chest, his arms corded with muscles, the skin-tight breeches that molded his thighs.

Her eyes widened as she realized that she'd caught him undressing.

"Forgive me, Campbell. I did not mean to interrupt—"

"You interrupt nothing. I am not abed yet."

Color flooded her cheeks. "I was so eager to share my news with you, I did not think."

As she turned away in embarrassment he touched a hand to her shoulder to stop her. At once they both felt the flare of heat.

His voice lowered. "I'm honored that you would share your happiness with me."

Just standing here, being touched by him, she knew that there was so much more she wanted to share with him. So very much more.

She stood unmoving, her back to him. "How could I not be happy when I hear once again the sounds of voices and laughter in Inverene House? Is it not a wondrous sound?"

"Aye." He kept his hand on her shoulder, though the heat was swiftly becoming an inferno.

"And it is all because of you...."

"Shh." In one smooth motion he lifted the heavy hair from her nape and pressed a kiss to the back of her neck. He hadn't meant to. It had happened so naturally, so spontaneously. But now that he was kissing her, he couldn't stop.

With a little moan she leaned into him and realized that he was fully aroused. His strong arm came around her to mold her to the length of him, while his other hand twined in her hair and he continued raining kisses along the back of her neck and across her shoulder.

With a sigh of pure pleasure she turned her face slightly. He nibbled at the corner of her lips while his arms enfolded her.

As he moved his lips over her cheek and along the curve of her jaw, he murmured, "Oh, my lady. You feel so good, so right, here in my arms. All day I have tried to avoid you, to deny these feelings I have for you."

Her heart soared at his admission. It was not really her he'd been avoiding; it was his passionate feelings for her.

With his teeth he tugged at her lobe, before his tongue darted inside her ear to tease and taunt. His big, work-worn hands began to weave their magic, as well, cupping the fullness of her breasts, while his thumbs found her already hard nipples.

"Stay the night," he whispered against her neck, as his mouth trailed moist, hot kisses across the pale line of her shoulder.

She should be able to think of a score of reasons why she must go. But her mind refused to cooperate. All she could do was move in his arms and revel in the pulse of desire that shuddered through her. She wanted him as much as he wanted her. Nothing else mattered.

He turned her in his arms and covered her mouth with his. Needs, desires, seemed to explode within them, driving them to the edge of madness.

Lost in their passion, they were aware of nothing except their need for each other.

The door between their chambers was suddenly thrown open, and a woman's voice called, "Shall I help you undress before I retire, my lady? Oh! Forgive me."

Two heads came up sharply. Still clinging together, Merritt and Shaw turned toward the servant who stood in the doorway, her hand at her mouth to stifle her gasp of dismay.

It was Merritt who found her voice first. "Aye. Thank you, Dulcie."

Like a splash of frigid water, she realized the depth of her weakness for this Campbell. Even the approach of a servant could not break through his allure.

The servant turned away, mortified by her lapse.

Merritt swallowed and took a step back, as if to prove that she was still in control of herself. "I will leave you now to your rest."

"That is indeed wise, my lady." Shaw caught a handful of her hair and watched through narrowed eyes as it sifted through his fingers. Lowering his gaze to her mouth, he tasted her as surely as if he were still kissing her. "And infinitely better for both of us."

She turned and fled.

For long minutes after she left, he stood very still, staring at the closed door. He felt cold and empty, and more alone than he had ever known.

At last he walked to the balcony and studied the shadowed loch below. God in heaven, what was he to do? His desire for Merritt Lamont was becoming an obsession.

When, a few minutes later, he poured wine into a goblet, he noted that his hand was still trembling. And his pulse had still not returned to its normal rhythm.

Despite the work he had done this day, he was certain sleep would evade him this night.

Chapter Eighteen

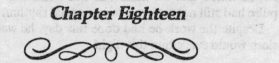

Shaw lay upon his pallet, hovering in a twilight world somewhere between sleep and wakefulness. All night he had slept fitfully, his troubled thoughts centered on Merritt. Merritt. How he ached for her. This need for her was far from simple. It complicated everything. The woman had become a hunger greater than food or drink, a need deeper than life itself.

He resented this intrusion into his well-ordered, disciplined life. Always before, his needs had been simple, his goals direct. Now, for the first time in his life, he felt lost, adrift. The feelings she had awakened in him were humbling. Always, he had believed himself above the things of this world. Now, he realized, he was a mere man, with all of man's weaknesses, all of man's appetites.

Moonlight streamed through the balcony window, casting the room in light and shadow. The door between their chambers opened. An ethereal figure drifted toward him, shimmering in a gown as delicate as a butterfly's wings.

He tried to order her to go, but his voice was strangely silent. She continued moving toward him, hands outstretched.

He knelt up, catching her hands. At once he experienced a shock. His hands were empty. His eyes blinked open. There was no one there. He was alone. In his troubled state he'd imagined her, warm and real and seeking him out as a lover.

He passed a hand over his eyes. His forehead was beaded with sweat. His heart was racing as though he'd climbed a rugged Highland mountain peak.

With a sigh of self-loathing, he tossed aside the bed linens and strode to the settle, where his clothes had been carelessly dropped the night before. He dressed in haste, then glanced at the dawn light streaking the horizon. The servants would be up and about in the kitchen. He would break his fast with them and join the men in the fields. If he worked long enough and hard enough, he might even be able to erase the image of Merritt Lamont from his mind for an entire day, though, in truth, he knew such a thing was unlikely.

"Here you are." Merritt poked her head around the doorway of her mother's old sitting room, where Shaw and Edan were engrossed in their books. "I have seen you not at all in the past few days, Campbell."

"There was much work to be done." He glanced up in time to see a vision in a velvet gown the color of dark forest foliage. At once he ducked his head and fixed his gaze on the book in front of him. The words ran together in a blur.

"Will you join us in the great hall for a midday repast?" She felt ashamed of herself for this ploy, but it was the only excuse she could think of. She'd had a burning need to see him, and he had avoided her at every turn.

Shaw shook his head. "I requested that one of the servants bring our meal in here, so that we may continue with our lesson."

"Aye. There is so much to learn," Edan put in excitedly. "And Shaw says I have a fine mind."

"You do indeed," Shaw confirmed, "though your education in some areas has been sorely neglected. You are clever and bright. I see a lad who shall one day assume his father's position as leader of his people."

The boy beamed under such lavish praise.

Merritt's heart swelled with joy for her brother. "Oh, Edan, I am so happy for you."

She glanced again at her brother's tutor, who had been studiously evading her. Was it because of what had happened in his chambers? Could it be that, in the cold light of morning, he regretted his actions? It was obvious that he was uncomfortable in her presence. He had made it plain that he preferred the company of anyone else to her, seeking out the servants from sunup to sundown for the past several days. Now he had locked himself away with his books and her little brother, shunning her even at meals.

Oh, if only she could confide in Sabina, and partake of her wisdom. But her older sister had far too many duties to concern herself with such foolishness. Besides, Merritt could hardly tell a member of her own family that she was in such a turmoil over a Campbell.

Was she losing her mind or—Sweet Virgin!—her heart? Was that what was happening? She could not. She must not. Still, if truth be told, the Campbell was on her mind, day and night. She had barely had a moment's rest during the last few nights, knowing that only a door lay between her and the man who occupied all her thoughts. Once she had even padded to the door and stood uncertainly, her fevered forehead pressed to the cold wood. In the end, she had returned to her bed and lay huddled beneath the covers, praying for the dawn.

"Edan," Shaw said, breaking through her musings, "would you like to display your newfound skills?"

"Aye," the boy cried at once.

"Then," Shaw said softly, handing him a scroll, "you may read aloud to your sister."

As the boy's voice washed over her, reading from the Book of Genesis, Merritt turned away and restlessly began to circle the room. The evidence of the servants' diligence was everywhere. Dozens of precious parchments and scrolls had been dusted and placed on open shelves. The windowpanes had been polished to a high shine, allowing sunshine to spill into the room, forming patterns of light and shadow on the freshly scrubbed stone floor. Though the room was still sparsely furnished, the table and chairs gleamed with polish, and a new settle, draped with animal hides, had been positioned in front of the fireplace. A fire blazed on the hearth, lending its cozy warmth to the room.

At a knock on the door, Merritt opened it to admit Astra and a young serving wench. At Astra's direction, the servant placed a silver tray on the table, then arranged the food and filled goblets.

"Will you stay and eat with us, Merritt?" Edan asked.

Shaw was about to protest when he reminded himself that this was the lass's home and he, after all, was the uninvited guest. Reluctantly he held his silence.

Embarrassed, Merritt seemed about to refuse when she caught sight of the little frown line between Shaw's brows. Her anger suddenly surfaced. So, he resented her intrusion here, did he? That was all she needed to goad her into accepting.

"Aye. I would like that." She turned to the housekeeper. "If there is enough for three of us."

Astra nodded. "More than enough, lass. Now that we have our larder stocked, we have ample food for everyone."

"Then I will be pleased to stay and sup with you." Merritt was rewarded with another frown from Shaw before he turned away and replaced the scroll on a low shelf.

"Come, lad." Shaw easily lifted Edan in his arms and carried him to the table, where he settled him on his chair.

"My lady." Shaw held a chair for Merritt, and as she sat down she felt the brush of his hand against her back. She stiffened, keeping her head high, her gaze averted.

"There is so much to learn," Edan said between mouthfuls of steaming meat pie. "Shaw says that in time I will read every book in this room."

"Truly?" Merritt glanced at the piles of books, then studied her little brother with new respect. "That is quite a feat."

"It must be done if I am to have the knowledge necessary to lead our people."

"Lead our people." Merritt smiled. "I like the sound of those words, Edan."

She returned her attention to a biscuit still warm from the oven. After spreading honey on it, she popped it into her mouth.

Across the table, Shaw watched as she licked at a drop of honey. His throat went dry at the sight of her tongue moving seductively over her lower lip. Was the female doing this on purpose, just to taunt him?

Feeling the heat of his gaze, Merritt flushed and looked away.

"I have learned much about our family from the many scrolls on those shelves," Edan said.

At once, both Shaw and Merritt turned to the lad, in the hope of calming their inner turmoil. It was far easier to converse with Edan than it was to deal with each other.

"Father was once considered closer than a brother to Shaw's father, Modric," Edan explained. "The scribe who recorded their friendship called them true brothers, who would lay down their lives for one another."

Merritt's brow arched. "Do you know this to be true, Campbell?"

He nodded. "The same is recorded in our family history."

"How, then, did they become enemies?" she asked.

"Pride," Shaw replied. "Your father swore he would never bend his knee to another."

"You are wrong," Edan said quickly. "'Twas love."

"Love?" Both Merritt and Shaw stared at him in surprise.

"Aye. According to the scribe, in his youth Father was in love with a maiden, but she gave her heart to another. Grief sent him into a black, raging fury that drove him to battle both friend and foe alike." The boy, seeing that he had their complete attention, took a second portion of meat pie and savored another bite before continuing. "Father spent years traversing the Highlands, leaving behind him a path of pain and destruction. Then, while visiting the keep of Galen MacArthur in Argyll, he discovered an innocent lass who could erase the other from his mind."

"Our mother, Brinda, was a rare, gentle beauty," Merritt explained to Shaw, "who could have tamed the heart of a wild beast."

"Aye, a wild beast would have described our father in his youth," Edan added. "According to the scribes. And only with Brinda did our father find peace and contentment. And that, in turn, led him to regret his earlier attacks on his neighbors."

"I must differ," Shaw said. "For I have read our inscribed family history, and nothing is said about a lost love. The only reason given for your father's rage against his people is pride."

Quick as a wink Edan slid from his chair and scooted across the floor, calling, "I shall retrieve the scroll that you may read for yourself."

Merritt's eyes were filled with love as she watched her brother. Knowing he was out of earshot, she turned to Shaw. "I haven't a care about our history, but I care deeply for my little brother. For so long now Edan has languished in a prison of sorts. With these books, and someone to teach him how to use them, the walls of his prison are being lifted." She caught Shaw's hand. "And you made it possible." Her voice was soft, her eyes dreamy.

"Nay, my lady." Though he tried to resist her touch, he couldn't help turning his hand palm up, and closing his strong fingers around hers. At once he felt the unwelcome heat that always flared when he touched her.

Merritt watched as a strand of pale hair dusted his forehead. She longed to reach up and brush it aside. Her fingers tightened in his.

He answered with a tightening of his own callused palm and cautioned himself against prolonging this agony. The mere touch of her had him wanting more.

"Edan is too bright, too quick, to remain in darkness for very long," Shaw whispered, staring into her eyes. "Even without my help, in time he would have found his way to the light."

"But you took the time with him, when no one else would or could. And for that, Campbell, I shall always be grateful."

He allowed himself but a moment's pleasure, then scraped back his chair and stood. His voice was rough with impatience, for he despised this weakness in himself. "I do not do this for your gratitude, my lady. It merely passes the time until I can return my own brother to our home."

She watched him stride across the room and open another book, shutting her out. She had to bite her lip to keep it from trembling. Why had her gratitude angered him so?

"Do you wish to read the scroll?" Edan asked.

She forced her attention back to her brother. "Nay. Perhaps another time."

When, a few minutes later, she slipped from the room, neither Shaw nor Edan seemed to take any notice. But Shaw had to concentrate all of his energies on the boy's lesson, for his mind was greatly troubled.

"Shaw Campbell." Sabina's voice trembled with anxiety. "You must come at once and dissuade your brother from his foolishness."

Shaw looked up from his place at table in the great hall. Astra and the servants were just about to begin serving the evening meal.

"What foolishness would that be, my lady?"

"Please," she said, catching his hand and urging him away from the table. "We will talk as we climb the stairs, for I fear that unless we hurry, he will surely fall."

"Fall? He is standing?" Shaw's eyes lit with pleasure as he raced up the stairs.

Beside him, Sabina lifted her skirts and nearly ran in her haste to keep up with him. "Not only standing. He ordered a servant to bring him his clothes. Had I known, I would have forbidden it. But now that he is dressed, he insists that he is strong enough to join us below stairs to sup.''

"This is wonderful news." Shaw threw open the door of Sabina's chambers and came to a sudden halt.

Across the room, Sutton was leaning against the back of a chair. Even from this distance, his brother could see the effort such a feat cost him. Sutton's knuckles were white, and his face bore the tight, pinched look of pain.

"So," Shaw called in a cheerful voice. "Your strength returns."

"Aye. And with it, my determination to leave these four walls. I crave the company of others."

"You see," Sabina cried as she followed Shaw into her chambers. "You must convince him of the foolishness of such a thing, for he is far too unwell."

Shaw grasped his brother's hand and could feel the weakness in that once viselike grip. It would be a long while before Sutton was strong enough to undertake the journey home. But for now, he was standing. For Shaw, that was enough.

"He is not sick. Merely weakened. Come, my brother. This is a time of great rejoicing. We will descend the stairs together. It is time you met the rest of the Lamonts."

With his arm around Shaw's shoulders, Sutton brushed past Sabina and made his way slowly, painfully across the room. It was a faltering, torturous descent to the great hall. But as they entered, and everyone in the room turned to watch their progress, Shaw felt his brother square his shoulders. And though Sutton continued to cling fiercely to Shaw's strength, he managed to hold his head high while he made his way to the table.

When they paused beside his chair, Sutton did not immediately sit. Instead he stood very tall, and turned to face his host.

"Upton of the Clan Lamont," Shaw said politely, "my brother, Sutton of the Clan Campbell, would sup with us."

"Aye. And welcome," Upton said, pulling himself painfully to his feet. If the Campbell would show no weakness, neither would he.

At once Merritt and Sabina took up a position on either side of their father, in case he should stagger. But he waved them off and continued standing straight and tall. The two men cast long, measured looks at each other. Almost at once a half-forgotten image floated into Sutton's mind. While he had lain helpless upon his pallet, he had seen this man standing over him, flanked by these females. That time, too, he had flung off their arms, as if determined to strike. But strangely enough, he had merely stared down at Sutton for long, silent moments, before turning away.

"You have met the lady Sabina, and this," Shaw said, "is her sister, Merritt."

Sutton detected a slight change in his twin's voice when he spoke the lass's name. Perhaps another would not have noticed, but he and his brother were, after all, finely tuned to each other's mood changes. Sutton made up his mind to ponder this at another time.

"My lady." He acknowledged this fiery-tressed lass with a slight bow and noted that she was studying him with great curiosity.

"And this is their brother, Edan."

The lad smiled broadly at the man who looked so much like the one beside him, despite the bushy red gold beard that covered Sutton's lower face.

This one, too, Sutton could vaguely recall. He tried vainly to piece together the images that had floated in and out of his consciousness immediately after his attack. He remembered the lad seated beside his pallet, staring directly into his face. But instead of walking away as the others had, the boy had seemed to crawl away like a wee bairn. Sutton dismissed such a thought. Surely his memory had been dulled by pain.

With the introductions concluded, Sutton sank gratefully onto his chair. Upton did the same. At once Astra directed a serving wench to approach, bearing a tray of steaming venison and mutton.

"Thank you, Astra." Shaw bit back a smile when he noticed that the housekeeper kept her distance. Apparently the arrival of his twin had brought all her fears to the surface once more.

"You are feeling restored?" Upton asked.

"Aye." Though he felt ravenous, Sutton was surprised to find himself unable to eat more than a few bites before he was forced to push aside his trencher. But even that little bit of sustenance seemed to renew his strength.

"Then my daughter is deserving of much praise, for we all thought your life was over when you were brought here. She alone fought to save you when we thought all hope was gone."

Shaw glanced at Sabina, who kept her gaze averted. But as she lifted her head, her eyes met Sutton's. In that brief instant Shaw saw a look pass between the lass and his brother. A look that spoke, more than any words, of a deep and abiding bond between them. And why not? The lass truly had saved Sutton's life.

"On the morrow," Edan said, breaking the silence, "I shall record this event in the scroll."

"What scroll do you speak of, lad?" Sutton asked.

"The scroll that records the history of the Clan Lamont. Shaw is teaching me how to read and write, so that one day I can assume the leadership of my clan."

"So, you would be a laird like your father. How old are you, lad?"

"I am ten and two," Edan said proudly.

"It is true that you must be educated if you are to lead," Sutton agreed. "But a lad of such an age must have skills beyond that of books. You should be receiving lessons in the use of weapons. Have you mastered dagger, sword and longbow yet?"

"Nay." The boy looked down at the table.

In the awkward silence that followed, Shaw said softly, "The lad was wounded in an attack. He has not the use of his legs."

Again Sutton recalled the image of Edan crawling across the floor. It would seem that his vision had not been distorted by the pain. The lad truly couldn't walk.

Sutton felt something lodge in his throat and had to swallow several times before saying, "So you cannot walk. You can still learn to wield a sword from your horse's back. If," he added, "you truly desire to be a Highland warrior and laird of your people."

"There is nothing I desire more," Edan said with feeling.

"Then," Sutton declared, as an idea formed in his mind, "your education must begin at once."

"My education?" The boy stared at this bearded stranger, so like the man he had come to admire.

"There is no one better to teach you to read and write than my brother," Sutton said with a trace of pride. "For he has the finest mind of any man I've ever known. But when it comes to the skills of a warrior, he will be the first to admit that he is sadly lacking."

Merritt opened her mouth to protest, intent upon relaying the story of Shaw's courage in the face of the thieves. But before she could speak, Shaw quickly broke in. "Aye.

Sutton's skills with weapons and horses upon the field of battle are legend."

"I would be more than happy to impart my knowledge," Sutton offered.

At once his brother said, "You are fortunate to have such a tutor, Edan."

The boy's eyes danced with eagerness. His fondest wishes were about to come true. "I would be grateful for your knowledge, Sutton. You will find me an apt pupil."

"That remains to be seen," Sutton muttered, feeling the weight of exhaustion. The shirt beneath his tunic was bathed in sweat. He knew he had asked too much of his battered body, but as a warrior he understood that the sooner he forced himself to act, the sooner his strength would return.

Beside him, Shaw had come to the same conclusion. It was time for his brother to begin to live again. And the best way to do that was to throw himself into something that was not only demanding but satisfying. While Sutton shared his knowledge of weaponry with Edan, he would be forced to push his own body to the limits, thus gaining strength.

He glanced at the thin, taut line of his brother's mouth, and knew that he was suffering greatly. "We will bid you good-even," he said.

Scrambling to his feet, he caught Sutton's arm and helped him to stand.

Before he turned away, Sutton nodded to those around the table. "I thank you for the food." He looked up and caught the old housekeeper's eye. "And you, good Astra."

The housekeeper flushed and turned away. But not before Shaw saw the look of stunned surprise on her face. And the softening look of pleasure in her eyes.

Chapter Nineteen

"**D**o you see the knot in yon tree, lad?" Sutton lounged on a fur robe beneath the shade of a tree. Though he had made it down the stairs without assistance, he found the effort so exhausting he'd been forced to sink to his knees as soon as he reached the stables.

"Aye," Edan called as Adair lifted him into the saddle and secured his legs with strips of leather. Each day the lad's skills with his mount had improved, until he no longer feared the movement of the horse beneath him. He had gone from walking his horse in a slow, cautious circle to a jarring trot around the fortress to a brisk run across the rolling hills, all the while managing to remain in the saddle and lift and wield a variety of weapons.

With each lesson his strength had grown, until now he could handle a sword and crossbow with ease. But because of his youthful stature, his favorite weapon was a small, deadly knife, which he kept tucked into his waistband.

"I want you to take a handful of dirks and see how many times you can hit that knot."

"That is easy," the lad said, as he began tossing the knives. Each one hit the target.

Though he was impressed with Edan's skill, Sutton merely said, "You did not let me finish. You will hit that knot while running your mount past it."

Edan swallowed. "A full run?"

"Aye." Sutton closed his eyes a moment against the weariness. He despised this weakness that continued to plague him. He could see that he was improving each day, but it was not enough to satisfy him. Deep inside was the nagging little fear that he would never have the strength he once had. To a Highland warrior, it would be a bitter defeat, worse than death.

At once he thought of the brave lad who was even now racing past him, tossing his dirks at the tree. How Edan must have despaired when he'd learned that he'd lost the use of his legs. But, from the tales Shaw had told him, the lad had never given up. He'd battled his fears and his weaknesses with a rare courage. And now, with just a little encouragement, the boy was struggling to regain the dream of every Highland lad.

Sutton watched as Edan went through his paces. Though several daggers missed the target, one of them struck a direct hit.

"Look!" Edan shouted. "I did it."

"Aye. That was fine, lad. But remember," Sutton said, recalling the words of one of his wise old tutors, "the tree is not tossing knives at you as you approach. Think how much harder it would be if you were forced to evade returning weapons as you advanced."

At once the boy's smile of triumph faded and he attacked this latest lesson with a vengeance, imagining with each toss of his knife that the tree was fighting back.

Sutton thought about the mission that had brought him here. He had journeyed to Inverene House to confront Upton Lamont, an old enemy. Instead, he had found a man whose fortress had been invaded, his wife killed, his only son crippled. Sutton experienced a wave of annoyance at himself for his impatience with his own infirmities. How could he feel sorry for himself when these Lamonts had suffered so much more? Still, his loss of memory of that night plagued him.

"Look, Sutton!" the lad shouted.

Sutton counted four dirks within the small knot of the tree. His admiration for the boy grew. Edan was indeed an apt pupil.

"Well done," he called. "We will end the lesson for today. You may ride the hills now until you tire. As for me, I must go inside and rest. But on the morrow, I will think of something more challenging, for I can see that your skills are growing faster than the goals I have set for you."

With a victorious smile, Edan turned his mount toward the flock of sheep in the distance. As soon as he left, Sabina hurried toward the figure under the tree and helped him to his feet, then folded the fur robe.

With reluctance, Sutton slipped his arm around the lass's shoulder, feeling the delicate bones beneath his touch. They walked slowly toward the scullery door.

"I thought Adair was going to assist me," Sutton muttered.

"He was needed to help with the new shed in the pasture."

"And my brother?"

"Shaw directs the workers from the village." She held the door and waited until he was inside, then took up her position beside him.

When Sutton's arm draped around her shoulder, she steeled herself against the feelings that began, low and deep, and spread through her veins like liquid fire. It happened each time he touched her. This man, this rugged

Campbell warrior, must never know the depth of feeling he stirred in her. For if he guessed at her reaction to him, she would be lost.

Beside her, Sutton climbed the stairs and fought his own demons. All his life women had been attracted to him, and he to them. His enjoyment of them had been as easy, as natural, as his enjoyment of good food or fine ale. He had never questioned his right to sample their charms, as long as they'd been freely given. But this woman was unlike any he'd ever met. The more he came to know her, the more he realized that she was not a woman he could love and easily walk away from. She had let him know, by both word and deed, that she was not the least bit interested in him as a man, but saw him merely as a wounded animal that needed her care. That intrigued him, for he liked nothing better than a challenge. But that was a mistake. When he thought about seducing her, he discovered that he could not, for he knew instinctively that this woman, once tasted, would linger on his tongue for a lifetime, making all other women seem unimportant by comparison. To love her was to lose himself, his own identity. His days of womanizing would be over. He would become that which he'd vowed never to become, a man weakened by—nay, chained by—love. And that he must never allow.

As they reached the top of the stairs and headed toward her chambers, he risked a glance at her lovely profile. The truth was, the sight of Sabina Lamont took his breath away. She was by far the loveliest female he had ever seen. And not only lovely to look at, she was a thing of beauty inside, as well. Her devotion to her family was unquestioned. Her kindness to all, even the most lowly servants, was a joy to behold. And her attention to him, though he'd made it as difficult as possible, had been unwavering.

"At last. You will find rest." She opened the door to her chambers and helped him inside.

As he eased himself down upon the pallet, she knelt beside him and spread the fur robe over him. Before she could get to her feet he caught her hand in his.

"Thank you, my lady. I could not have made it without you."

She dimpled at the seriousness of his tone. "I think there are strengths within you that you are not aware of. I have no doubt that even without my help, you would find a way to your pallet."

She started to pull her hand away, but he held her fast. "Perhaps, my lady. But you make my journey easy."

She stared down at his offending hand. "And you, sir, make mine difficult."

He shot her that charming grin that had melted the hearts of so many maidens across the Highlands. "Is my company so painful to endure?"

"Aye." She spoke the word vehemently.

In the next instant she surprised them both by bursting into tears.

"Oh, my lady." Sutton knelt up and caught her by the upper arms.

Humiliated, she covered her face with her hands.

"Tell me what I've done to cause your tears," he murmured as he gathered her into his arms and began to stroke her hair. "For I will do anything to make amends."

At his tender ministrations, her tears increased and her body shook with sobs. And all the while, he stroked and soothed and whispered words meant to comfort.

When at last her crying subsided, he held her a little away and said, "Can you tell me now what I have done, that I may atone?"

"It is not you," she said haltingly. "It is I."

"I do not understand."

"I wanted to hate you, for you are a Campbell. And I think, for a little while, I managed to remember that. But soon I found myself forgetting. And now, when you are so kind to Edan, I find myself wishing..."

"Wishing what, my lady?"

The tears started again, and she said between sobs, "Wishing that you would never get strong enough to leave. And that is a selfish wish, unworthy of me. And wishing that you would stay, and defend us against our enemies. But that is a foolish wish, for our enemies are your clan, the Campbells."

"Oh, my lady." He framed her face with his hands and bent his lips to her cheek.

With great tenderness he kissed away her tears. He heard her little intake of breath and knew that he'd overstepped his bounds. But it was too late. His lips moved over her face with exquisite care, tasting, nibbling at the corner of her brow, her forehead, even the tip of her nose.

Sabina had never known such feelings. Confusion. Elation. Wonderment. And slowly, ever so slowly, an awakening to a need deeper than any other. She could wait no longer to taste his lips.

With a little moan of pleasure she lifted her face and offered her lips. His mouth moved over hers, seducing, then devouring, as her hunger fueled his own.

For Sutton, all weariness vanished. The pain of his wounds no longer tormented him. All that mattered, all that he was aware of, was this woman in his arms. Her lips were the sweetest he'd ever tasted.

He had not planned this; had not wanted it. But now, as she moved in his arms and offered him the greatest gift of all, he knew he was lost. From this moment on, there would be no other woman. From this moment on, he was hers, and hers alone.

Shaw and the men trooped into the great hall for their midday repast. The work in the fields had gone well. Several sheds had already been completed. It was hoped that by the time the flocks began their spring lambing, all the outbuildings would be repaired.

Shaw watched as Sutton entered the room, leaning heavily on Sabina. As they walked, the two looked into each other's eyes and shared whispered words that made them both smile.

Shaw was puzzled. What had transpired between these two that they should suddenly feel so at ease?

Almost at once, the truth dawned. He watched them more carefully, as if hoping to deny what his heart already knew. But the more he watched them, the more he was convinced. His brother and Sabina had become intimate. There was no other explanation for their behavior.

He glanced at Merritt and saw that she, too, was watching. She happened to turn and meet his gaze. At once her cheeks colored and she looked away.

Aye, he thought. The lass sees, also. And knows.

Shaw felt a welling of anger. His brother's wenching had always been a matter of much discussion in their family. And they had long looked the other way, rather than condemn him for his obvious weakness. But this was different. Sabina had dedicated herself to Sutton's care. She had endured his cruelty when he was in a fevered state, and had gone without food and rest to see to his recovery. And now, while a guest in her house, he had dared to repay this sweet creature by seducing her.

As they took their places at table, Shaw crossed the room and caught Sutton's arm roughly. "I would have a word with you."

"Can it not wait until after we have eaten?"

Astra directed the wenches to begin serving the meal.

"Nay," Shaw said angrily. "We must resolve something between us—"

Before he could say more, one of the servants burst into the great hall shouting, "M'laird. They've stolen the lad."

All heads turned toward him. It was Shaw who demanded, "What are you saying?"

"Young Edan. He was riding near the forest, when a score of men on horseback burst from their hiding places and snatched him from his horse."

Upton leapt to his feet, clinging to the table for support. "A score of men, you say? Did you recognize any of them?"

"Nay, my laird. But I know they were not from our village."

"Campbells," one of the serving wenches cried.

"Aye," came the voice of a villager who was seated at a table. "Was it not Sutton Campbell who suggested the lad ride today?"

Sutton was about to speak in his own defense, but before he could say a word, Sabina commanded imperiously, "You will be quiet."

All eyes turned to this normally docile creature, but her eyes blazed in anger, and Shaw knew in that moment that she had not merely been seduced. She was a woman who was indeed in love, for her defense of her man was fierce and all-consuming.

"Sutton and Shaw Campbell have done everything they can to help us in our need. I will not hear another word against them."

Merritt joined her sister. "We must not become divided in our loyalties. Shaw, we must go after him," she cried. "You know what they will do to him."

"Aye." Shaw touched a hand to her arm. "I will go."

"You?" Sutton could not hide his astonishment as he gripped Sabina's arm for support. "Brother, this calls for warriors. I am the one who must lead this charge."

"If you but had your strength, I have no doubt of it," Shaw said with sudden calm. All his earlier anger against his brother had faded, to be replaced with a burning hatred for the men who had abducted Edan. "But it is impossible for you to sit a horse in your present state."

"The lad is my only son," Upton shouted. All eyes turned to him as he added, "His protection is my responsibility."

"Nay, my laird," Shaw said as firmly as he dared. "Like Sutton, you have not regained your strength for such a difficult undertaking. This I pledge. I shall see to him. And I give you my word. I will not fail."

As Shaw began striding from the room, Merritt started to follow. He turned on her. "You will remain here with your father."

She refused to be deterred. "I do not take orders from you, Campbell. You have no right to keep me here."

His hands shot out, catching her roughly by the upper arms. His voice was a low rasp of fury. "I leave you no choice. I cannot afford to worry about you while I search for your brother."

She struggled to pull free. "You do not know the forest as I do. Without me you will become hopelessly lost."

"You heard me, my lady." He pushed her aside and strode from the room. Over his shoulder he called, "I ride alone."

The others in the great hall had fallen deathly silent. This savage, ferocious, intense warrior was a side of Shaw Campbell that none had ever seen.

As Shaw raced up the stairs to retrieve his traveling cloak and weapons, Merritt heard him calling orders to a servant to saddle his mount.

She stood uncertainly for a moment, gazing first at her sister, who clung to Sutton's arm as if clinging to life itself, and then at her father, who sat slumped in his chair, his head bent, eyes downcast. He had lost so much in his life. His wife, his clan, his purpose for living. How could he survive the loss of his son?

"Please," she prayed fervently. "Let the Campbell get there in time to save Edan. And please," she added as tears stung her eyes, "bring them both safely home to Inverene House."

For she knew, in that instant, that both her little brother and Shaw Campbell were equally important to her. Both owned her heart. And the loss of either of them would leave a void in her life that would never be filled.

Chapter Twenty

Darkness came early in the Highland forest. Though the valleys below were still bathed in a glorious sunset, here in the dense woods, the tallest of the trees blotted out all light.

Shaw moved slowly, slipping often from the saddle to the ground to look for evidence that the group of horsemen had passed this way. Crumpled underbrush, broken branches, hoofprints in the earth were all indications that he was on the right path.

While he tracked the band of thieves, he found himself recalling bits and pieces of his early childhood spent with his father. The warrior skills he had thought lost came rushing back to him.

Modric had been known as a fierce warrior, as well as a protector of his people. His skill at tracking invaders who snatched innocent women and children had become legend. It was said that Modric could ride the length and breadth of Scotland without taking time to rest, to assure that the innocent were returned to their families and the guilty were punished. His justice was swift and final. But he was also known as a fair and just leader, slow to anger, quick to forgive.

How fortunate, Shaw mused, that when their parents had been wrenched from them, he and his brothers and sister had been taken in by the good monks of Saint Collum. What would their lives have been like without that charity? Shaw could still recall those first days and nights, having suffered the loss of all that was familiar. Clinging to their older brother, Dillon, they had felt alone, bewildered, adrift. But at least they had had each other.

Edan was alone. Without the use of his legs, he was quite helpless. What torments must the lad be suffering?

That thought drove Shaw as he slid from the saddle once more and, leading his mount, trudged through the tangled vines and dense growth of the forest, searching for a trail. He must not fail the lad. Edan's life depended upon it.

He had lost their trail.

Shaw knelt on the bank of the river, swollen with spring rain, and peered through the darkness. He had wasted precious time crossing from one side of the river to the other. But he could find no trace of the horsemen. He knew they had entered the water at this point, and had remained in the water, hoping to elude capture. But had they fled upstream or down? More precious time would be wasted while he searched for tracks.

He cursed and pulled himself into the saddle. The choice was his to make. If it took him until morning light, he would search first downstream and then up, until he found their trail.

He shook off the weariness that threatened. He would not rest, could not, until he found the lad. He urged his mount into the water and headed downstream.

At a sound behind him, he drew his sword and wheeled his mount. A cloaked figure leading a horse stepped from the cover of darkness.

"You!" he roared, as he recognized Merritt, dressed in the garb of a stableboy. He returned his sword to the scabbard.

"Aye, Campbell. I see it is as I'd predicted. Without me you are lost."

"And how would you know such a thing?"

"Because I have been following you. You did admirably," she added, "until now. I have waited and watched, hoping to keep my presence unknown, while you frantically crossed the river and back. But now I see that I must take matters into my own hands."

"How noble of you. Are you suggesting that you know which way the knaves went?"

"Aye," she said with a smug smile. "I have only now realized. They went upstream."

She saw the look of disbelief that crossed his face. "Why upstream?"

"Because," she said, pulling herself into the saddle, "that takes them deeper into Campbell terrain, where they will be offered protection for their deceit. If they go downstream, they risk running into villagers loyal to my father."

Shaw knew at once that she was correct. He had still been mentally denying that these villains were loyal to one of his own clan. "Aye. Of course. Thank you, my lady. Now take yourself back to your father's fortress at once."

As he turned his horse she reached out and caught his reins. "You do not really believe that I came all this way just to be sent home like some helpless female?"

Anger and frustration surfaced. "We waste time. You heard my command earlier. I do this thing alone."

Her eyes blazed. "I do not obey commands from a Campbell. It is my brother we seek. And I will not return to Inverene House until he returns with me."

"Little fool," he muttered. "I will not have you exposed to danger, too." His hand tangled in her hair and he pulled her face close. "It is bad enough that Edan is in the clutches of those villains. I could not bear it if you suffered the same fate."

At his outburst, all the fire seemed to go out of her. She surprised him by touching a hand to his cheek. "Aye, Campbell," she whispered. "I do understand, for I know that same fear for you. But know this, also. I am handy with sword and dirk, and I know this forest. With me at your side, you stand a better chance of rescuing Edan. And his safety must be the only thing that matters. Not even our... feelings for each other can matter at such a time."

He took a deep breath, then brought her hand to his lips and pressed a kiss to the palm. "Let us ride, then. For the night is swiftly passing. And darkness is our best hope of surprise."

"Listen. Up ahead."

At Merritt's words, Shaw reined in his mount and strained to hear anything out of the ordinary. At first all he could hear were the sounds of a distant waterfall and the cry of a night bird. But then he became aware of the muted sound of men's voices, low and deep, and the occasional burst of raucous laughter.

Without a word Shaw and Merritt slid from their saddles, tied their mounts and crept forward.

The villains had made camp in a small clearing. They seemed to have no fear of being discovered, since in the center was a roaring fire. The men, seated on logs or lounging in the grass, were feasting on a stag roasting on a spit. While they ate they passed a flagon of ale among themselves.

Shaw touched Merritt's hand and pointed. Following his direction she made out a small figure huddled beneath a tree. Edan's hands and feet were bound. Even from this distance, they could see that he was shivering. Despite the damp cold, the villains had taken his cloak. One of them wore it tossed rakishly over his shoulder.

At the sight of it Shaw's anger surfaced. He pulled out his dirk and started to rise. Merritt yanked him back down and pointed to a tree a short distance away. Surprised, he looked up to see the shadow of a man holding a cross-bow.

"It is no wonder they appear so relaxed," he observed.

"Aye," Merritt said in a low voice. "They have posted a guard. There will no doubt be another guarding the far side of the encampment."

"This is the second time you have saved me from my folly," he whispered.

"I'll not let you forget it, Campbell."

He squeezed her hand. "I am certain you will not, my lady." He returned his attention to the thieves. "We must eliminate their guards before we attempt to rescue Edan."

She nodded.

"You remain here," he said softly. "I will crawl to the far side and locate their other guard."

"How will I know when you have found him?"

"A dove will coo thrice. That is the signal to take out this guard, as well. When both men are eliminated, we must attack with such force that the thieves believe there is an army. Can you do that?"

"Aye."

He paused a moment, studying her in the darkness. She was the most magnificent woman he had ever known. She had not paused or questioned, but had immediately accepted a course of action that could mean great danger. "Take care, my lady."

He crawled away, and within minutes she could no longer see him in the tall grass.

She lay, unmoving, her gaze fixed on her little brother. She took no notice of the chill of the night, the dampness beneath her. Nor did she consider the evils that lay ahead. She knew only that Edan had already been made to suffer more than most lads. There would be no more sorrow in his lifetime, she vowed. If necessary, she would lay down her life for him that he might be returned, unscathed, to their father.

The soft cooing of a dove was carried on the night air. At once her attention shifted to the men seated around the fire. In their merriment, they took no notice as the dove cooed a second and then a third time.

Merritt pulled a knife from the waistband of her breeches and aimed it at the figure of the man in the tree. She was so intent upon her task she never even heard the soft rustle of movement behind her. A ragged figure sprang to his feet and clamped a big hand around her wrist with such force that her dagger dropped uselessly to the ground. Caught unawares, she managed to bring her elbow back with enough force to be rewarded with a grunt of pain before he wrapped his other arm around her throat and pressed with all his might against the delicate flesh. She pried at the arm, desperately kicking and clawing, but her strength was no match for his. With such strength, he would surely break her neck. She could feel her life ebbing as darkness seemed to descend like a heavy cloak over her eyes. Her hands fell away limply. She slumped unconscious in his arms.

* * *

Shaw led his mount and Merritt's toward the villains' camp. He knew he'd wasted precious time retrieving the horses, but he had to improvise some sort of distraction. Working quickly, he plucked a handful of thistles and placed them beneath the saddles.

He disposed of the guard with ease, taking him from his perch in the tree with a single toss of his dirk. As the villain pitched forward, Shaw gave the signal, then raced toward the clearing, leading the horses. He kept his eye on the leader, Lysander, who was busy tipping a flagon to his lips. This time, Shaw vowed, he must take out the leader first, and the others would be dispatched with little effort.

As he looked toward the far side of the clearing, he was surprised to see the other guard still sitting in his tree. Had the lass missed her target? It seemed unlikely. She was as skilled with a dirk as any man. Unless . . .

He felt a chill along his spine. Without waiting to consider the darker side of his question, he took aim with his crossbow. An arrow sang through the air. The shadowy figure of the guard toppled, landing silently in the damp moss below.

At once Shaw slung his bow over his shoulder and retrieved his sword from the scabbard. Leading the horses, he lifted his weapon high and raced the remaining distance to the edge of the clearing, intent upon attack. But when he came within sight of the encampment, he skidded to a halt and watched in shock and disbelief as a ragged villain made his way into the camp carrying a limp, unmoving Merritt. Suddenly all Shaw's carefully woven plans lay in tatters. The woman he loved had been captured.

From a great distance Merritt could hear her little brother's voice calling to her.

"Merritt, please, please awake. Do not give up. Please. Open your eyes. You must not die."

She drew in deep drafts of air through lungs that were starved for it. With each breath, her throat constricted with spasms of pain. Her mind refused to obey her. Her eyes were closed, the lids too heavy to lift.

"Merritt, speak to me. Tell me you are alive."

At her little brother's voice, closer now than it had been a moment ago, she struggled upward, though her mind still seemed clouded with layers of damp, heavy wool.

"Ah. You are breathing," came Edan's voice beside her. "You are not gone from me yet. Awake, Merritt, and speak to me."

With a tremendous effort, she broke through the confusion and surfaced. Her lids fluttered, then opened wide. Edan, though bound, had managed to scoot close enough to lie beside her. She realized her own hands were also bound, as were her feet.

"Edan." Even that whispered word caused her pain, and she was forced to swallow several times before she could say more. "Have they harmed you?"

"Nay. But they leave little doubt of their intentions. Their leader said I will be killed."

"Have they said why?"

He shook his head. "They said only that the Black Campbell ordered it."

"Is he here with these men?" she asked.

"Nay. Their leader is the one who attacked our home and killed Mother. It was he who bludgeoned me, and threatened to cut off my legs." He swallowed back the tears that threatened. Highland warriors did not cry. But his heart was heavy. Not for himself, though he feared dying, but for his beloved sister, who lay bruised and helpless beside him. He had never before seen Merritt looking so wounded, and the sight of it frightened him. "And now, he will harm you, as well."

"Nay." She struggled against the vines that encircled her wrists, only to have them contract and tighten until they drew blood. "I am not alone, Edan. The Campbell is with me."

Edan felt his hopes rise, but only a little. "He is one against ten and two."

"We are three," she corrected. "You and I may be bound, but until we draw our last breath, we are never helpless. Feel in the dirt for sharp stones or anything else that can relieve us of these bonds."

Edan began to take heart. Merritt was right, of course. As Sutton and Shaw had taught him, there were many things a warrior on the field of battle could do to save himself. This was his first real test since his lessons had begun. He must not fail his tutors. But as he struggled to cut through his bonds with the rough edge of a stone, his hopes were dashed once more. His heart plummeted as the leader of the villains approached and hauled Merritt roughly to her feet.

"So, woman, you have returned. You cannot stay away from me, it seems," Lysander said with a cruel laugh. With one hand at either side of her tunic, he tore it away, and the shirt beneath, revealing a pale, creamy chemise that barely covered her heaving breasts. His eyes gleamed with undisguised lust.

"Now that I have filled my belly, there is another hunger to feed. This time I will not be denied my pleasure, woman. And 'twill be greater," he called to the others who had joined in his laughter, "knowing the lad will be forced to watch."

Edan's eyes filled with tears that he could no longer hold back. And though he tried to look away, he found himself watching the brutality unfolding before him with horror and revulsion.

A great black wave of fury swept over Shaw. Whatever plans he had made were forgotten. The only thing he could see was Merritt in the clutches of that brute. All that mattered now was the woman he loved.

Instinctively he brought his fists down hard on the saddles and released the reins. The two horses burst into the clearing, bucking and rearing.

Startled, the thieves who had gathered around Lysander and Merritt were forced to leap out of the way of the crazed animals. Using those few precious moments, Shaw tossed his dirk with such skill it landed at Edan's feet.

"Free yourself and hide in the woods," he shouted.

Without even pausing to look back, he flung himself into the throng of men and hauled Lysander away from Merritt, sending the thief sprawling in the dirt with a powerful blow to his face. In an instant the other villains leapt into the fray with fists, knives and swords.

For a moment Merritt lay, shaking her head to clear her confusion. She was startled to find herself free of Lysander's cruel hands.

Gathering her wits about her, she ran to her little brother. But as she bent to lift him in her arms he cried, "Nay. Take up a weapon and join Shaw. I can crawl to safety."

"You are certain?"

"Aye," he shouted. "Leave me."

Edan watched as Merritt retrieved a sword from one of the fallen thieves. His heart swelled with pride as she bravely faced two men who towered over her. And though they were skilled fighters, she soon managed to disarm them and turn her attention to Shaw, who was surrounded by a pack of armed villains.

"Behind you," Edan shouted, and Merritt turned in time to hold off a surprise attack by one of the thieves.

She shot her little brother a look of gratitude as she continued the skirmish.

From his position on the ground Edan glanced toward the safety of the forest. He had been raised to obey without question. And he knew the wisdom of Shaw's order. At any moment one of the villains could capture him. That would force Shaw and Merritt to surrender, and all of the efforts to rescue him would have been in vain. He dared not place his sister and Shaw Campbell in any more peril.

Scooting across the clearing, he disappeared in the tall grass. From his position of concealment he watched the fighting and realized that more than half the villains already lay dead or wounded. But those who remained were fighting for their lives against Shaw, who seemed to be battling with all the strength and cunning of a madman.

"The leader flees," Shaw shouted, as Lysander raced toward a thicket. "He must not be allowed to escape again." He turned away, in an attempt to follow Lysander. Thus distracted, two of the villains were able to come up behind him. One of them swiped at his arm with the blade of his sword, causing Shaw's weapon to fall from his hand. Unarmed, blood streaming from his wound, he turned to face his attackers.

"Now shall you die," called the swordsman.

"Aye. As surely as I stand here." The second villain, determined to see that Shaw did not escape his fate, drew an arrow into his bow. If the swordsman failed to kill him, his arrow would seal Shaw's doom.

Merritt, caught in a duel with a sturdy young peasant determined to run her through, could not come to Shaw's aid or her own life would be forfeited.

With rare courage, Shaw stood facing his attackers. Although he knew that he had little chance of fending off both men, he would not back down.

The swordsman lifted his weapon and advanced. At the last moment Shaw surprised him by bending low and flinging himself forward with all his might. The two men fell to the ground and rolled around, fighting for control of the sword, while the archer, arrow at the ready, could not fire, lest he kill the wrong man.

Merritt found herself backed up against a tree, her attacker poised to thrust his blade into her heart. With one last flash of her blade, she found his shoulder and managed to disarm him. Surprised by her skill, he backed away for a moment. That was all the time she needed for her blade to find his heart.

She turned, ready to come to Shaw's aid. But to her horror she realized that, although he had managed to disarm his attacker, the archer stood poised to release his arrow into Shaw's heart.

Prepared to face death like a true Highland warrior, Shaw lifted his head high and straightened his shoulders.

As the archer triumphantly drew back his bow, his victorious look faded to one of stunned surprise. Before he could release his arrow, he suddenly stiffened, then fell forward into the dirt. In his back glinted the hilt of a small, deadly dirk.

Both Shaw and Merritt looked in astonishment to the figure standing stiff and unmoving across the clearing.

"I did not mean to disobey you," the boy said, his voice quavering, his eyes filling with tears. "But I could not flee to safety when those I love were in danger. I would have faced death, Shaw Campbell, rather than let him harm you."

"Praise heaven, lad," Shaw called. "For I was surely doomed."

"Edan!" Merritt clapped a hand over her mouth in stunned surprise. "You are standing!"

As the realization dawned that he was standing without support of any kind, the boy took a tentative step toward his sister before crumpling to the ground.

Chapter Twenty-One

"Edan. Oh, God in heaven, Edan!" Merritt raced across the clearing to kneel beside her brother's collapsed form.

"Are you hurt, lad?" Shaw asked tenderly as he knelt and cradled the boy in his arms.

"Nay. I was...overwhelmed," Edan whispered. "Did you see?" He suddenly brightened as the realization dawned anew. "I was standing."

"Aye."

"Without anyone's aid."

Merritt and Shaw smiled at each other over his head.

"I am sorry about their leader," he said to Shaw.

"Lysander? What are you sorry about, lad?"

"I could have stopped him with my dirk. Instead, I allowed him to escape. But I was forced to choose between stopping him and saving you. And even the hatred I feel for that villain was not as strong as the love I feel for you, Shaw Campbell."

Shaw had to swallow the lump in his throat before he murmured, "Would that love could always be stronger than hate." He gave the lad a gentle smile. "Do not fret about the tasks left undone. There will be another day to tend to them. This night you proved yourself to be a noble Highland warrior.''

"Am I truly?"

"Aye." Shaw saw the way the lad struggled against his weariness. "You have earned the right to rest now, Edan. We will make our camp here, and you and your sister will sleep until the morrow."

"And you?" Merritt asked.

"I will keep watch. And pray that Lysander attempts to return. For I would relish the chance to exact vengeance for his cruel deeds."

With great tenderness he wrapped Edan in his cloak and laid him near the fire.

Kneeling beside her brother's sleeping form, Merritt whispered, "Edan can stand. Praise heaven, he can stand. Do you think it is wrong of me to believe that he might also one day walk?"

"Nay, my lady. For now that I have seen, I, too, believe that he will walk."

He drew a fur robe around Merritt. The sight of her torn tunic and shirt, and the bruises at her throat, had his eyes darkening with temper.

Seeing his fierce look, she murmured, "Your twin does not know you as I do. He thinks himself a warrior. But tonight I saw the bravest Highland warrior of all."

Shaw's voice was a fierce whisper. "When I saw Lysander's hands upon you, I fell into such a black rage, I have little recollection of anything except the need to rescue you from those brutes."

"Hush. It is over, thanks to your courage."

"And yours, my lady."

She touched a hand to his arm and felt the sticky warmth of his blood. "You are wounded, Campbell. Let me cleanse and bind it."

Oh, the touch of her. It sent a fire raging through his loins that had him burning with need.

"Nay." He pulled away roughly and got to his feet. "Take your rest, my lady, while I retrieve the horses, for they have been caused enough discomfort."

She watched his lithe, pantherlike movements as he stormed away from her. Almost as though, she thought, he were an angry, stalking beast and she a trap that had been set to ensnare him.

When he'd been swallowed up by the surrounding forest, she drew the fur around her. Huddled deep in the folds, she turned to study her little brother, who slept as peacefully as if he were in his own pallet. If truth be told, he had not slept this peacefully in all the years since the attack upon their family.

She whispered a fervent prayer that all their troubles were over. Perhaps now that Lysander had lost his band of villains, he would let go of this hatred against her family.

Studying the flickering flames of the fire, she listened to the quiet, peaceful sounds of the forest. She felt no weariness, only a strange sense of hushed expectancy. As though something rare and wonderful were about to occur in her life.

With a fur around his shoulders, and his tunic and shirt removed, Shaw leaned his back against a boulder and struggled to tie a strip of linen around his arm, to stem the flow of blood. His sword and dirk lay in the grass beside him. Nearby the horses were tethered.

The fire had burned low; glowing embers shone in the dark of the night.

Hearing the rustle of footsteps, he looked up to see Merritt approaching.

She frowned and dropped to her knees beside him. "Why did you not ask me to help you with this?"

"I . . . thought you were sleeping."

"Do you know you are not a good liar, Campbell?" Without waiting for a reply, she took the linen from him and began to tie it around his arm.

As she did, her hair swirled forward and he had to close his eyes against the sudden desire to twine his fingers in it.

"Does this hurt?" Her fingertips moved over his arm, across his shoulder, filling him with a need so deep, so sharp, he caught his breath.

"Nay." He leaned back, breathing in the woman scent of her.

"And this?" She shocked him by pressing closer, spreading her hands to roam across his naked chest.

At once his eyes blinked open. His voice was a low growl. "Do not play games with me, my lady. Return to your brother's side, where you will be safe."

She smiled at him. "Does that mean I am not safe here?"

"That is exactly what I mean."

"Ah." Her smile grew. Boldly she touched her lips to his. "As you may have noticed, Campbell, I thrive on danger."

His hands gripped her shoulders painfully as he knelt and started to push her away. "This is not a game. And I am not some village lad who can be teased by the lady of the manor."

Her voice lowered. "I do not tease."

"Nay?" His eyes narrowed. "Then what is this?"

"It is what I feel for you, Shaw Campbell."

"I know what it is you feel. Gratitude for saving your brother."

"Aye. Gratitude. And . . . more."

His voice roughened with emotion. "Do not let your heart rule your head, my lady. On the morrow, when you have returned safely to your father's house, you will regret what you say and do here."

"Do you believe that? Have you no heart, Shaw Campbell? Can you not see the love that is shining in my eyes?"

A little thrill shot through him and still he struggled to resist. His voice grew stern. "Leave me now. If you are testing me, you are being cruel, for I am quickly losing my honor. If truth be told, I am losing my pride, as well, my lady." He would beg, he would crawl, to take what she offered.

When he tried to push her away she cried, "Aye, I have cast aside my pride, as well. I have ne'er felt for any man the things I feel for you. I want to lie with you, Shaw Campbell. And hold you. And love you." Her eyes filled with unexpected tears, and she blinked in vain, hoping to stem the flow. "I will ask nothing of you. But now, for tonight, let me show you the depth of my feelings."

She heard his quick intake of breath. "God in heaven, what am I to do with you?" He drew her roughly into his arms, his hands bruising in their intensity. "I have tried for so long now to be strong." Against her temple he murmured, "I thought I could resist you. But I cannot. I cannot."

His mouth savaged hers and he kissed her with a passion, a thoroughness that left them both gasping. Almost at once, as if regretting his lapse, his touch gentled as did his kiss. "On the morrow," he murmured against her lips, "you will turn away from me, and wish you could be as you are at this moment. Innocent. Untouched. Unspoiled."

"Nay," she whispered between kisses. "This is all I desire. You are all I desire, Shaw Campbell."

He could feel the heat building, and still he held her a little away, gazing deeply into her eyes. "If it is so, then let me . . . let me fill myself with you, Merritt."

Her eyes widened. It was the first time he had ever spoken her name. Always before he had avoided it, as though by saying it, he would somehow acknowledge that she was special.

"Say it again," she whispered.

"What?"

"My name."

"Merritt. Merritt." He ran nibbling kisses across her cheek, along her temple, over her closed eyelids. And with each kiss he chanted her name. "Merritt. Merritt." It was a litany of love that he knew he would hear in his mind for a lifetime.

His mouth moved over hers, slowly, deliberately, until hers parted for him. His tongue met hers, teasing, tempting, until she sighed and gave herself up to the pleasure of his kisses.

His lips skimmed over the line of her jaw, across her cheek to her ear, where his tongue traced the soft curve, before darting inside to send her pulse racing. When he tugged on her lobe, she shivered and moved in his arms. He ran a trail of hot, moist kisses down her throat, then froze, remembering her bruises.

"When I think of that brute choking you, hurting you . . ."

"Shh." She touched a finger to his lips. "We will not speak of it now, love."

Love. The word sent his heart soaring. "Oh, Merritt. Merritt." With exquisite tenderness he touched his lips to her throat, then pressed a line of kisses across her shoulders.

When she swayed in his arms he lowered her to the fur robe and murmured, "Even now I would not hold you if you desire to flee from me."

At the dangerous look in his eyes she felt her breath hitch in her throat. She touched a hand to his chest. His heartbeat was as unsteady as her own.

"I could not leave you, Shaw Campbell." She twined her arms around his neck and drew his head down for another kiss.

"Nor could I make you go, Merritt Lamont." The words were spoken inside her mouth as he covered her lips with his.

The moon was a golden crescent hanging low in the midnight sky. A million tiny diamonds winked their light against the darkened backdrop.

The breeze had grown still, as though even the very air held its breath. The rush of a nearby waterfall added to the symphony of insects and forest creatures who lent their voices to the night.

Consumed with heat, Shaw struggled to hold his own needs at bay, cautioning himself to go slowly, in order to make this first time as pleasurable as possible for Merritt. It was, after all, the only thing he could give her.

With exquisite tenderness he undressed her. His hands skimmed her shoulders, sliding the torn tunic and shirt from her. His fingers fumbled with the ribbons of her chemise until it parted and slid from her shoulders. In the dim light of the fire he studied the way she looked, naked and vulnerable.

"Oh, Merritt, you are so beautiful." His work-roughened fingertips felt wonderful as they glided over her flesh. His hands were strong, his touch tender, patient. He was soothing her, she knew. And leading her. But she was already willing to follow without question.

He kissed her with a gentleness, a reverence that had her pulse racing. With lips and tongue and fingertips he explored her face, her throat, the sensitive hollow between her neck and shoulder. And with each brush of his lips he felt her body grow more tense, her breathing grow more shallow.

He would not dwell on the future, though it loomed, empty and endless. For now, for tonight, there was only Merritt. Her arms, her lips, her body and the pleasure he could give her. For now, she was all that mattered.

As her blood heated and her body throbbed with need, Merritt felt the fire seep through her veins. The dangers that lurked beyond the circle of firelight were forgotten. As was the future. She would not think about what her life would be like when Shaw left. For now, all that mattered was this man, this moment.

Locked in his embrace, she felt enveloped in a cocoon of pleasure. His kiss, his touch, his caress eased her tension and calmed whatever fears remained. With whispered love words and gentle sighs he led her, always allowing her to set her own pace.

Trust. As he deepened his kiss she realized that she had complete trust in this gentle Highland warrior. He would not take her where she did not wish to go.

Shaw felt the subtle change in her and thrilled to it. It was not surrender. A firebrand like Merritt would never simply surrender her will. What drove her was passion. A passion that had long slumbered within her. And now that he had awakened it, he could taste it on her lips, feel it in the press of her body to his. Hot and wild and free of restraint.

With unexpected tenderness he skimmed his hands across her rib cage, then lower, to find the fasteners of the breeches she wore.

"I will forever praise the stable lad who loaned you these," he muttered with a low chuckle. "For I find them far more erotic than any feminine frill."

As he tugged them loose, he shocked her by pressing his lips to the flat planes of her stomach. "Far more erotic, my lady," he whispered as his lips moved lower.

She had never known such feelings. Like a slave to her newly discovered passion, all she could do was give in to the rapture brought about by his hands and lips. Her fists clutched at the fur robe beneath her as she gasped and reached an unexpected peak of pleasure. She could wait no longer to be joined with him.

Shaw felt his heart thundering as she reached for the fasteners at his waist. When his clothes joined hers, she knelt up, skimming her lips across his chest, until she was facing him.

With his hands on either side of her face, he studied her in the light of the fire. Passion darkened her eyes. They smoldered with an intensity that excited him.

Tangling his hands in her hair, he bent her head back and savaged her mouth with his. At once she sensed the change in him, and felt a thread of alarm. Gone was the gentleness, the tenderness. In its place were wild, primitive needs that struggled for expression.

Her alarm gave way to comprehension. For the first time she understood why, for all this time, he had held himself aloof. There was, carefully hidden behind a man of books and letters, another, more carnal creature. For the first time she glimpsed the dark side to her gentle warrior. This was the shadowy world of passion, of desire, that could make a man desperate.

The unleashing of his deepest needs released her own, as well. It excited her to know that they were about to taste the forbidden fruit that, once shared, would leave them forever changed.

With a boldness that surprised her, she brought her lips across his shoulder to his hair-roughened chest. At his low moan of pleasure, she grew even bolder, and with lips and tongue and fingertips she began to explore his body as he had explored hers.

Shaw's body was alive with need. It had been a tremendous struggle to go slowly, to allow her to set the pace. But now that her passion had been unleashed, he was free to give her so much more. It was no longer enough to satisfy her, to make this first time pleasurable. He would make this night a celebration that would last them through all the lonely, empty nights that stretched out endlessly before them.

For this night, there was no past, no future. There was only now. This moment. And this woman, who had brought him to the edge of insanity.

With his needs quickly building, he laid her down and brought his lips to her breast, nibbling, suckling her, until the nipple hardened. He moved to the other, feasting on her breast until she writhed beneath him and moaned with pleasure. Her hands fisted in the fur, and she arched toward him, but still he held back, unwilling to give her the release she sought. With lips and tongue and fingertips he moved over her, drawing out every sensual pleasure.

The wind sighed in the trees, but it could not cool their overheated flesh. Heat rose between them, around them, filling their lungs, dampening their skin with sheen.

Merritt was beyond thought. Now there was only Shaw. He tasted dark and dangerous, like his rugged Highland forests. She inhaled the musky male scent of him, mingled with the scents of evergreen and horses. The touch of his fingers against her skin was more heavenly than the finest cloth spun from her loom.

She trembled and strained as he slid along her body, moist flesh to moist flesh.

He struggled to hold back, to savor the moment. But he felt her stiffen as he moved his lips down her body.

At the exquisite pleasure bordering on pain, she cried out as she reached the first crest. He gave her no time to recover as he brought his lips back to hers. She whispered his name as he entered her. It didn't seem possible to want more, but she did. She wanted all.

This deeper arousal startled them both. Her eyes opened wide, focusing on his, as she wrapped herself around him.

He filled himself with her, with the clean, fresh taste of her, which he knew would linger forever on his tongue. Her special fragrance, the scent of heather and evergreen, would always remind him of her.

He knew that in the long, joyless nights to come, he would examine this memory from among his heart's treasures and be warmed by it.

Needs clawed at him, desperate for release. He whispered her name as his lips closed over hers and he slipped beyond the edge of sanity.

And then she was moving with him, racing toward a distant light. Their bodies trembled and shuddered, and still they soared until at last they broke free and drifted among a million bright stars.

They lay, still joined, their breathing shallow. Shaw pressed his lips to Merritt's forehead. "I am too heavy for you."

"Nay." She wrapped her arms around his waist, unwilling to move, lest it break the spell.

They lay in silence as their breathing slowly returned to normal. At last she gathered her courage.

"Is it always like this?" she asked.

He levered himself on his elbows to kiss the tip of her nose "Like what?"

"So... wondrous. Like a glimpse of heaven."

"Ah." He smiled, loving her description. "I know not. I know only that I, too, glimpsed heaven in your arms."

She smiled, then her eyes snapped open in surprise. "You know not? What does that mean? Have you...ne'er loved a woman before?"

"You are the only one," he said, touching his lips lightly to hers. The first, the last, the only, his heart promised.

"Truly?" She lay very still, absorbing the shock of his admission. For some strange reason her heart had begun a wild dance of joy inside her chest. Could it be that this strong, brave warrior could hold no other woman up for comparison? In his heart were there no lingering memories of another? But he had said as much, and he had no reason to speak a falsehood.

She felt a thrill unlike any she had ever known. "But you were so... skilled."

"Thank you, my lady. As were you." He chuckled, and the warmth of it wrapped itself around her heart.

He rolled to one side and drew her into the circle of his arms, folding the fur around them both to stave off the night air. "Perhaps it is like eating," he murmured against her lips. "When one is hungry enough, it requires little skill to satisfy." He traced a finger across her shoulder, then gathered her hair in one hand and bent his lips to her neck. "But then," he murmured against her delicate flesh, "after such a fine, satisfying meal, the mind begins to ponder... fruit tarts and fine pastries."

How was it possible that he could want her again so soon? But the touch of her skin, the taste of her lips, had him fully aroused.

He moved his mouth lower, to the soft swell of her breast. "I should warn you, I do love...fruit tarts and fine pastries."

"As do I," she whispered.

Her laughter turned into a gasp as he trailed his lips over the length of her body, and then began working his way back up.

Her eyes darkened with passion. Her arousal was instantaneous. But this time, as they came together, there was no fire and flash. Instead, there was slow heat and the easy knowledge that they had all the time in the world. They slipped into a kingdom of whispered promises and sensuous delights. A realm of dark passion and primitive needs. A place where only lovers can dwell.

Chapter Twenty-Two

Shaw lay very still, studying the woman asleep in his arms. All night they had loved, at times with slow, lazy thoroughness, at other times in a wild frenzied dance, as if to hold back the fleeting hours. Already the horizon was streaked with faint light. So little time, he mused, to catch up on a lifetime.

There was so much he wanted to know about her. So many things he hoped to ask. And much about himself he wished to share. But each time they started to talk, they ended up speaking with their bodies instead.

While Merritt slept in his arms, he'd had time to ponder his future, and her place in it. But there were so many complications.

Merritt lay a moment, savoring the feel of Shaw's strong arms around her. Strange. Even with her eyes closed, she knew him. Knew him as intimately as she knew herself. All night, as they had loved and exchanged whispered secrets, she had come to realize that this Campbell owned her heart completely.

He'd been an amazing lover, at times gentle, at other times almost savage. The depth of his passion had surprised her.

Her eyes flickered open and she lifted a finger to the little frown line between his brows. "Do I make you so unhappy?"

He caught her hand and lifted it to his mouth, pressing a kiss to her palm. "Oh, lass, you make me happier than I have ever been."

"Then what is it that makes you frown so?"

"The thought of leaving here."

"Aye." She thought how wonderful it would be if they could stay here, hidden away in the forest, far from the bloody battles that had divided their two clans for a lifetime.

"There is something I must tell you," Shaw began, for he had carefully thought over the words he would say. He needed to explain about his pledge to serve the Church, and his promise to an old monk. "Have you not wondered why there was no other woman before you?"

"Aye." She sat up, shoving the heavy hair from her eyes. "Though I must admit, it pleases me mightily. But first, there is something important I must tell you. For it lays heavy between us, and I love you too much to allow anything to divide us."

Love. At her easy use of that word, he felt his heart nearly burst with happiness. How could he deny her anything?

"Aye, love. Tell me what you will." He twirled a strand of her hair around his finger. "And then I will share my secrets with you."

She bit her lip. Though she had tried to think of a way to break it gently, she had only the cold truth, and she feared how he would receive it.

"You asked how your brother came to be wounded, and at Inverene House. And the tale that Sabina and I told was true..." She sighed. "But there is more. Sabina and I were up in the meadow that night."

"Searching for a lost sheep," he amended.

"Aye." She looked away. "For many lost sheep."

"So, you were stealing." He tugged on the lock of her hair to force her to look at him. "I suspected as much."

"We were merely taking back what belonged to us."

"And on the way home you crossed paths with the Avengers?"

She shot him a dark look. "Is this my tale, or yours?"

"Forgive me, my love." He trailed a finger across her shoulder, tracing the path of several fascinating freckles.

She took another deep breath. "The villains who had stolen our sheep awoke and began to follow. We did not fear them, since we had often outrun peasants before. But this time, there was something different. As we approached the loch, a second party of scoundrels took up the chase. Almost as though they had been alerted that we would be there. But that was impossible. Only Sabina and I knew that we would be out that night."

"Perhaps it was just ill-timed."

"Nay. They were well armed, and as soon as they saw Sutton's tall form, they began to attack. I suspect that they knew the Avengers would be out that night, and they lay in wait. That is why Sutton was so gravely wounded. I believe they mistook him for one of the Avengers."

Shaw nodded thoughtfully. "And since they seek justice against those who rob and kill and burn the cottages of helpless peasants, they sought his death."

"The Avengers do not do those things," Merritt cried vehemently.

"As you have always insisted. But someone has been killing and looting and burning. If not the Avengers, then who is responsible?"

"I know not. But I would venture a guess that it is this Black Campbell who directs all the villainy. The only victims are those who refuse to denounce my father."

"And who is to say that he and his cohorts are not the Highland Avengers?"

"Nay. The Avengers are not villains. They merely fight against villainy."

"Why do you defend them, love?"

She bit her lip and held her silence.

Hoping to make it easier, he whispered, "I have long suspected that you and Sabina know the identity of these Avengers and are trying to shield them. Is this so?"

"Aye. That is it."

"They are men of your village, perhaps?"

"Nay. The truth is..." Her voice trembled, and she watched his eyes as she finally managed to say, "Sabina and I are the Highland Avengers."

It took Shaw several minutes before he could find any words to speak.

"You and Sabina."

"Aye."

"But why?"

"We did it for Father, and for Edan. There was no one left to help us. You saw what the thieves did to our stables and our flocks. We were desperate."

"And so you looted and pillaged and burned—"

"Nay. Those are lies that were spread to dishonor us. Each time they were repeated, they grew, until it was impossible to tell fact from falsehood. All we did was retrieve our flocks. But the thieves did not want to admit that they had stolen them first from us. So they invented tales that would make them look heroic and the Avengers look evil."

Instead of the anger she'd expected, Shaw threw back his head and began to laugh. This was not the reaction she'd anticipated. "What is so amusing?"

"Oh, lass," he said, resting his forehead against hers. "How could I have been so blind?" He trailed a finger across her shoulders, up her throat, along her jaw. "The garb of a stableboy."

He traced the outline of her lips with his fingertip. "Your skill with weapons." He seemed fascinated with her lips. His finger probed inside her mouth and she playfully bit it. "Your knowledge of the forest. It all makes perfect sense."

She pulled back. "You . . . are not angry?"

"Angry? Oh, lass. How could anything you do make me angry?"

She released the breath she had been unconsciously holding. He knew, and he didn't hate her.

His smile faded as he brought his lips to her throat, where he tried, with gentle butterfly kisses and murmured words, to make up for the bruises that still marred her tender flesh.

She moaned softly as they came together in a storm of passion that had them both breathless. And as the morning dawned, gilded with sunlight sparkling on dew, they slipped once more into a world that only lovers know.

"'Tis time to awake, my brave Highland warrior." Merritt touched a hand to her brother's shoulder.

Edan yawned and stretched, then tossed off his cloak. Morning sunlight streamed into their forest clearing. Above them birds chirped. A fresh log crackled on the fire.

He glanced toward Shaw, who was just returning from the stream. His wound had been freshly dressed. Droplets of water still glistened in his hair.

Merritt's cheeks glowed, and it was obvious that she, too, had just returned from a morning swim, for her fiery hair hung down her back in a riot of damp curls.

"I had not one unpleasant dream last night," Edan said softly. "Nor did I even once reach for my sword or dirk."

"That is a good sign." Merritt handed him a joint of roasted deer, then began to roll their furs and clear their campsite.

As she worked she glanced often at Shaw, who was busy saddling the horses.

"But I did have a strange dream," Edan continued. "I heard the sound of much laughter from the far side of the fire. And I thought I heard voices whispering. But of course I must be mistaken."

Both Merritt and Shaw stopped in midstride to turn their heads and study the lad.

His eyes twinkled with merriment. "Mayhap I should tell Astra of my dream. She will surely explain what it means."

Shaw's eyes were equally filled with humor. "I see you have learned many new things on your journey, some of which would have been better unknown. Mayhap, instead of sharing them with old Astra, you should record them in a scroll for later generations to peruse."

"Aye. A very good idea," Edan said with enthusiasm. "I can write about my abduction, and the bravery of my sister and my tutor."

"And about your own bravery, as well," Merritt put in.

"And about the first steps you took," Shaw added.

"And about the way my sister looks at my tutor whenever she thinks no one is looking," Edan said with a laugh. "And about the way my tutor returns such looks. I think I was not dreaming last night."

"Enough," Merritt commanded, her cheeks flaming.

Shaw turned away to hide his grin. "I think our brave young warrior is strong enough this morrow to ride his own mount, and Merritt can ride with me. That is," he added, "if you are ready to begin the journey home."

"Aye," Edan shouted. Tossing aside his cloak, he struggled to stand.

Beside him, Merritt reached out her hands as if to help him, but he evaded her touch, determined to do it alone.

By the time he was standing, sweat beaded his upper lip. He remained still, getting his balance, then lifted his foot and took one tiny step. At once he dropped to his knees.

He was so elated by his small success he failed to see the tears of joy that sprang to Merritt's eyes. But Shaw saw. And shared her jubilation. Neither of them had a doubt that, in time, the lad would walk again.

"Inverene House," Edan called as his mount broke free of the forest.

Behind him, Merritt and Shaw strained for a glimpse of the familiar fortress.

Long before they arrived, the cry had gone up from the servants in the fields that they were approaching. By the time they reached the courtyard, it was filled with a cheering throng. The villagers milled about, shouting words of greeting.

"Oh, my lady," old Astra cried. "Your father's heart has been so heavy."

Just then Upton pushed his way through the crowd, assisted by Sabina and Sutton, who stood on either side of him.

Behind him, much to Shaw's astonishment, stood Dillon, and his man-at-arms, Walcott Maclennan, and their cousin, Clive, along with Dillon's army, all standing at attention.

"Dillon," Shaw cried from the back of his mount. "How did you come to be here?"

"When we returned from Edinburgh and saw that you and Sutton were not yet at Kinloch House, we came in search of you." It would not do for the laird of the

Campbells to show his relief at the safe return of his brother, but Dillon's heart was filled with joy at his good fortune. He would not have worried nearly as much if it had been Sutton who was trailing the villains. But all the Campbells knew that Shaw was not a warrior.

Shaw slid from the saddle and helped Merritt to alight. At once she flew into her father's arms and hugged him fiercely, while Shaw greeted his brothers and cousin warmly.

"As you can see, Father, we are here, and we are unharmed," Merritt said, kissing Upton's cheek.

"Aye." He held her a little away, studying her carefully. How grateful he was to see this lass who was so dear to his heart. There was a bloom on her cheeks that he had ne'er noted before. And a look in her eyes...much like the one he'd seen in his own Brinda's, when first they'd loved.

"Assist my son from his horse that I may have the privilege of greeting him," Upton called to a servant.

"Nay." Edan waved the peasant away. With his gaze fixed on Upton he called, "I have brought you a gift, Father."

Puzzled, everyone watched as the lad slid to the ground. For a moment he stood, clinging tightly to the saddle. Then, taking a deep breath for courage, he released his hold and stepped away. At first he wobbled, and it appeared that he would fall, but, as the crowd grew deathly silent, he took a step toward his father, and then another.

Upton, tears streaming down his face, broke free of Sabina and Sutton and ran forward before dropping to his knees, arms outstretched. With one last burst of strength Edan fell into his father's arms. The old man drew him close and clung to him, weeping for joy.

All around him, servants and villagers cheered and wept.

Astra turned to Shaw, dabbing at her eyes. "Bless ye," she said as she lifted herself on tiptoe to press a kiss to his cheek. "For there is no finer gift ye could have brought m'laird."

Upton got to his feet, lifting his son in his arms. At once two servants positioned themselves beside him, in case he should falter. But the old man's strength seemed to have blossomed at the first sight of his son's newfound skills. It was as if the frail old man he had become had been pushed aside in favor of the strong, proud warrior he had once been.

He felt no shame at the tears that flowed freely from his eyes. Fixing Shaw with a look, he said loudly, "Shaw Campbell. I had believed my daughter and my only son to be gone from me forever. Instead, you have returned them to me, not only unharmed, but stronger than ever. It is truly a miracle. Hear me. All that I have, all that I shall ever have, is pledged to you and your clan. For you have returned to me all that matters in my life."

"Come," he then called to the assembled. "We will feast and rejoice."

As Upton led the way inside, he was followed by the cheering throng. And though Shaw and Merritt peered around, trying vainly to return to each other's side, they were helpless against the villagers that swept them along toward the great hall.

The feast was a magnificent affair. The servants carried platters of roasted deer and sheep, fish and fowl, along with great quantities of wine and ale. There were trays laden with tarts and puddings and every manner of fancy sweet.

The entire village had been invited to share in the laird's celebration. And while they feasted, they watched in astonishment as the Lamonts and their hated enemies, the Campbells, sat side by side.

Shaw was flanked by Dillon and Sutton. Like his brothers, he wore a shirt of softest lawn and a tunic of deep green. Across his shoulders was tossed the green-and-black plaid woven by the women of his clan.

Across from him sat Merritt, in a gown of crimson velvet, her fiery tresses pulled to one side in fat ringlets that streamed across her breast.

Since their return to Inverene House, they had not had a moment alone. And now, as the meal wore on, along with the endless speeches, he gazed at her with a look filled with longing. She seemed to sense his eyes on her and, lifting her head, gave him a shy smile. At once his heart seemed lighter.

Dillon scraped back his chair and stood, holding aloft a goblet of ale. A hush settled over the crowd.

"As laird of the Campbells," he said loudly enough for his voice to carry through the huge room, "I accept the gratitude of Upton, laird of the Lamonts, for that which my brothers have given him. And I add my thanks for the care given my brother, Sutton, by the lady Sabina. Her solicitude was such that Sutton is fully restored from his wounds. And he has come to me with an unusual request." Dillon glanced around the great room before adding, "Our families have long held enmity between us. But my brother would heal these wounds by asking the lady Sabina to be his wife."

At once the throng broke into a chorus of exclamations. Everyone was speaking at once.

Dillon waited a moment, then continued, "I have given my permission for this union, as has your laird."

The crowd erupted into shouting and applause, the men thumping their tankards loudly on the wooden tables.

Merritt, seated beside her sister, threw her arms around Sabina's neck and hugged her fiercely. "Why did you not tell me?" she whispered.

"There was no time. It has all happened so quickly."

"Oh, Sabina. I am so happy for you. Later, when we are alone, you must tell me everything." With a shy smile she added, "There is much I must tell you, as well."

The two sisters clasped hands as Upton got to his feet and the crowd fell silent. "The Campbells leave on the morrow, and my daughter will accompany them."

"So soon?" Merritt cried.

"Aye," Sabina whispered. "The laird of the Campbells has commanded it."

Merritt's lower lip trembled, but she kept her head high, her eyes fastened on her father.

"It was not easy knowing that Sabina would be so far away," Upton continued. "But I have given my leave for the marriage, since I will not be left alone in my old age. I still have my beloved daughter Merritt at my side, as well as my son, Edan."

Across the table, Shaw looked thunderstruck as his eldest brother stood and touched his goblet to Upton's. "We will form a new alliance," Dillon said firmly. "Between the Campbells and the Lamonts. It will begin with Sutton and Sabina. And I know that it will continue with my brother, Shaw, a man of peace, who has pledged his life to serving the Church."

At that Merritt's eyes filled and she went deathly pale.

"What is it?" Sabina whispered.

But Merritt had already pushed away from the table. She dared not glance at Shaw or she knew she would fall into a fit of weeping. With her hand at her mouth to stifle her cry, she ran from the room.

Shaw pushed back his chair so quickly it fell over. He took no notice as he strode quickly from the room. Behind him, the crowd fell silent. Upton and Dillon exchanged puzzled looks.

* * *

Shaw caught up with Merritt on the stairs but she pulled her hand away when he tried to stop her.

"Merritt, you must listen," he said, but she continued on until she came to her chambers. When she tried to close the door on him, he shoved it open with such force the sound reverberated through the upper hallway. Servants, fearing his wrath, scurried away.

"Now," he said, leaning against the door, "you will listen."

She shot him a hateful look and flounced across the room, putting as much distance between them as possible. Crossing her arms over her bosom, she shouted, "You lied to me. You led me to believe that you loved me. And all the while, you knew that you had already pledged your life to the Church. You are no better than a man who takes a mistress while concealing the fact that he has a wife."

"That would be true, had I already taken my vows."

She looked up, then narrowed her eyes. "What are you saying?"

"It is true that I intended to spend a lifetime serving the Church, in payment for the kindness shown by the good monks who raised me. I had intended to tell you of it this morrow."

Merritt thought back to the scene at dawn, when Shaw had seemed anxious to tell her something of importance. But they had become...distracted by their lovemaking. Her cheeks flamed.

"That is why there has been no other woman in my life. I have tried to prepare myself for a life of service to the Church."

"You have taken no vows?"

"Nay. And now that I have discovered your love, my lady, there will be no vows except those I make to you."

It took several moments before she felt the full impact of his words. "Oh, Shaw Campbell." She rushed into his arms and buried her lips against his throat. "When will you speak to my father?"

"Now, with your permission."

"And when will we wed?"

"When I return."

She went very still. "Return?"

He nuzzled her ear while he murmured, "I must first go to the monastery of Saint Collum, to break the news to Father Anselm. Then I will return, to claim you for my bride."

"Truly?" Her tears had become tears of joy. "Then let us go to Father with the news."

"Aye." He swept her into his arms and carried her down the stairs. But when they reached the great hall she whispered, "Put me down. Else I will be laughed at by all the villagers."

"Let them laugh, love. For I cannot bear to let you leave my arms again."

With that he walked into the great hall, still carrying Merritt in his arms, and approached the table where Upton and Dillon were seated.

The crowd fell silent, but around the room many heads craned for a better view.

"What is this?" Upton Lamont asked. "Has my daughter hurt herself?"

"Nay, my lord. But she was wounded by my brother's words." Shaw turned to Dillon. "It is true that I have always intended to pledge myself to the Church. But, like Sutton, I seem to have lost my heart to a Lamont. Merritt Lamont. And I would ask for her hand in marriage, and for your blessings upon that union, my brother."

Astonished, everyone at table stared at Shaw and the lass in his arms.

"Do you know what you are saying?" Dillon thundered.

"Aye. I am declaring my love for Merritt Lamont."

"And what of Father Anselm?"

"I will go to him and explain. Then I will return to claim the lass for my wife."

"You would take my last daughter from my side?" Upton demanded.

"Nay, sir. If you agree, I will live with her here in Inverene House and continue Edan's tutelage until he grows to manhood and can assume the leadership of his people."

Merritt couldn't hide her elation at his announcement. Wrapping her arms around his neck, she hugged him.

Upton glanced from Merritt to Shaw, and then to Dillon Campbell. "'Twould seem that the bonds between us grow stronger with each passing moment."

"Aye."

"Does this mean that you will grant your permission?" Shaw asked.

The two men nodded their heads. And while the entire assembly cheered wildly, Shaw set Merritt on her feet and bowed grandly over her hand. Above the din he muttered, "When the others have retired, I will come to you in your chambers and speak to you of my love."

With a sly smile she whispered, "You will do more than speak of your love, Shaw Campbell. You will show me. For it will have to be enough to hold me until you return."

Chapter Twenty-Three

Two columns of mounted Highlanders awaited a signal from their laird. Sabina and her family stood in a tight circle, saying their last tearful farewells, while, at a nearby wagon, Astra issued orders as the last of her mistress's trunks was handed up.

For long minutes Merritt clung to her older sister, allowing her tears to fall freely. "I cannot bear the thought of our separation."

"Nor I, Merritt. My heart is breaking at the thought of leaving all of you, and my beloved Inverene House. But, though I tremble at the thought of what awaits me at the end of my journey, I must be with Sutton. Surely you know how I feel."

"Aye." Merritt's gaze trailed Shaw as he made his way through the throng of villagers who had assembled in the courtyard. In her eyes was a look of love. "It is strange how these feelings fill our lives. My heart will be empty until Shaw returns."

"And mine is filled to overflowing," Sabina whispered as she gave her sister a final kiss and allowed Sutton to lead her to her mount.

Shaw made his way to Merritt, who stood beside her father and brother. All through the night they had said their final, tender goodbyes in her chambers.

Shaw offered his hand to Upton Lamont, and then to his son. "Farewell, my friends."

"When will you return?" the lad asked.

"I will be gone perhaps a fortnight, for the journey to the monastery of Saint Collum is a long one. But know that while I am gone, my heart is here with all of you."

Shaw turned to Merritt, and a smile lit his eyes at the sight of her in feminine frills, with not a single weapon in view. Leaning close he whispered, "Have the Avengers been banished from the land?"

She glanced toward her sister, whose hand was held firmly in Sutton's. "Aye, my lord. So it would seem."

"Then farewell, my lovely avenger." He lifted her hand and brushed his lips over the back of it.

She felt the heat dance along her spine. "Safe journey, Shaw Campbell. I am already impatient for your return."

"No more than I, my love."

Merritt felt a rush of pride at the sight of him, so tall and handsome, as he strode away. He was hers, her heart whispered. And soon he would be her husband, her lover, for a lifetime.

As he pulled himself into the saddle, Shaw was surprised to see his cousin standing in the courtyard. Clive wore no traveling cloak. Turning to Dillon, he called, "Is Clive not returning with us?"

"Clive has generously offered to remain here. In your absence he will tutor Edan, and offer a measure of safety to the Lamonts."

"Why was I not told?"

Dillon gave him a gentle smile. "I went to your chambers last night to share the news. You were not there. And when I learned from old Astra that the lady Merritt's chambers adjoin yours, I decided it best not to... disturb you."

Shaw laughed. "A wise decision, my brother." He watched as Clive crossed the courtyard to stand beside Upton Lamont and his children. "See to their safety until I return, cousin," he called.

"Aye. I shall see to them." Clive lifted a hand as the columns of soldiers began to move smartly away.

Shaw turned for a last glimpse of his beloved. She waved and forced a smile through her tears. Shaw's gaze was drawn to the man beside her. In the sunlight, they stood in sharp contrast. Merritt's hair glinted like fire. His cousin's hair gleamed black as a raven's wing.

"You are quiet, my brother."

Shaw turned to his twin. "Aye. It was in this forest that I discovered I was a warrior."

"So, now you have a fondness for fighting."

"Nay." Shaw glanced up at the thin rays of sunlight that filtered through the canopy of trees. "I will ever be repulsed by it. But evil must be stopped. And the villains I encountered in this forest were truly evil." Despite his heavy traveling cloak, he shivered. "I feel their presence now, as if they were all around us."

Sutton cast a sidelong glance at the underbrush. "Mayhap we are both fools, but I feel it, as well."

The two had always known they shared a gift. At his brother's ominous words, Shaw nudged his mount into a gallop and raced between the lines of soldiers until he reached Dillon. "Have some of your men ride ahead. I sense a trap."

"But this forest is Campbell land. We are among our own kinsmen. They would not dare to attack their own laird."

"Aye, that I know. But I tell you, Dillon, something is amiss."

Before Dillon could issue a command, they heard a cry and watched as one of their soldiers took an arrow to the back and toppled from his horse. Amid a flurry of arrows from the trees overhead, a swarm of ragged men dropped to the ground brandishing swords and knives. The air was alive with the cries and screams of battle as horses fell, crushing their riders, and dust swirled around the figures of men who stood sword to sword.

"We must protect the lady Sabina," Shaw cried. "For surely she is their target."

At once Sutton and several soldiers formed a protective ring around the lass to ensure her safety.

As the battle continued, Shaw realized that he'd been wrong. These villains were not merely after Sabina. Seeing the number of men, and the quantity of weapons with which they were armed, he knew they had come prepared to eliminate an entire company of soldiers.

Though the villains were many, they were no match for the skilled warriors who fought beside Dillon Campbell. Soon the ground beneath their feet ran red with blood. The grass was littered with the bodies of the dead and dying.

Out of the corner of his eye Shaw saw the leader, Lysander, lift a sword against Sutton. At once Shaw tossed his dirk. Though his aim was true, Lysander turned at the last moment, taking the dirk to his arm instead of his heart.

Cursing his luck, Shaw raced to his brother's side.

When Lysander saw the two, his eyes widened. Then his lips curled into an evil smile. "So. It is as I was told. You two share the same face."

"Who told you of us? Who is this Black Campbell, who bribed with gold our own kinsmen?" Shaw challenged as he thrust his sword, missing Lysander's arm by a mere fraction.

The villain merely laughed and drove Shaw against a tree. Neatly dancing away, Shaw avoided a thrust that would have cost him his life.

"Answer me." Shaw lunged, and this time his sword tip caught Lysander just above the heart.

Stunned and gravely wounded, the man cried out, then, clutching the blade that protruded from his flesh, he dropped to his knees. At once Shaw pulled his sword free and pinned the man to the ground by pressing his knee to his chest. Unsheathing a dagger he whispered, "Give me the name of the Black Campbell or my blade will slit your miserable throat."

Lysander clutched his coarse tunic, which was quickly becoming saturated with his own blood. He knew the wound was mortal, and that his life was slowly ebbing. "It no longer matters," he said with a harsh laugh. "You are too late to stop him. By the time you can return to Inverene House, he will have succeeded in killing all who dwell therein."

"Inverene House?" As the truth dawned, Shaw cried, "God in heaven." Visibly shaken, he scrambled to his feet. Turning to Sutton he cried, "I must ride to Inverene at once. The Black Campbell is there, intent upon killing the Lamonts."

"Our cousin, Clive, will protect them," Sutton said, hoping to soothe his brother's fears.

"You do not understand." Shaw pulled himself into the saddle. "How could we have been so blind? Clive is the Black Campbell."

"I have read all of the Book of Proverbs. And these scrolls." Edan hobbled toward a low shelf. Though he could take no more than a few steps before pausing to rest, he could hardly contain his joy at each small success.

"My cousin must have spent a great deal of time with you, if you are as proficient as you claim."

"He spent more time with me than anyone ever has. He is a fine tutor." With his back to Clive, Edan was unable to see the dark look that crossed the man's face.

Edan picked up several scrolls and hobbled toward the table where he and Shaw had spent so many pleasurable hours poring over the Lamont family history. "Would you like me to read to you?"

"Aye. A fine idea." Behind him, Clive touched a hand to the dirk at his waist. Oh, it had all been so easy. And now that he was in control, they were like lambs to the slaughter.

Without warning the door burst open and Clive whirled.

Merritt entered, followed by Astra and a serving wench. In her earnest attempt to prepare herself for her new role as wife and mistress of Inverene House, Merritt wore a new gown of emerald velvet, with a low, rounded neckline and narrow, tapered sleeves. The billowing skirt was gathered here and there with matching ribbons to reveal three petticoats beneath, each a lighter shade of green. Though the effect was stunning, it made walking perilous, and she found herself taking small, dainty steps. She was grateful that she no longer had need of a weapon, for the gown left no place on her person to conceal even a tiny dirk.

"I thought you and Edan might enjoy taking your midday meal here by the fire. Shaw often did, so as not to interrupt the flow of the lessons."

"Then I shall do the same." Clive watched as the servant set a silver tray on the table and poured wine into goblets.

"Will you stay and eat with us, Merritt?" Edan asked.

"If you like."

"Nay," Clive said quickly. Then, seeing the look that the old housekeeper gave him, he explained, "I am not yet accustomed to the tutelage given by my cousin. 'Twill take a day or two before I determine just how much young Edan knows. I think 'twould be better if we worked alone."

"As you wish." Merritt found this dour man a sharp contrast to the laughing, teasing man she loved. But he was, she reminded herself, Shaw's trusted kin. She would give him the respect due him.

She crossed the room and touched a hand to her little brother's shoulder. "Do not tire yourself, Edan. Promise me you will rest."

"Aye," the boy said distractedly.

With a kiss to his cheek, Merritt followed Astra and the servant from the room.

When they were alone Clive picked up a goblet and tasted the wine.

"Would you like me to read this scroll?" Edan asked.

"Aye. Read to me, lad."

"The battle was in the year of our Lord..."

As the boy's voice washed over him, Clive circled the room, draining the contents of his goblet. It would be an easy matter to torch such a place. The scrolls and books would burn quickly. He glanced up toward the massive wooden beams. They would take some effort, but it could be done. And when those in the surrounding villages saw the rubble that had once been Inverene House, they would know and fear the might and power of their new laird, the Black Campbell. And all would bend their knee and swear allegiance. Or share the fate of these fools. As for him, he would return to Kinloch House. It would suit his needs well. He'd spent a lifetime coveting the power and possessions of his cousins. And now, all would be his.

"What think you?" Edan asked.

"About what?" With an effort, Clive shifted his attention back to the lad.

"About the battle. Shaw said that a warrior can learn much by reading about past battles. For 'tis the past that shapes our future."

"Aye. 'Tis so. We cannot escape our past." Clive slipped the dagger from its place of concealment at his waist and held it up, so that the sunlight streaming through the windows glinted off the blade. He advanced on the boy, his eyes glittering with hatred. "Prepare to die, Edan Lamont. For the things of my past are about to strip your future from you forever."

"I do not much care for Shaw's cousin," Merritt said to her father.

Upton tried to pull himself back from his own dark thoughts. He missed Sabina. And, though he was loath to admit it, he missed Sutton and Shaw. Especially Shaw. There was a wisdom and goodness in the lad far beyond his years.

"He will be good for Edan," her father muttered. "The lad needs a man around."

"He has a man," Merritt said, closing her hand over his big, rough fist. "You, Father."

"I meant one who is not too old and tired to share his life."

"You are neither old nor tired. You are the best father in the world. And Edan is devoted to you. He spends hours going over the scrolls that describe your many battles."

Upton beamed with pride. "Does he?" He tugged on his beard as a new thought struck. "Do you know that I have ne'er heard my own son read?"

"Would you care to?" Merritt asked.

Upton nodded. "Aye. I would like that very much."

She caught his hand and helped him to his feet. "He and Clive are in Mother's sitting chambers. You will be pleased to see how the servants have restored it."

Edan stared in disbelief at the knife in Clive's hand. "Why do you wish to kill me?"

Clive took a step closer, feeling a rush of power. "Because you are Upton Lamont's only son. Your death will cause your father great pain."

"Then it is my father you hate."

"Aye."

Edan's mind was working frantically. Shaw had taught him that a truly great warrior, in order to best an opponent, should know the mind of that opponent. He needed to keep Clive talking. He swallowed and forced back the terror that threatened.

"But you never met my father before. How can you hate a man you do not know?"

"My father, Thurman, knew your father. And grew to despise him."

"Why?"

Clive's fury erupted. He grasped Edan by the front of his tunic and hauled him to his feet. "Stop asking foolish questions. I am weary of the sound of your voice. Now will you die, so that my mission can be fulfilled."

As he lifted the dagger, Clive was stunned to feel a big hand at his shoulder, flinging him aside like a helpless whelp. He fell in a crumpled heap against the wall. His knife, he noted numbly, had slid across the floor, landing in front of the fireplace. In a daze he turned to see Upton Lamont on his knees cradling his son in his arms.

"You will leave my house at once," Upton commanded. He continued to hold his son to his chest, as if to assure himself that Edan was truly unharmed. "Because you are kin to my daughters' betrothed, I will let you live.

But you are banished forever from Inverene House, and from Lamont land. If you return, you will forfeit your miserable life."

"I understand...and obey." Clive darted a glance at his knife, to gauge how many steps he would need to reach it. Drawing himself up to his full height, he started to cross the room.

Merritt, seeing the direction of his gaze, began to race toward him, cursing her useless gown and lack of weapon. "Nay, Father!" she shouted. "He is not to be trusted."

But before she could reach him, Clive made a frantic dash and scooped up his knife. "Now," he said, "we will see who gives the commands in Inverene House."

"You have but one puny knife against three Lamonts?" Upton taunted as he rose up and started forward.

"One knife is more than enough, old man." Clive lifted his hand above his head and took aim. "Since it is pointed at your beloved son's heart. And hear me, Upton Lamont. When I toss my dirk, I never miss."

Upton froze in his tracks. He cared not for his own life. But he could not bear the thought that his carelessness might cost the life of his children. "Let Edan and Merritt live," he implored. "Take my life instead."

"Do not tempt me, old man."

Seeing the danger to his father, Edan was determined to distract this madman from his mission. "Clive said his father's name was Thurman, and that he knew you."

At once Upton reacted with stunned surprise. For long silent moments he peered at the man who stood before him. His voice was a strangled whisper. "Aye. I should have seen the resemblance. Not to Thurman, but to his wife, Aldora, for you are very like her."

"Clive said his father hated you," Edan put in.

"Nay, it is not true," Upton protested. "When we were young warriors, we were as close as brothers. But... something happened to end our kinship."

"Aye. You left the circle of friendship rather than bend your knee to another." Clive's eyes narrowed. "'Twas what my father also wanted to do, but because he was determined to win the love of Aldora over all other men, he acceded to her wishes and remained under the protection of his clan. But as years went by, my father saw the way you prospered, while he was never anything more than a loyal man-at-arms to his cousin, Modric. And all because he listened to his woman." Clive's voice rose. "A woman who never loved him. A woman who loved you, Upton Lamont."

At his words, Merritt and Edan turned to stare in shock and surprise at their father.

Upton's tone softened. "'Tis true that Aldora loved me, and I loved her when we were very young. But she chose Thurman over me. And I swear to you, I never saw her again. She was never disloyal to your father."

"You think not. But I know that she never forgot you. And as news of your conquests grew, so did her regret that she had not risked all for love." Clive's eyes darkened. "All my life my father told me the tale, and made me promise on his grave to avenge his loss and have what was rightfully his."

"Rightfully his? He may have been bitter, but your father was not a thief and a murderer. If you do this terrible deed, you will be hunted until the day you die."

"Nay," Clive said with a bitter laugh. "You see, there will be no one left to tell what happened here. After I force you to watch the murder of your son and daughter, I will end your miserable life, as well, Upton Lamont."

"You do not think your cousin Shaw Campbell will spend a lifetime searching for the one who destroyed his happiness?" Merritt asked sharply.

"Shaw Campbell." Clive's voice was filled with scorn. "The perfect son. The perfect brother. The perfect cousin. And to you, the perfect warrior and lover, is he not?" His lips twisted with anger. "But he will love you no more. My men were lying in wait for Shaw Campbell and his brothers."

"Your men?" Merritt felt a shudder pass through her. Then her voice broke. Not Shaw. Not her beloved. "God in heaven, what are you saying?"

"I am saying that right now they lie dead in the forest. All of them, including the pretty Sabina."

At Merritt's startled gasp, Edan began to cry softly. Upton became deathly quiet.

The silence was suddenly broken by the familiar sound of Shaw's voice. "Your well-laid plans went awry, cousin. It is your men who lie dead in the forest. But before he gave his life, the leader, Lysander, revealed the truth. I know now that you are the traitorous Black Campbell."

Everyone turned with relief toward the tall figure who stood in the doorway, his sword at the ready.

Shaw's eyes blazed with fury. "Now I have the answers to all those puzzling questions. On the night Sutton was attacked, it was not the Avengers those swordsmen sought." He turned the full force of his wrath upon his cousin. "It was you who told the villains where Sutton would be."

Though he said not a word, Clive's eyes glittered with fury. His fingers tightened on the hilt of his knife.

"How you must hate us, that you would do such an evil deed," Shaw said.

"Aye," Clive thundered. "I hate all of you. I am sick to death of your talk of honor and courage and duty to your country. What of your family? What of me? When would I ever have a chance to be laird? The only one who ever cared about me, the only one who ever loved me, was my father. It was he who insisted that I take what was rightfully mine."

"It was not love that Thurman gave you," Upton said sadly. "It was hatred, jealousy. Aye, and a compelling need for vengeance."

"But why?" Merritt asked, turning toward her father.

The pain etched in his face was almost more than she could bear.

"Because," he said, turning his full gaze upon Clive, "Thurman carried a terrible secret in his heart. And that secret must have tormented him for all his life, until it drove him into madness. That is why he has taught Clive to hate. For you see, Thurman knew he was not Clive's father."

"What are you saying?" Merritt demanded. But even as the question slipped from her lips, the truth dawned.

Everyone turned to Upton Lamont, who was staring at Clive with tear-filled eyes.

"I had not thought I could suffer a worse pain than that of knowing that Aldora would not leave the safety of her people. For years the knowledge that she was another man's woman drove me to cruel, barbarous acts for which I am now ashamed. But even that pain cannot be compared to this." His voice nearly broke, but he forced himself to continue. "You see, when I left, I knew that Aldora carried my seed. You are not Thurman's son, Clive. You are mine."

At his words, Clive's eyes went wide with a look of shock and disbelief. "Nay! Never! You are my enemy. And you must die," he shouted as he bent and snatched a flaming stick from the fire. "Else my father's vengeance will never be complete. Die, Upton Lamont. Die, Shaw

Campbell, with the woman you love. Then I will be laird and all knees will bend to me."

In one quick motion he tossed the burning stick among the books. Flames leapt and danced, quickly turning the shelves of fragile scrolls into a wall of fire.

While Upton and Shaw raced across the room to drag Edan away from the flames, Clive made a dash toward the door, in the hopes of sealing them in a fiery grave. But Merritt, seeing what he was about to do, made a desperate leap and landed against him, knocking him to the floor. As his knife slipped from his hand, both he and Merritt scrambled to retrieve it. When her fingers closed around the hilt, he swung his palm in a wide arc and slapped her so hard her head snapped to one side. At once the knife slipped from her nerveless fingers.

Merritt watched in horrified fascination as, in one quick motion, he snatched it and pressed the finely honed blade to her throat. "You will do just as nicely as the lad. For it will give me the greatest pleasure to forever deny your father your love and my cousin the pleasure of your charms."

As he pressed the knife to her flesh, he suddenly stiffened. His evil smile was replaced by a look of stunned surprise. His blade clattered harmlessly to the floor. As he pitched forward, Merritt scrambled out of the way and he slumped in a heap. Embedded in his back was Shaw's jewel-handled sword.

Flames erupted perilously close to the wooden beams. Shaw scooped Merritt up into his arms and, together with Upton and Edan, they fled the inferno. In the hallway, a line of servants was already hurrying forward, armed with containers of water and heavy hides to snuff out the blaze before it could spread through the rest of the fortress.

"Oh, my love," Merritt cried as she clung to Shaw's strength. "I feared I'd lost you."

He would not speak of his own deep fear, which had driven him to race through the forest like a man possessed. Instead he touched his lips to hers and whispered, "The fates could never be that cruel. We have only just found each other, my love. And I make you this solemn promise. We will never be separated again."

Epilogue

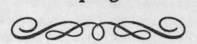

Father Anselm watched as Shaw paced back and forth in the knave of the chapel.

For at least the hundredth time, Shaw peered out at the assembled. His eldest brother, Dillon, and his wife, Leonora, were seated in the first pew, along with Robert the Bruce and his entourage, who had journeyed from Edinburgh. Behind them sat Sutton and his bride, Sabina, both of whom wore identical smiles of pure bliss.

In the third pew sat Shaw's sister, Flame, who looked somehow different since her journey to Edinburgh. There was a polish, a sophistication, that had not been evident before. But beneath the latest gown and perfectly coifed hair, he could detect the impish gleam that still lurked in her eyes.

Across the aisle sat Upton Lamont, his hair and beard trimmed, his scarlet tunic and cape as fine as any king's. Beside him sat Edan, who seemed to have grown overnight from boy to man. He had even assisted the workmen in the restoration of the burned-out chamber, which was now a magnificent library.

"I know you are restless, but sit a moment, Shaw," the old monk urged. "'Twill be our last chance to talk, for I must soon return to the monastery."

"Aye." Reluctantly Shaw sat in a chair and accepted the goblet of wine the old priest held out to him.

"Despite your nerves, you appear happy, lad."

"I am, Father."

"I had a chance to visit with your lass. She is, as I expected, quite special. Though I must admit, I was certain the lass didn't exist who could tempt you."

Shaw smiled then, and the old monk saw the love in his eyes. "Aye. Merritt is unlike anyone I have ever known."

The priest decided to broach an important subject. "Before you wed, would you like me to hear your confession?"

Shaw's smile deepened. "You'd like that, would you? To know how many commandments I've broken since I've been away?"

Father Anselm's eyes twinkled with a hint of mischief. "You cannot blame an old man for trying to live through another. It's been too many years since I dreamed a young man's dream, or followed a young man's course."

Shaw set down his wine and adopted a more solemn pose. "Then hear me, Father, for I ask your blessing."

Father Anselm clasped his hands in prayer and lowered his gaze.

"I have killed," Shaw said softly, "not once, but several times. I've stolen sheep and horses." He saw the monk's eyes widen, though he said not a word. "And I've taken the virginity of my enemy's daughter, though it was done for the noblest of reasons—love. Thus, I am a sinner. And, if truth be told, an unrepentant one, for, though I have remorse for those I've killed, I feel not a shred of regret for my other transgressions. As Merritt so often pointed out, it was not stealing to retrieve sheep and horses that had originally belonged to her family. As for the other, how could I regret loving Merritt Lamont?"

"Aye," the old monk said with a sigh. "How indeed?" He paused a moment, then lifted his hand in a blessing. "For those sins for which you ask pardon, I grant it, in the name of our heavenly Father."

They heard the sound of the heavy chapel doors being thrown wide and got to their feet.

"It is time, Shaw. Have you any doubts?"

Shaw chuckled. "None. Let us make haste, for I have waited a lifetime for this moment."

As they made their way to the altar, the strains of a lute filled the air and a vision in a gown of white satin and lace began to walk slowly up the aisle.

The old priest turned to Shaw. "The Church has lost a man of vision and courage, who would have made a splendid leader."

"Rome holds no appeal for me," Shaw whispered, his gaze fixed on Merritt.

"Aye. I can see that."

When she paused beside him, Shaw turned to greet his bride, and lifted the veil away from her face. As he took her hand in his she murmured, "Has the good priest persuaded you of your folly yet?"

"He has tried. But I have told him that it would be impossible to leave all this excitement for the quiet life of a monk. Besides, my lady, if I am to begin my life with you honestly, I must admit I love you far too much to leave you ever again. Let our love seal the pact between the Campbells and the Lamonts forever."

Forever, his heart sang as the vows were pledged between them. He had come to this place to find his brother, and to exact justice of the notorious Highland Avengers. But what he had found had shaken him to the very core. His father's enemy, who had become a trusted friend. A lad who had taken all of life's cruel blows and risen above them. Two women who had done anything necessary for the survival of their family, and one of them this amazing woman, who had taken his quiet, careful life and turned it inside out. And with her fire, her zeal, her courage, had filled all the empty places in his heart.

* * * * *

Harlequin® Historical

WOMEN OF THE WEST

Exciting stories of the old West and the women whose dreams
and passions shaped a new land!

Join Harlequin Historicals every month as we bring you
these unforgettable tales.

Don't miss any of our Women of the West!

Harlequin® Historical

THE LION TRILOGY

The new series from popular author
Suzanne Barclay.

If you enjoyed LION OF THE NORTH,
be sure to watch for the dramatic
conclusion to Suzanne Barclay's
saga of the powerful, passionate
Sutherland clan:

LION'S LEGACY, available in early 1996

And if you missed the first book in the trilogy, it's not too late to
order LION'S HEART from the address below.

Suzanne Barclay Brings the Highlands to Life!

To order your copy of *Lion's Heart* HS #252, please send your name, address, zip or
postal code, along with a check or money order (please do not send cash) for $3.99
for each book ordered ($4.50 in Canada) plus 75¢ postage and handling ($1.00 in
Canada) payable to Harlequin Books, to:

In the U.S.	In Canada
3010 Walden Avenue	P.O. Box 609
P. O. Box 1369	Fort Erie, Ontario
Buffalo, NY 14269-1369	L2A 5X3

Please specify book title with your order.
Canadian residents add applicable federal and provincial taxes.

HLT-2

ANNOUNCING THE

FLYAWAY VACATION SWEEPSTAKES!

This month's destination:

Beautiful SAN FRANCISCO!

This month, as a special surprise, we're offering an exciting FREE VACATION!

Think how much fun it would be to visit San Francisco "on us"! You could ride cable cars, visit Chinatown, see the Golden Gate Bridge and dine in some of the finest restaurants in America!

The facing page contains two Entry Coupons (as does every book you received this shipment). Complete and return *all* the entry coupons; **the more times you enter, the better your chances of winning!**

Then keep your fingers crossed, because you'll find out by June 15, 1995 if you're the winner! If you are, here's what you'll get:

- • Round-trip airfare for two to beautiful San Francisco!
- • 4 days/3 nights at a first-class hotel!
- • $500.00 pocket money for meals and sightseeing!

Remember: The more times you enter, the better your chances of winning!*

*NO PURCHASE OR OBLIGATION TO CONTINUE BEING A SUBSCRIBER NECESSARY TO ENTER. SEE REVERSE SIDE OR ANY ENTRY COUPON FOR ALTERNATIVE MEANS OF ENTRY.

VSF KAL